This isn't a romance about chiseled, lantern-jawed college kids boasting V-cut abs. There are no marathon steamy sex sessions, not without having at least one nebulizer on standby anyway.

Marcel Giresse, the thirty-six-year-old Director of Finance at the French Ministry of Justice, is happy to leave all that nonsense to his oldest friend Lucien, the sixteenth Earl of Rossingley. In fact, Marcel is too short of breath and too set in his nerdy ways to ever think about sex at all. Which is a shame because the prisoner serving a sentence for murderer that he's just interviewed is smart, intriguing, and hot as hell.

Guillaume Guilbaud is approaching forty and has wasted his best years rotting in a prison cell. The only interesting thing that has happened to him since his best friend Reuben was released is taking part in a series of interviews with a disarming and charismatic civil servant named Marcel. As if *that* friendship could ever materialize into anything, especially as he feels so ill-prepared for his imminent life on the outside.

But after a chance meeting at Rossingley, Guillaume finds himself renting Marcel's annex and desperately falling for his sweet, chronically ill landlord. Which is crazy, because Marcel is celibate, posh, clever, and fundamentally out of Guillaume's league. Furthermore, Marcel also has far too many interfering friends and concerned relatives determined to ensure he doesn't become any more attached to the mysterious ex-con he's shyly let into his life.

To Take a Quiet Breath is a slow-burn romance because Marcel is too breathless for a romance at any other speed. It's about two men finding that love can quietly creep up on you no matter how many obstacles are thrown in its path and discovering that as long as an inhaler is readily at hand, anyone can swing from the chandeliers.

TO TAKE A QUIET BREATH

BREATH

Rossingley, Book Three

Fearne Hill

A NineStar Press Publication

www.ninestarpress.com

To Take a Quiet Breath

© 2021 Fearne Hill

Cover Art © 2021 Natasha Snow

Edited by Elizabetta McKay

ISBN: 978-1-64890-422-6

First Edition, November, 2021

Also available in eBook, ISBN: 978-1-64890-421-9

CONTENT WARNING:

This book contains sexually explicit content, which is only suitable for mature readers. Warning for an MC with serious chronic asthma and scenes of breathing crises; social reintegration of an ex-con MC who was imprisoned for murder, now rehabilitated; description of a prison rape (past and off page).

To RRH, with love

Chapter One

Guillaume

The man from the ministry was not at all what I expected. Although I knew him to be in his midthirties, his pale skin was unlined, and he had the gaucheness of a younger man. He had also dressed that morning without the benefit of a mirror. The brown tweed jacket, with a red fleck, while old and comfortably worn, neither complemented the blue flowery shirt nor the dark grey chinos.

Notwithstanding, the whole package worked.

He was oddly out of breath, too, full pink lips slightly parted as if he'd climbed a flight of stairs, even though the visitors' room was located on the ground floor. After unwrapping a multicoloured striped scarf from around his neck, he perched his slender frame on the edge of the uncomfortable orange plastic chair across from mine, then leaned forwards and breathily introduced himself.

"*Monsieur*, so good of you to agree to meet me. I'm Marcel Giresse."

I couldn't recall the last time anyone had called me *mon-sieur*—prisoners weren't afforded that luxury. As we shook hands across the table, his hand smaller than mine, soft and cool, his blue eyes studied me owlishly from behind wire-framed spectacles. In spite of myself, and not entirely sure why, I was mildly intrigued by him. Possibly, it was his slightly flustered air or the way he curled the edge of the scarf around his fingers. Or perhaps because his pale face with its delicate features, framed by haphazardly cut glossy black hair, was extremely pretty. Even so, I had no intention of making this easy for him. I acknowledged his polite greeting with a curt nod.

"Guillaume Guilbaud, how do you do. I've been incarcerated for fourteen years, eight months, and three days. Before answering any of your questions, I have some of my own. Why has the Ministry of Justice sent its director of finance to visit me?"

My tone pitched somewhere between accusatory and defiant. I wasn't the most intimidating inmate in here—far from it—but outsiders were generally wary, and my criminal record spoke for itself. Yet this guy only fidgeted some more on the unforgiving plastic seat and surprised me with a delighted, genuine smile.

"Oh, we're starting with the easy questions!"

In a conspiratorial fashion, he leaned even closer. "It's a rather odd one this. Let me explain. I spend an awful amount of time with my niece, Clara, who is eight, by the way, and super bright. She quite rightly pointed out to me recently, 'Uncle Marcel, how can you possibly allocate the budget appropriately if you've never actually met any of the prisoners? After all, they will know more than anyone where the money is needed the most.'"

He relayed this in a high-pitched, little-girl voice, which threw me slightly. Thankfully, he quickly returned to his own deeper, refined tones.

"And do you know, Monsieur? It occurred to me she was absolutely correct. But, let's keep that little bit of truthfulness between us, yes? It can't get out that I make national policy decisions based on the insight of my eight-year-old niece."

Hitching his glasses up his nose, he continued, "Mind you, perhaps I should consult her more often as, let's be frank, she's come up with a more sensible proposal than I've heard at any of the dreary board meetings I've had to attend. Don't you agree?"

Whoa, who the hell was this guy? I'd been anticipating a nervous pen-pusher in a dull suit, clutching a clipboard, not some anti-establishment beatnik with startlingly clear blue-grey eyes. And he was still talking.

"I'd like to take this opportunity to apologise right now for the sheer arrogance of all my predecessors in assuming they can make decisions about you, without you! And you have my assurance that I have instructed my juniors to pay visits to other long-term inmates over the coming months, at a variety of penitentiaries around the country, so that I'll have a range of views prior to making my recommendations. Not only your personal insight, though I sense that yours will be as valuable as anyone's."

Was that the end of the spiel? Could I get a word in edgeways? Seemingly not.

He paused, only very briefly, in order to hitch his glasses up his nose again with the knuckle of his left hand.

"So, on seeking the prison governor's recommendation regarding whom to visit, he suggested you immediately because

a) you hardly have visitors, b) you have been stuck here a dreadfully long time, and c) because—ah…his words, not mine, so forgive the rather indelicate use of language—because you… are…ah, 'one of the few fucking blokes in here who can hold a decent conversation, and that includes the staff too'."

The profanity sounded so wrong coming out of his pretty mouth, and he winced as he said it. After he'd listed each point, reeling them off on his fingers, he then added apologetically, "But I have to say, the prison officer who showed me in seemed awfully pleasant and quite capable of chatting, albeit on a superficial level."

His speech came to an end, and he sat back, seemingly exhausted.

Somewhere in between leaving his plush Paris office and travelling down to the island, he must have lost the memo on political evasiveness. I hadn't needed to look up to see which officer had shown him in and was observing us with interest from the doorway—Antoine always had an eye for pretty men, despite being married with two children. Something I knew as well as anyone. Slightly off my stride, I had a further question for him.

"Your surname is Giresse. Are you related to Alain Giresse?"

He wouldn't have been expecting that curve ball, but still, he displayed neither surprise nor wariness. I must have lost my touch; I could strike the fear of God into some of the newer inmates with only a firm stare.

"Now, Guillaume. Ah…may I call you Guillaume? You must call me Marcel. Monsieur Giresse has me imagining the ghost of my dead father looming over my shoulder."

I found myself nodding in acquiescence, slightly bewildered.

"This is more interesting. Alain Giresse. Hmm. My aforementioned father has an extensive family tree, plotted back to circa 1800, which I can draw for you if you would like me to, at least, branching out to the first cousin of each generation. Any further, and I confess I would have to consult the copy in my desk drawer. But I'm afraid, unless I'm mistaken, which would be unusual to say the least because my memory rarely fails me, your friend Alain and I are not closely linked. So, no, I conclude that this particular Giresse and I are not related."

"He's not my friend," I pointed out. "He's a famous footballer, three times French player of the year in the 1980s, and an attacking midfielder for Marseilles. I asked because your surname isn't that common, that's all."

Having planned my surly opening gambit, my even surlier follow-up responses, and several sarcastic put-downs smattered in between, I was rapidly losing control of the conversation. He regarded me apologetically.

"Oh, I'm terribly sorry for my ignorance; I don't know anything about football. Never even watched a match from start to finish, I don't think. But I'm happy to give it a try if you think it will assist me in understanding you better."

A further adjustment of the glasses up his nose, accompanied by a hamster-like twitch and another guileless smile. Determined to regain the upper hand, I tried a different tack.

"I'm wary of visitors, Marcel Giresse, so I've done my homework on you. Thirty-six years old and born near Versailles, you are the youngest person since 1945 to hold such a senior position in the French civil service. Your wealthy parents, now deceased, educated you at Eton in England, where you excelled, thus ensuring you were trilingual from an early age as your mother was of German descent. You then completed a degree at the Sorbonne in what can only be described as rather tricky sums, gaining the highest score ever recorded in the final paper before winning a scholarship to study economics—some even trickier sums I imagine—at Harvard, where you also won the academic prize before BNP and Amundi headhunted you. You declined both offers, taking up a position with Intrexis in London instead.

"After five years—during which time you were credited with increasing the value of Intrexis's worth by 200 per cent when they floated on the London Stock Exchange, securing yourself a small fortune in the process—you turned your back on the financial markets and took up a position within the civil service, where you steadily climbed to your current lofty heights. Not surprisingly, on your present trajectory, you are tipped to be Head of the Civil Service before you reach forty. You have never married and have no children. Your academic citations are lengthy and frequently quoted by others. Congratulations, Marcel Giresse, on being dealt such an exceedingly good hand in life."

If he was at all shocked by my background checks on him, and my withering put-down at the end, he hid it well.

"Oh, I love these sorts of games, Guillaume! My turn!"

Wriggling in his seat as if settling in, accompanied by another push of the glasses, he continued.

"You, Monsieur, are Guillaume Guilbaud, aged thirty-eight. You were born and brought up in L'Estaque district of Marseilles by your mother, Claire, who is half-Moroccan. Your Tunisian father left home when you were three, and I believe you haven't had any contact with him since. Your older cousin,

Bruno, took you to the local football club from an early age, where you quickly excelled, eventually leaving school at sixteen to play for second division Nîmes Olympique. You had trials for Olympique de Marseilles, which, I have learned, is a prominent first division club. On the cusp of signing a three-year contract, you returned home from training one day to find your mother's boyfriend allegedly raping your youngest sister, who was only fourteen. The following day, you killed him with a blow to the head and subsequent strangulation. There were witnesses to your attack; the rape was difficult to prove as your sister has learning difficulties, and you were sentenced to fifteen years in prison for first-degree murder."

He smiled at me gently. "Did I leave out anything important?"

This stranger, with his soft breathy voice and delicate features, was unlike anyone I had ever encountered. In three simple sentences, he had summarised the single, most defining event of my life. Without a trace of accusation, pity, hatred, or even fear at being in the presence of a cold-blooded killer. He could have been recounting my professional career highlights, as I had done to him.

Returning his smile with a faint one of my own, my voice broke slightly as I answered his question.

"No, Monsieur Giresse. I think you have…succinctly covered everything."

"Then I am so terribly, terribly sorry that, in contrast to me, you have been dealt such an exceedingly bad hand in life, Guillaume. While it is too late for you, as your sentence is nearly at an end, I hope very much to do everything within my power to improve the lot of many others who have been dealt such a bad hand. That when they have served their time and paid their dues, the French state does all it can to ensure they re-enter the world equipped to forge competent, law-abiding lives."

If it were only that simple.

"Why have you come all this way to ask me my views on failings in the French penitentiary system? Could you not have picked someone in a prison closer to home?"

He laughed easily. "Any closer to home and you would be living on my front doorstep!"

My confusion no doubt showed on my face. I had been informed that morning that a very senior figure from the Ministry of Justice was coming from Paris to talk to me. Why the point of where he lived was bothering me more than the fact that he was here at all was as strange as the whole situation. As if reading my mind, he explained further.

"My home is here on the island, about a ten-minute walk from the prison, though I have to commute up to Paris fairly frequently. Those infernally dull board meetings I mentioned."

He smiled at my raised eyebrows. "It is unusual, I know, but I am given…ah…a degree of leeway, probably on account of my uncanny ability to perform those really tricky sums you alluded to better than anyone else. And also because of my, ah…uncanny disability."

I found myself smiling back, even if I couldn't for the life of me fathom what his disability could be, and I was damned if I was going to ask. He'd walked into the room unaided, and his ears and eyes appeared to be in excellent working order, especially his eyes, which were a hypnotically brilliant blue-grey behind the thin glass lenses. And his brain was obviously tip-top too.

"So what do you want to know?" I asked coolly.

He laughed. "Oh, my goodness, where do I start? You are the expert on failings in the French justice system, not me."

I was no less immune to flattery as the next man, particularly when the flatterer was so pretty. I endeavoured not to show it, but I hadn't set eyes on a man as cute as him since my friend Reuben graced the prison cells. Buying myself a few seconds of thinking time, I let my gaze roam the visitors' room.

"Okay, Monsieur Giresse. Why don't we start here, in this room? You were right when you mentioned that I don't receive many visitors. We'll come to that in a moment. But the man sitting to our right—" I pointed to a young Somalian prisoner at the next table gesticulating wildly to a nervous-looking woman opposite him. She balanced a grizzling baby on her lap while a grubby toddler of indeterminate sex crawled at her feet.

"That man is named Asad. He is the father of three children. His family live less than an hour away and would like to visit him more often. Whatever bad he has done, he would like to be a part of their lives; he loves his children. Pictures of them cover the walls of his cell; he phones whenever he can. He is entitled to three visits per week, each lasting up to an hour, in addition to a six-hour private visit in a family room three times a year. So far in the last twelve months, he has had one four-hour stay in a family room—supervised by a guard and not private—and his wife has been allowed to come here once a week. Did you know that only 22 per cent of prisoners achieve their allocated visiting hours?"

I sat back, folding my arms, eyeing him. Once again, if my aggressive approach flustered him, he didn't show it. On the contrary, he leaned forwards and frowned slightly.

"If I'm not mistaken, you have taken your figures from the 2016 report by the European Prison Observatory; I have access to the more up-to-date ones—not yet published—which show the data to be much worse, I'm afraid."

He adjusted his glasses before continuing. "The reasons for the decline are multifactorial, which is an explanation but not an excuse. Believe me, I am not here to make excuses."

After jotting something on a lined pad in indecipherable loopy handwriting, he looked up at me.

"I think the reason you don't have visitors is multifactorial, too, but I'm guessing one major inhibitor is that your mother lives 850 kilometres away and is now in her late sixties. Am I wrong?"

Staring at him, I debated how to respond. Should I continue with polite verbal sparring and pretend some of this would make a difference? Or should I terminate the interview and walk away? Because it just became a little too personal, and to survive somewhere like this, personal is not up for discussion. But this sweetly odd man, with his kind eyes and lofty ambition, was a world apart from the guys in here, and I'd probably never see him again anyway.

"Monsieur Giresse, there are many men like me. Over a quarter of sentenced prisoners are housed more than 100 kilometres from family. And when your family is already a smidgen ashamed of you, to say the least, an expensive journey across France to spend an hour sitting with someone you thought you knew but obviously didn't, and having a total stranger monitor your conversation anyway, well, it all becomes a bit of an effort. My family abandoned me several years ago."

He regarded me carefully for a moment, the bitterness in my voice all too apparent.

"Monsieur, I cannot even begin to imagine how that must feel, how you must feel, after all this time. And I am sorry your family no longer wishes to see you. But I want you to help me to try to understand so I may help others. Like Asad over there, for instance."

Mentioning my family, my mother especially, had been too much. I stood abruptly. Feelings I'd pushed aside for so many years threatened to surface.

"Can we continue some other time? I'm…I'm done for today."

He stood, too, putting out his hand for me to shake again. "It would be my pleasure, Guillaume. You have given me much food for thought."

I held his hand a little longer than necessary, wanting a last look at those eyes and that mouth. Now the interview was over, I was sorry I'd terminated it. He hitched his glasses up awkwardly.

"You…ah, you…you're not as…ah, rough as I was expecting," he blurted, and his cheeks turned a delicate shade of pink. "Sorry, that sounded dreadfully rude."

I winked at him. "I can be rougher if that's how you like it?"

Fuck, where did that come from? I didn't wink at blokes, especially posh blokes from the Ministry of Justice. And I certainly didn't come out with lines like that! If he was blushing before, it was nothing compared to the positively crimson flush on his face now. I made a desperate attempt to cover my tracks.

"What I mean is we're not all rough. Don't assume that because we're criminals. My mum didn't have much money, but she brought us up right. I nearly didn't play football professionally at all; I was planning on college until Nîmes wanted me."

Even to my own ears, I sounded lame. Why the fuck did I feel the need to explain myself to this posh stranger? I carried on anyway.

"My upbringing isn't to blame for…for what I did. That was all me. And only me."

A lump of shame in my throat prevented me saying anything further. Without a backwards glance, I strode away.

Predictably, Antoine was waiting for me as I returned to my cell, all leery smiles and nudge-nudge wink-wink. He was an attractive man—tall and trim, with an easy smile. He'd been a guard here for around four years, and most of the time, I was quite pleased to see him. Already having got rid of the guy with whom I was currently sharing, he locked the door firmly behind both of us.

"Not quite my type, Guille, but I know your tastes by now. That posh bloke ticks all your boxes. Fancy sucking me off to get rid of that build-up of sexual tension?"

That's not what Antoine wanted at all; I knew him too well. My strange meeting with the peculiar Monsieur Giresse, however, had left me in an equally peculiar mood and, yes, vaguely turned on. I decided to indulge him.

"How about, Antoine, you kneel at my feet, and I let you choose your current favourite scenario?"

Sometimes I wondered how the hell I had got involved with Antoine, and then I reminded myself that he gave truly excellent head. If, in order to receive it, I had to growl at him in my most evil, criminal voice that he was a very bad boy and should be at home with his wife and kids, then so be it. It was a harmless kink, and one to which I was usually amenable, although achieving maximum pleasure while simultaneously fake reprimanding a grown man was sometimes a challenge.

Today we were playing naughty vicars. Shit, not one of my favourites. Theology and homosexuality weren't natural bedfellows.

I pushed my jeans down as he knelt at my feet and got to it.

"You pretend to be the bishop, Guille," he breathed around his licking and coaxing. *God, this man has a good tongue.* "I'll be a young verger that you caught pinching money from the collection box."

Christ, whatever. Having given his instructions, Antoine stopped talking and concentrated on the job at hand, going deep effortlessly. The hectoring words fell easily from my lips as he expertly started bringing me to climax, his own hand flying over his cock.

"You know what I do to naughty, thieving vergers, don't you?" I began in my most spiteful voice, cringing even as my balls tightened. In these weird moments, I found it helpful to channel my inner brute. "I strip them and whip their naked arses with the leather belt of my cassock until they cry out my name and beg me to stop."

I was only peripherally aware of Antoine's responding moans of ecstasy around my cock. To be fair, we'd done this scene a few times, and I'd honed my script, so I could mostly switch off and concentrate on the fabulous feel of my shaft in his hot, slippery mouth. The one thing they can't control in prison is your thoughts; I used to drum that into Reuben.

Which was a good thing because, right now, the head bobbing up and down on my cock didn't belong to a pleasant yet sexually confused blond prison officer but to a sharp-eyed, breathy, slender civil servant wearing mismatching clothes and a shy smile.

Antoine hung around for a while afterwards, which was unusual. Sitting on the bed, he fidgeted while I cleaned up.

"You all right?" I asked when it was clear he wasn't going to leave any time soon.

"Yeah," he nodded. "Thanks, that was perfect. Particularly when you threatened to tie me up with a bell rope."

He coughed nervously. "I…er…I wanted to ask you something."

I raised my eyebrows expectantly. We'd chatted over the years about this and that, nothing in particular. I knew he was bisexual, although I was uncertain anyone else did, and I knew he was unhappy in his marriage and wanted out. In his turn, he knew I missed Reuben, had lost touch with my family in Marseilles, and didn't have a clue what I was going to do when I was released.

"There's a coaching job for you at Saint-Martin football club if you want it. When you get your marching orders. The men's team. A couple of the guys who work here suggested I ask you."

The main town on the island, Saint-Martin, was still very small, and the prison stood at the edge of it. Our inmate football team had thrashed the local men's team. I sat down on the opposite bed and rested my elbows on my knees. We avoided eye contact.

"And my cousin runs the PMU bar on the port front. He could get you a few shifts there too. Between us, we could easily find you somewhere to live."

I said nothing for a moment. So far, my plans after my release extended to visiting Reuben for a couple of weeks and, afterwards, perhaps heading back to Marseilles. Or maybe another big city. Staying here on the island hadn't occurred to me.

"Can I think about it?"

He looked relieved. "Yeah, sure, take your time."

Chapter Two

Marcel

Oh, my goodness! A real, live murderer winked at me! And I might be dreadfully out of practice, but even I recognise sexual innuendo. My cheeks heated again at the memory. I should have delegated this type of thing to my junior colleagues and stayed at my desk. Computers don't flirt.

The prisoner, Guillaume Giresse, was not what I had expected at all. Demonstrating precisely how I needed to quash my preconceived ideas in order to make sensible allocations regarding my enormous budget responsibilities. Guillaume was clearly highly intelligent, and I was flabbergasted when he parroted my background to me in that musical southern accent, although I hoped I hid my surprise by continuing to prattle on. Handsome, too, not that I dwelt much on that sort of thing these days, but I admired his form, much as I might admire a life drawing or a Renaissance sculpture.

Lean, strong, and very athletic-looking, his physique fit with his history as a professional footballer and his ongoing coaching of the prison team. His neatly cut, thick hair, roughly hewn cheekbones and strong nose were only eclipsed by his striking and watchful dark eyes, gilded by impossibly long black eyelashes. The North African heritage from both his parents was evident in his smooth brown skin. As we talked, I tried to subtly decipher the swirls of a tattoo reaching up from his shoulder to his neck while also trying not to be distracted by flashes of his silver tongue stud.

I had imagined I'd find him intimidating, and he was, up to a point. Proven murderers probably have that effect on most people, and he had done his level best to ignore my warm overtures. I planned to persist, however, because his sharpness would be to my advantage.

My island home was fabulous. Friends have told me I have the best location on the Ile de Ré. As I strolled around the quaint port, past fishing boats on one side and brightly coloured cafés and restaurants on the other, I struggled to disagree. It was bizarre that this ever-popular holiday destination was also home to one of our country's largest prisons, but that was how history evolved sometimes. One hundred years ago, the star-shaped fortress was temporary housing for convicts awaiting deportation to French overseas territories. After the abolition of deportation, it morphed into more permanent accommodation, over the years developing into the huge prison complex from which I'd returned. The prison authority's attempts at disguising the buildings as government offices were so impressive most tourists had no idea it existed, even as they stood on the front lawns photographing the imposing architecture. And it was certainly never mentioned in guidebooks.

My three-storey stone house stood at one end of the port, with splendid views across the small harbour towards the city of La Rochelle on the French mainland. The same friends who adored my house, also warned me I was mad to buy somewhere so grand and tall, what with my health problems, but I bought it anyway and haven't regretted it for a second. Even if I did sometimes have to crawl up the stairs on my hands and knees.

Humming as I let myself in via the wrought-iron gates, I was slightly out of breath, but not unpleasantly so. As I wandered through to the kitchen, I was pleased to see that my sister had made use of her key and was rummaging through the fridge. My niece, Clara—she of the precocious interest in prisoner's welfare—was colouring at the kitchen table and gave me a gap-toothed grin.

My older sister, Sabine, had insisted on her own key to my home ever since I'd suffered a serious hospital admission several years ago, and being a bossy deputy headteacher, she'd got her way. Most of the time, I haven't minded, especially on days like this when she'd refilled my freezer with home-cooked dinners for one.

"You sound happy," she remarked, standing straighter to look at me properly. I must have passed muster, as she nodded with satisfaction. "And you have some colour in your cheeks."

"I am happy," I declared, ruffling Clara's hair. "I took this young lady's advice and arranged an interview with a prisoner. It was extraordinary! He was extraordinary! He's called Guillaume, and I'm going back next week to visit him again."

"Why's he in prison?" asked Clara, casting her colouring aside and carefully recapping her felt-tip pen.

I shook my head. She might be the smartest eight-year-old I'd ever encountered, but I wasn't about to divulge the horrid details of Guillaume's crime.

"I'm not allowed to tell you, I'm afraid, *ma chérie*. Top secret."

Unimpressed, Clara selected another felt-tip and resumed colouring.

"What made him extraordinary?" Sabine asked as I followed her into my study and watched idly as she began tidying up.

"I'm not sure, really," I mused, settling at my desk. "I think perhaps his thoughtfulness—about his life and the lives of other prisoners. And that he'd researched me beforehand."

"That's a bit creepy."

"No. It didn't come over as creepy. It was sensible really. After all, I'd come to his home with a long list of questions and expected a welcome."

"And did you get one?"

I thought back to Guillaume's forceful dark gaze as we shook hands. "Yes, I think so."

For the next hour or so, Sabine pleasantly fussed over me, and I equally pleasantly ignored her, already replaying my meeting with Guillaume in my head. I was itching to make some notes, desperate to immerse myself in those tricky sums, devise spreadsheets, create projections—indulge in all the stuff that got me off, to put it bluntly. So if I sounded like an incompetent adult by allowing my sister to cook for me, and generally check up on me each day, then it was because I totally was.

For me, real work meant choosing which breakfast cereal to eat, making small talk with the gardener, remembering to pay the electricity bill on time, taking my varied medications. In contrast, fun time was opening up my laptop, creating bar charts, becoming lost in the world of Excel and two-tailed

Mann-Whitney U-tests, floating away on a wave of economic manipulations. Sabine fell into the role of caregiver because she worried incessantly about my health and whether I'd bothered to cook a square meal over a bank holiday weekend. Whereas I wasn't playing a role at all. This was me, in all my happily inadequate glory. One boyfriend, years ago, when on his way out of the door, suitcase in hand, had moaned that my brain cells were so focussed on higher plane economics they didn't have any energy left for the mundane day to day, which he sensed included him. And anyone else who had auditioned for that position in my life since.

Disappearing into my studies, I scarcely noticed when Sabine planted a kiss on my cheek and made to leave, promising to call me tomorrow.

"Have you set your alarm for dinner?"

I nodded in the affirmative, still engrossed in the laptop screen in front of me.

"And for eleven tonight?"

I nodded again, absentmindedly. Her voice was annoying, like a mosquito buzzing around my head. I made a Herculean effort not to show it. After patting my shoulder and calling to Clara, she walked away.

"Simon says he's popping in tomorrow too. Be nice to him! Text him beforehand if you want any groceries from Intermarché."

I groaned as the front door closed behind her.

Not closed enough, evidently.

"I heard that, Marcel! And Dominic is coming over for chess on Wednesday!"

Double groan.

"I heard that too!"

Not only did my sister feel the need to ensure I ate, slept, and changed my underwear at generally acceptable intervals, she'd also recruited some clean, single, homosexual men to keep an eye on me, too, in the hope I'd fall madly in love with one of them, and they'd take me off her hands. But she must have unwittingly selected a dating agency exclusively for creeps and people with odd grooming habits because celibacy was infinitely preferable to either of her two current protégés. Simon had stalkerish tendencies—giving him a key when I was last discharged from hospital had been a monumental mistake, and Dominic, sweetie that he was, sported a thick monobrow and...

"You need to see beyond that hairy wart, Marcel. And the eyebrow thing! Don't be so superficial!"

Silence at last, broken only by my contented humming and my fingers tapping on the laptop keys. Occasionally, I succumbed to the urge to rock in my chair, something I only did when I was in a really good mood. And alone. People didn't need to discover I was any more peculiar than they already believed.

When the first of Sabine's alarms sounded at 7:00 p.m., I obediently heated up a portion of spaghetti bolognese and imbibed a glass of orange juice before returning to my work. Following the second alarm at eleven, I took my medication, did the bathroom stuff, and got into my pyjamas. With the midnight alarm, I laid aside my current choice of light reading, *Microeconomics of Complex Economies (First edition)*, and extinguished the light.

Chapter Three

Guillaume

Despite the ungodly hour and cooler weather, attendance at early morning football practice was better than expected, I thought as I packed away the training gear. When the boys focused properly, we were a decent side, runners-up in the local league last year. Naturally, the opposition teams moaned about home advantage, seeing as, for obvious reasons, we never played any of our matches away. I'd coached and played pretty much since the day I arrived, and while it wasn't exactly Olympique de Marseilles, coaching kept me occupied. And, more importantly, fit. As I was no longer the spring chicken of fourteen years ago, some of the younger lads had worked out they could give me the runaround.

"I'm invigorated from merely watching you," said a refined voice. Looking up, I spied Marcel Giresse beaming at me from his seated position on one of the benches lining the pitch. He'd looped that colourful scarf around his neck once again, the rest of him bundled up in an expensive-looking, long charcoal-grey woollen coat, exactly the sort I would expect a businessman of his status to wear. The tatty pair of Adidas gazelles and mismatching socks poking out from underneath slightly ruined the debonair look.

"Visitors aren't usually allowed this far in," I responded, aware of two prison officers watching our interaction with interest and subtly ensuring some of the more 'forceful' inmates left him alone.

"Oh, I pulled a few strings. I'm quite important, you know."

This last comment was delivered in a false whisper, heavily laden with irony, and I smiled back at him despite myself.

"I asked if I could have a tour of the prison and suggested that one of the longer-term inmates conduct it. I, ah…I may even have mentioned you by name. My delightful new friends here—" He nodded his head towards the guards. "—can clarify that you have permission to join me for the next hour. Free range over the campus; I'm informed you are a low-security threat, what with being only a few weeks away from walking out the front door forever and all."

"Campus!" I snorted. "That's a new one on me. You make it sound like a university."

"I think, Guillaume, you'll find it's the Ministry's preferred term for an establishment such as this," he replied snootily, then ruined the effect by giggling. For a brief moment, I wondered if the chief minister for justice had any idea about the man behind the brain whom he employed.

"Do I have time for a quick shower first?"

As if to compound my theory, and out of earshot of the guards, Marcel murmured, "I could make so many comments about hot, sweaty men, but I shall manfully refrain for the sake of my professional status."

And in a much louder tone, "Of course, Guillaume, go right ahead."

I was on the verge of giggling myself as, fuck, he'd just blown his professional status big time. And he'd confirmed my assumption that he was gay, not only from the lack of kids and a wife but because he was too damned pretty to waste on women.

Freshly showered and changed into a tracksuit in record time, I found Marcel exactly where I'd left him, no doubt charming his escorts. We fell into step, and I began the tour with an overview of the whole 'campus' from the highest point of the recreational area, which was up a set of stone steps, originally part of the inner walls of the citadel. He surprised me by taking my arm.

"I hope you don't mind; my chest is quite tight this morning—it's the cold air. I would also appreciate if we could… ah…walk a little slower? It's rather a bore, but I'm not very good with stairs."

After fishing in his overcoat pocket, he withdrew a blue inhaler and took a couple of puffs. Not knowing how to respond, I kept quiet, and we resumed a slower pace. Any lurking snails would have overtaken us.

However, the slow pace gave us an opportunity to talk, and one thing I had begun to realise was that Marcel loved to chat. And that I hugely enjoyed his company.

Marcel declared the prison had been a source of fascination for him ever since he'd made the island his home several years earlier.

"Tell me, Guillaume, how does this beautiful island, with its reputation as a holiday haunt for the rich and famous, manage to perform such a sleight of hand as to hide a prison in plain sight? It's always puzzled me."

A rhetorical question, he shrugged his shoulders. "Most of the tourists don't know of its existence, even though they wander the grounds and pet the donkeys grazing on the lawns. It towers over Saint-Martin port, yet no one has any idea that behind its stone walls are four hundred of France's most dangerous criminals!"

He went on to describe how, on entering Saint-Martin by road, signposts pointed to the majestic seventeenth-century citadel, home to all those aforementioned prisoners. Visitors were encouraged to stroll the grounds and admire the turrets, the fortified harbour views, the huge earthen dykes that bore witness to the island's chequered military history. I'd have to take his word for it; I'd travelled along that road only a handful of times—once when I arrived in a prison van at night, and another memorable occasion as I lay in agony, strapped to a stretcher in the back of an ambulance, having dislocated my shoulder on landing heavily after a rather fierce football tackle. During none of journeys was admiring the scenery a high priority.

That was not to say I had never left the prison at all. In the last few months, they'd let me out a few times on expeditions laughably described as part of my gradual rehabilitation into society. I was about as prepared to re-enter society as a three-year-old child starting high school. They'd permitted a select group of us to walk into Saint-Martin—discreetly escorted, of course, so as not to draw attention. We'd even had a round of drinks in a bar down one of the cobbled side streets and enjoyed an ice cream from the huge parlour on the port. Hell, I might even have walked past Marcel's house.

"But a penitentiary sheltered behind the citadel's high walls?" he continued animatedly. "Who would believe such a thing?" He shrugged. "Sure, there are signs saying, Ministry of Justice and No Entry and Private Property. But very few tourists, after a bottle of Rosé des Dunes and a plate of oysters, will join the dots."

I'd never thought of any of this before, and I enjoyed hearing his conspiracy theories as to why the prison had succeeded in maintaining utter discretion.

"The last seven prison governors all have homes on the island," he declared with a hint of mischief. "None of them would imperil the value of their extortionately priced properties by allowing dissent amongst the prison staff, let alone the prisoners themselves! Hence, the staff here are paid better than their compatriots in other institutions so they don't complain loudly. And though you may disagree—and knowing you, my friend, no doubt you will—statistically, the conditions for prisoners are better here than on other 'campuses' too."

He was right; I wasn't going to let that comment go. A heated exchange followed as we perambulated around the grounds, occasionally stopping so I could point out particular facilities, or lack of them. Thanks to the two officers following us at a discreet distance, we were not interrupted by any inmates; nevertheless, we received our fair share of curious looks and whistles, especially as Marcel still clung to my arm. He quoted facts and figures, I lobbed back a few of my own, and we finally reached the prison library.

"The source of all my facts and figures," I said, seeing the shabby room and its paltry collection of books as if through the eyes of a stranger. I'd instilled in Reuben the importance of knowledge and education if he wanted to make a life for himself after prison. I'd taken my own advice and read almost every word of every book in this room, several more than once. Though I'd made him read the newspapers with me, Reuben had stuck mostly to carpentry and gardening books. This musty room felt as close to a home as anywhere. "It's not much, but it's better than nothing."

Back on even ground, and his breathing steady, I reluctantly disentangled my arm from my companion's.

"It may be small," observed Marcel, "but it has served you well. You are articulate and informed."

He hesitated, chewing on his lip. The guards waited outside, gossiping to each other.

"You have impressed me very much, Guillaume. You give me a lot to think about and have changed my perceptions massively. Thank you for that."

His easy praise shouldn't have affected me as much as it did. Feeling myself reddening, I turned away, gesturing to the shelving.

"This room is much smaller than the recommended size for a prison library and has fewer books, too, though they are changed reasonably frequently. There should be ten books per prisoner and a copy of a current newspaper between twenty, which is a joke."

I shrugged. "To be honest, size is unimportant as very few of us use the library anyway. And there are actually enough newspapers as only a handful of us can read them. Many inmates do not have French as a first language, and I can't recall ever seeing a foreign language book or newspaper on the shelves."

Sighing heavily, Marcel patted my shoulder. "It is too late in the day to embark on a discussion regarding education, Guillaume. Rest assured, I'll be fascinated to hear more of your thoughts when we do. Next time, perhaps? Our tour has worn me out."

He glanced at his watch. "Can we walk back via the living quarters, please? We have enough time, and it's the only area I've yet to visit."

After a brief discussion with the two, by now, very bored officers, it was agreed we could walk through Block D, which would be mostly empty as it was their staggered mealtime. The older officer gave Marcel a quick lesson in how to negotiate the double sets of security doors and advised him to avoid eye contact and not to respond to abuse should he receive any.

"They can be unpredictable with strangers," he warned darkly. "We had a Sikh electrician in recently, doing something with the lighting. We passed a couple of guys playing pool, as calm as you like, and as we walked by, one of them, out of nowhere, grabbed him and yanked off his turban. Scared the living daylights out of him—and me."

Marcel nodded anxiously, wordlessly taking up my arm again. His fingers curled pleasantly around my bicep.

We paused outside an empty cell as Marcel took in the ragged posters, a pile of dirty laundry, paltry toiletries, and a worn, grey towel. With a neutral expression, he studied the two narrow beds topped with grubby, thin duvets.

"Is yours like this?" he asked in a low voice.

I nodded. "Almost identical. I'm much tidier though. The guy I'm sharing with at the moment doesn't have much stuff either."

He gave my arm a quick squeeze. "I'm so sorry for you, Guillaume. I'm glad you're getting out soon."

Continuing the tour, we followed the stink to the depressing toilet block and the grimy open shower stalls. Marcel wrinkled his nose as we walked along a row of toilet cubicles. None of them had doors, many had towels draped across the opening instead, makeshift attempts at privacy. Not a bog roll in sight.

"Is this…ah, do you…what I mean is, do you have anywhere more private for…ah, you know, a proper trip to the loo?" he asked, blushing slightly.

I laughed. "Nope, this is it. For shitting and shagging."

I'd embarrassed him with my crudeness and immediately wished I hadn't. For some reason, I desperately wanted him to think well of me.

"Goodness, you probably think I'm dreadfully naïve, don't you, Guillaume?"

I glanced across at him, still wrapped up in his thick scarf and expensive coat. "You are very naïve," I replied. "It's nice that you can be. In some ways, you remind me of a friend I once had in here. He was naïve too."

Marcel frowned. "You, ah, you mentioned, ah, shagging. Sorry, but I…ah, have I misunderstood something?"

I shook my head gravely. "No, no misunderstanding. It's a popular pastime. Toilets are the best place for it; spread a towel across the front of the cubicle, shut your eyes, and try to ignore the stench."

He winced, but his eyes widened. "And do you, ah…have you…?" He stopped. "Sorry, I'm so sorry. It's none of my business. Let's carry on."

"I don't mind answering," I said, surprising him. "You're here on a factfinding mission—you might as well find out about everything that goes on here. And the answer is yes, I do, and no, I don't. I don't do it here in the toilets. I have a… um…a more hygienic arrangement with one of the prison officers. It's to our mutual benefit."

Marcel gave the toilets a last horrified look. "Again, it's really not any of my onions, as my niece would say, but I'm glad to hear it."

He sounded relieved on my behalf, which was nice. "So, ah, are you a, ah…a homosexual?"

Faggot, poof, shit stabber, bum bandit. No, I couldn't imagine any of those terms on Marcel's lips.

"I've had both," I replied shortly. "I had girlfriends prior to being here. I probably favour men more."

"Is he nice?"

"Who?"

"Your prison officer."

I exhaled deeply and shrugged. "He's willing, available, and clean. And married and confused. We're sort of friends. As I said, mutually satisfying, that's all."

We'd reached the end of the row, and the two officers were making noises suggesting we move it along. Marcel and I parted company outside the visitors' room.

"I've arranged one more visit. I want to discuss educational opportunities with you. I don't know the exact date, but it will be before you leave at the end of the month."

I smirked. "It will be a short conversation. There aren't really any."

"Then we shall talk about something else, Guillaume. Conversation with you flows very easily."

He had an extremely sweet smile, not shy exactly, but almost tentative and slightly mischievous. We shook hands, and if he held mine for a fraction longer than necessary, I wasn't complaining.

"It's odd to think you have lived here, about two hundred metres away from me, for all these years," he remarked softly. "We're practically neighbours. Look after yourself, Guillaume."

"You, too, Marcel."

Chapter Four

Marcel

The vast gulf between the ragged prison toilet block and the picturesque port of Saint-Martin, merely a stone's throw away, would be impossible to comprehend unless I had seen it with my own eyes. The air seemed cleaner out here too. I'd left the prison complex wishing I could whisk Guillaume away with me. I'd bring him to my home, and we'd sit together at the kitchen table. Maybe I'd prepare him a meal, and afterwards, we would take a stroll and share a *café gourmand* in one of the port cafés. Two old friends enjoying each other's company on a cool sunny day.

Even if I could spirit him over the prison walls, my flight of fancy was ridiculous. Not least because I couldn't cook.

Simon was in my kitchen, ostensibly checking through my cupboards to see what I needed from the supermarket but more likely using it as an excuse to loiter and poke around. For the hundredth time, I wished I had the fortitude to ask for my keys back. Keen to disappear to my study and lose myself in work, it now looked like that would have to wait. He made a show of regarding me critically.

"Overdoing it again, Marcel? You look peaky."

"Hello, Simon. Nice to see you too."

Nothing irritated me more than constant references to my health, as though that was the sum of my entire existence on this earth. I could have retorted that he looked sour-faced, but that would have been childish and confrontational. When the occasion called for it, I could be extremely childish, but confrontation exhausted me, thus I tended to avoid it.

"I'm fine. Frightfully busy, that's all. And I've had a rather brisk—well, brisk for me—walk back from the prison. The breeze was against me."

He sniffed. "I hope you stayed away from those ghastly inmates. They'll be harbouring all sorts of strange germs. You can't afford to catch anything, not with the state of your chest at this time of year."

"My chest is fine," I snapped. "And I've spent the last hour or so with a very clean, helpful, intelligent man, so I'd rather you didn't refer to the inmates that way. Not everybody has had our advantages in life."

Simon rolled his eyes. "You and your bleeding heart, Marcel. Whatever shall we do with you?"

Stop being so dreadfully patronising, and get out of my house, for starters, I thought, but I bit my tongue. My kitchen smelled of coffee from the recent *grand crème* he had brewed for himself, and a used dinner plate and empty coffee cup sat as evidence, next to the sink.

Simon worked as a freelance journalist, and from the parlous state of his finances, not a very good one. Scrounging food from me had become the norm, although I was too polite, or arguably too weak, to mention it.

"I picked up your dry cleaning, Marcel," he stated, noticing the direction of my pointed gaze. His subtle way of reminding me that I needed him, ergo, it was perfectly fine for him to make himself at home. Comments like this were usually delivered after I had achieved something without his assistance, such as my pleasant stroll back from the prison.

"The bill came to seventy-five euros, if you have the cash."

I could easily afford it; however, I couldn't help thinking that dry cleaning was becoming more expensive by the week. It felt churlish to ask him to provide receipts; we were supposed to be friends after all. And he checked up on me almost daily, albeit in a way I disliked but kept my sister happy.

"And Henri, the gardener, wants paying; he's done sixty euros worth this week. Give it to me, and I'll make sure he gets it, if you like."

I did like, and Simon knew it. The cleaning lady, the pool man, the gardener. I had nothing against these people I employed; by all accounts, they were very nice. But I preferred my own company, and they disrupted my thought processes, interrupted my hours of work. And I was truly dreadful at small talk. Simon had readily volunteered to manage them, while I paid the bills.

Having handed over the necessary funds, I headed for my study. "I have a video conference with the Paris office in five minutes, and I'll be writing a report after that. Can you let yourself out?"

This was about as pointed a comment as I ever made. Fortunately, on this occasion, Simon took the hint.

"I'll be in again tomorrow. Make sure you don't forget to eat, Marcel. We don't want you wasting away."

"I've set an alarm," I responded irritably. "And I'm sixty-two kilos, with a BMI of 20.1."

So, that was Simon successfully negotiated, and I forgot about him soon enough anyway. After enduring my meeting and completing my report, I rewarded myself by finishing the cryptic crossword I'd been compiling and emailed it to my friend Lucien to complete. Lucien was one of the precious few people in my life who didn't behave like the most important thing about me was my brittle asthma. We'd been friends since we were spotty teenagers. Well, I was a spotty teenager; he was a young Adonis, and he knew how much I loathed any reference to it. The asthma, not the spots.

Within minutes, he'd replied by text. *Marcel, darling, you're slipping. I've already completed numbers seven down and three across. Are you being distracted by a gorgeous man? I do hope so.*

A vision of Guillaume, all hot and rumpled after his training session, crossed my mind. With no one around, I briefly hummed and rocked in my chair. *Possibly, Lucien, but only in an abstract sense. You know me better than that.*

Gosh, how thrilling! Looking forwards to seeing you on the eighteenth, darling. You can tell me all about him then. Perhaps we can plot how to turn abstract into actual. xx.

★

I worked happily at my desk for the remainder of the afternoon, only stopping when my alarm sounded, prompting me to eat. As I continued to respond to emails, I hoovered up a portion of my sister's delicious beef stroganoff and then settled down again with my prison report. The doorbell chimed as I was in the midst of changing my Mekko chart into a box and whisker plot, the better to illustrate my point to colleagues less mathematically astute than myself (those tricky sums again). Ignoring it, I hoped whoever it was would get bored and go away.

They didn't.

"Hello, Marcel."

"Hello, Dominic. I see you've brought over your chessboard."

"Yes, Marcel. I thought I'd let you beat me again."

He smiled at me, or rather at a spot on the wall a few centimetres above my left shoulder. I returned his smile. It was difficult not to, even though I had to make a conscious effort, when I looked at his face, not to zoom in on that *thing* on his chin.

Dominic was another of my sister's hopefuls for me, and I had a soft spot for him as he was totally harmless, lonely, and slightly pathetically in love with me. And once, when I'd suffered a moderately unpleasant asthma attack, he had calmly sorted out my nebulisers and stayed with me the whole night, thus avoiding a trip to the hospital. If Simon or Sabine had been present, they would have panicked and called for an ambulance. For that, he had my sincere gratitude.

Our chess evenings followed a predictable course—Dominic was a man of routine. Occasionally, I'd let him win because that was the polite thing to do, but generally, I beat him soundly. After the game, he'd compliment me on my tactical skills, fidget around a bit like a small child needing a wee, and then ask me if I'd like to go out for a drink with him sometime. I always declined, hopefully sounding regretful, while definitely avoiding looking at the hairy warty thing.

Tonight was no different.

"Have you…ever…ah, have you ever considered asking anyone else out for a drink, Dominic?" I broached gently, keeping my gaze fixed on the chess pieces.

He shook his head, embarrassed. This time, he stared over my right shoulder. "Not for a while, Marcel. I…um…I don't know any other homosexuals, apart from you and Simon."

"That's a pity, Dominic."

"Yes, Marcel. I think it's a pity too."

"And, ah…no luck with Simon either?"

"No, Marcel. He doesn't like me very much, I don't think."

We almost gave each other a look of deep understanding. At least, I looked somewhere in the region of Dominic's monobrow so that my eyes had plenty of room to manoeuvre above his chin, and Dominic focused somewhere approximating my upper chest.

"That's a pity, Dominic."

"Yes, Marcel. It is a pity."

Simon and Dominic had not hit it off, to put it mildly. When they had first met, Simon had been overbearing and supercilious, and Dominic had retreated into his shell. Not the best at picking up on subtle and not-so-subtle cues, Dominic had masochistically repeatedly asked Simon out for a drink, and Simon had repeatedly responded in an overbearing and supercilious fashion. As I said, Dominic was a man of routine.

"Keep looking," I reassured him, not feeling very confident at all. "Something or somebody will turn up, you'll see."

★

Once I'd shuffled Dominic off towards the door, the only chore remaining was my sister's nightly phone call. For someone who craved solitude, I didn't often get much of it. I phoned Sabine from my desk, knowing if I left it any later, she would be contacting me at an inconvenient moment, such as halfway through a calculation of positive convexity in my share portfolio.

My niece Clara answered.

"Shouldn't you be in bed, *ma chérie?*"

"Shouldn't you, Uncle Marcel? You know that sleep deprivation is associated with nocturnal bronchoconstriction."

God save me from precocious eight-year-old girls. She'd definitely inherited the brainy gene.

"My alarm hasn't gone off yet," I answered smugly, and she snorted.

"You have another three minutes and forty-three seconds. I'll quickly pass you over to my mother."

Sabine sounded tired, which wasn't surprising, given that she juggled her full-time deputy head job with bringing up a very demanding child single-handedly, in addition to keeping a close eye on me. Her husband had walked out three years ago—the affair-with-a-younger-secretary-from-work cliché. Heteros really didn't have much imagination.

"Had a good day, Marcel?" she asked, and I gave her a brief run-through of my prison visit, omitting my increasing fondness for one of the inmates because that would make her worry needlessly. In return, she gave me a detailed account of her day in the classroom, and I confess that I switched off and started to complete a sudoku at the same time because, well, she couldn't see me.

"I'll pop in tomorrow after work." She yawned.

"You really don't have to. My peak flows are fine, my oxygen sats have been above 92 per cent all week, and you are already doing too much."

I could hear her wavering. "And Simon will be over anyway," I pushed. "Honestly, I'm feeling really well. The alarm system is a success; I'm sleeping longer, taking my meds, not working too hard (we both knew that was a lie), and I'm generally good all round."

"Well…if you are sure… I do have a staff meeting, and Clara has ballet…"

"I mean it, Sabine. I'm great. I can always call you if I feel at all chesty."

With a little more coaxing, she agreed to miss out a day, and we signed off with mutual "I love you's." And I did love her; I truly did. But occasionally, familial love could feel too claustrophobic, and the company of close friends didn't always feel like enough.

Chapter Five

Guillaume

"Nice fingernails," I remarked with a smirk.

It was Marcel's final visit to the prison, and we had spent the time talking together in a quiet corner of the visitors' room. Mostly about the paucity of educational opportunities available to prisoners and how ill-equipped the majority found themselves to rejoin normal society after release. Me included, although at least I had a few euros in the bank. Over the last few years, I'd enrolled in some long-distance courses—a bookkeeping one and a sports coaching theory course, but nothing that prepared me for an actual job. It was no wonder that, within a year, 39 per cent of prisoners were repeat offenders. Prison was the only world in which they knew their place.

Marcel self-consciously held out his hand, critically examining the alternating black-and-blue design. "Ah, yes, my niece, Clara. She likes to experiment on me."

"And you're a soft uncle."

"Very soft. Her father left my sister a few years ago, so the three of us stick together. We are very close."

"So, you are on your own, then, apart from your sister and niece?"

Christ, where did that come from? Who cared anyway?

"Not that it is any of my business. I apologise; I shouldn't have asked."

"It's fine, and, yes, I am on my own and have been for about eight years. It's my choice. I'm…ah, what people refer to as 'voluntarily celibate'."

Not the sort of people I know, I thought as I suppressed a snort. Some of the frustrated, involuntarily celibate blokes in here would have quite a lot to say about voluntary celibacy. He continued.

"I…ah, I'm quite difficult, you see, what with my health and my, ah, foibles. I tried to be with someone, but it…it regrettably didn't work out."

He inhaled deeply. "So now I'm on my own, and that's… fine."

Again, not that it was my business, but I had begun to form a picture of his health problems. Once more, he'd been short of breath when he arrived in the visiting room and had taken a discreet puff of his inhaler before he sat. I was guessing asthma, which wasn't an uncommon ailment, but perhaps his was a bad type. As to his foibles, I'd only seen a charming eccentricity, but to be fair, I didn't really know the man at all.

"I think, in another life, you and I could have become rather good friends, Guillaume," he observed gently, briefly touching my hand with his own.

If our situations had been different, if this were a cosy café or a bar, not a prison visiting room, I would have suspected him of flirting with me, suggesting maybe more than friendship. Which was an exceedingly lovely thought. Regretfully, I cast it aside.

"Somebody as well-to-do and upstanding as you would never be friends with someone like me." I laughed, smiling back to show I wasn't mocking him. I was going to miss our chats much more than he would ever know. He frowned, poised to disagree, and I clarified.

"I'm a bad person, Marcel; you know that. A criminal. You're aware I murdered someone, but you've never asked me about it."

"I would if you wanted to talk about it."

I shook my head. "Not right now, no."

Studying his face, I tried to memorise every delicate feature, to recall after he'd gone. The way his overly long, glossy hair fell across his forehead and across one eye, and he didn't care or notice. The way he frequently and impatiently pushed his glasses up his nose. Those warm, blue-grey eyes. His kindness.

"There wouldn't have been a place for me in your rarefied world of economics and politics, Marcel."

He tutted at me disapprovingly.

"That's ridiculous, Guillaume. And I know you're not all bad, whatever you may have done in the past. The past is a foreign country, isn't that what they say? That person, fifteen years ago? It's not you, not the Guillaume Guilbaud I've come to admire. You set up the football team here for a start; that was the work of a good person, wasn't it?"

I laughed again, briefly. "I did that for me as much as anyone else. I'd have died of boredom if I couldn't have played football."

"Maybe, but I'm sure you have done some good for someone else while you've been here," he pestered. "I know you too well now, my friend."

He leaned back. "Come on; I'll wait while you think of something. I'm in no hurry."

My friend. I liked him saying that. I haven't ever had many of those. I have Reuben, obviously, maybe Antoine, but beyond that… I sat up straighter.

"Yes, Marcel, there is one thing in my life that I am proud of. It's not much, but it is something."

"Go on then," he urged. "I'm all ears."

Why not? It was unlikely I'd see him again, and a part of me wanted him to remember me not as an overly opinionated murderer he'd once interviewed for an economics report, if he remembered me at all, but perhaps someone who had made an effort to atone. I took a sip of my coffee, holding the cup close.

"I'd been in here about three or four years maybe, when a new guy arrived. He was very young, only eighteen, and he looked even younger still. Thin and puny, but nothing a good square meal wouldn't fix. Not junkie thin, just a teenaged boy who hadn't yet grown into his body."

I hesitated, unsure if should tell him everything. This was Reuben's story, not mine, not that they would ever meet.

"He was beautiful though; he had long, curly brown hair and big, frightened green eyes. Those eyes were almost haunting, as if he'd seen too much, you know? When I was that age, I was cocky and confident, invincible. Ready to take on the world! I was going to be the next Lionel Messi."

I laughed sheepishly. "But this poor boy looked like the world had taken him on, and he'd already lost."

If Marcel noticed the rush of emotion evident in my words and tone, he politely pretended he didn't.

"Anyway, this boy was fresh meat. All the blokes who were that way inclined wanted to have him. He was a marked man from the moment he turned up. And he knew it; he was petrified. You could see it in his eyes."

"Did you want him?" Marcel interrupted, regarding me curiously.

Again, I hesitated. "The truth? Yes, at first, of course, I did. He was much more attractive than anything else on offer. Anyhow, even though he was in here because he'd been caught up in a gangland killing, he seemed…innocent somehow…untouched by all the nastiness he'd grown up with. And so bloody young, very much a child who'd not had the luck of the draw."

I gave him a slight shake of my head, frustrated. "It's difficult to explain to someone who's never met him, but he had…a sort of otherworldliness. Untainted. I wanted to protect him. Yet he was scared shitless, obviously, and he might as well have had 'victim' tattooed on his forehead."

"Is this story going to upset me?" asked Marcel. "You should know that I only ever read stories with happy endings."

I grinned at him; he had a way of lightening the mood that managed to amuse without excessive flippancy.

"Don't worry, Marcel. Your sensitive soul is safe. This story has a very happy ending. Though I must warn you, as with all good stories, there is a sad bit in the middle."

I took another gulp of my cooling coffee.

"To cut a long story short, about two days into this new guy's stay, I wandered over to the shower block for a late-night wash-up and found him pinned up against a wall, being buggered by one of the known predatory bastards. A fairly unpleasant man called Andre, who'd spent almost all of his adult life in and out of prison. The new guy was too scared to scream or fight, and to be honest, it was the right thing to do, to let himself be taken because Andre would have likely tried to kill him if he hadn't."

Deliberately, I'd been brutally matter-of-fact because to sugar-coat the story would do Reuben a disservice. Why shouldn't the director of finance for the Ministry of Justice know exactly the scale of the problems he was dealing with? He'd come to me wanting stories and examples of areas where his money could be spent. I'd given him another one for his collection. More guards and more supervision, more separation of old lags like Andre, who were beyond saving, from new blood like Reuben.

Marcel's hand flew to his mouth in horror, his blue-grey eyes wide behind the glass lenses. I waved away his concern.

"Andre might have been a predatory bastard, but he was skinny and ill from too many fags. All talk and no trousers, any one of us could have taken him down, though the new guy didn't know that. He probably thought Andre was the devil incarnate. I pulled him off and beat him to a pulp. He learned his lesson—no one else was attacked, and he died of lung cancer not long afterwards."

Without noticing, Marcel had grabbed my hand and clasped it in his own across the narrow table. His voice had been reduced to a breathy whisper.

"Goodness, Guillaume, this is awful. And then what happened?"

I shrugged. "Nothing happened. I told you the story has a happy ending. The new guy and I became good friends, the best of friends. For almost ten years. We shared a cell for a lot of those years, except we did get moved around periodically."

"And did you, ah…did you…with him…ah, you know?" queried Marcel delicately.

I had begun to understand two things about Marcel. One, he never, ever swore or blasphemed, and two, he endearingly found mentions of sex and other bodily functions terribly embarrassing.

"No, I didn't," I replied firmly. "And neither did anyone else. That's what I'm coming to, the bit that makes me proud. For ten whole years, until he was released last year, I kept him safe and kept him innocent. He didn't always thank me for it— he reckoned he was going to be the first Frenchman ever to die of sexual frustration, but I was determined that nothing, or no one in here would taint him."

I gave a small smile. "As long as I had anything to do with it, my poor friend had to put up with 'involuntary celibacy'. He's almost forgiven me. He played football, took carpentry lessons, planted vegetables, and learned how to laugh again. I tried to give him the childhood or teenage years that he'd missed as best I could. He always said being in a cell with me was the nicest home he'd ever had, which is pretty rubbish really. Everyone thought we were a couple, and so they stayed away from him. If you met him, you would see it. He's never lost his spark, his enthusiasm for life. He's amazing actually."

I was aware that I spoke like a proud father.

"And where is he now? Is he okay?"

My lips quirked as I remembered all the treasured photos Reuben had sent me, the piles of letters, the cards, the emails. They were stored in shoeboxes under my bed, and I took them out and looked at them frequently. Cataloguing the changing seasons at this magical place called Rossingley. In the small hours of the night, when I lay awake in the dark, listening to snores and shouts and clanging doors, Rossingley took on the aura of an enchanted palace in a mythical wonderland. I slipped into proud parent mode again.

"Oh, yes, he's very okay. Doing wonderfully, in fact. He got out of here about two years ago. He's working as a gardener—he's passionate about gardening and is enrolled in a horticulture course at college part-time. And he has a rich boyfriend, who adores him. I'm going to stay with them for a couple of weeks when I'm released, until I get myself sorted."

Marcel still held my hand across the table, making no move to release it. It felt natural; I didn't want him to let go.

"You're very animated when you talk about your friend, Guillaume. He must mean a lot to you."

I nodded, my mouth suddenly dry. This gentle man sitting opposite managed to conjure emotions from me like a rabbit from a hat. "He means everything to me. He's all I've got."

The sentence hovered there, and once more, I sensed he was probing further, trying to gauge my feelings for another man. "Do you regret that you never took your relationship with him beyond merely friends?"

The million-dollar question, posed by someone I hardly knew.

My feelings for Reuben were complex. There were many times when I'd been tempted, the two of us alone in the cell together. I'd seen him happy; I'd seen him sad. I'd joined him in laughter and soothed his tears. I'd seen him naked; we'd shared many a chaste kiss and cuddle under a rough blanket in a narrow bed. But regret?

"My relationship with this man is more important to me than a love affair, or a…a quick release of sexual frustration," I eventually answered, feeling my face growing hot. "I'm not the right man for him. This way, I have him in my life forever."

A bell rang somewhere out in the hallway, signalling lunch and the end of the morning. Our two hours had flown by. I realised with a jolt that we'd shared some pretty intimate thoughts during our brief acquaintance.

"My cue to go." Marcel smiled, stood, and gathered together his belongings. I held out the colourful scarf.

"Don't forget this; you wouldn't be you without it."

Laughing with delight, he began wrapping it around his neck. "No, my mad professor look would be incomplete."

He hesitated, poised on the edge of asking me something. "Will…ah, will you be all right, Guillaume, after you leave here?"

Fuck knows. But he didn't want to hear that.

"Yes. Thank you. As I said, I'm going to stay with my friend for a while."

"I meant afterwards. Do you…ah, need anything? Don't take this the wrong way, but like…money?"

He leaned closer, lowering his voice. "Goodness, this is awkward. But I'm asking you as a friend, off the record. Not as a man from the Ministry. If there is anything I can do for you?"

Looking up at me, those blue-grey eyes met mine and held. I put out my hand, and he shook it. He'd done more for me already than he would ever comprehend, by talking to me as an equal, treating me as a person with an opinion that mattered. Treating me as a friend. I swallowed again.

"I'm fine. I'll be fine. But thank you."

Will I though? I'll stay with Reuben for a few weeks, and then what? Make a new life in England so I could be near him? But I didn't speak the language. Or I could take Antoine up on his offer, at least for a short time. And maybe, maybe, I would accidentally bump into Marcel one day in Saint-Martin port. And we would go for a coffee together, like the good friends we would become, and talk and laugh and… I pushed the thoughts aside. That way lay madness and disappointment. I was telling the truth when I said I believed there was no place for the likes of me in his world. Men like me did not deserve men like Marcel.

"Really, I will be fine."

I wasn't sure who I was trying to convince. "I earned some money when I played football, and I bought a house in Marseilles, which an agency rents out on my behalf. The most sensible thing I've ever done, in hindsight. It gives me an income every month, enough until I get myself sorted at least. And I have a few savings."

The goodbye hung between us awkwardly, both of us reluctant to deliver the final words. Eventually, it was Marcel who spoke, and he made me briefly rejoice that we were Frenchmen and could get away with such things in a prison visiting room.

"*On fait les bises*, Guillaume?" "I think we are good enough friends to kiss now."

Without giving me an opportunity to respond, he leaned across the table and rested both elegant hands on my shoulders. Pulling me close, he planted the softest of kisses on each cheek. For only a second, I breathed in clean warm skin, vanilla, and the tantalizing scent of freedom. And then he was gone.

Chapter Six

Guillaume

I'd deliberately damped down any emotions associated with leaving my prison home after fifteen long years. Given airtime, the overriding sentiments would have been regret and fear. Regret for the loss of my youth, my footballing talent, and what could have been. And paralysing fear of what lay ahead. Naturally, I've read widely on the topic, and it doesn't make for happy reading. Apprehension, confusion, depression, anxiety, guilt, shame, paranoia, and feelings of isolation featured heavily, making for one shitty word cloud. No small wonder that ex-prisoners became homesick and reoffended.

Antoine visited me on my last evening. He'd swapped a shift so that he could say goodbye, which was thoughtful, and the gesture brought an unexpected lump to my throat.

"One for the road?" he asked mischievously. "I'm going to miss our little sessions."

"You're not short on admirers. I'm sure you'll find someone else to play games with."

As he started to unbutton my jeans, he made a face and sighed. "Yeah, I suppose. I've already made a move on the guy in 33M. You know who I mean? Short, slightly Neanderthal-looking? Quite cute?"

How anyone could put cute and Neanderthal together was beyond me. Only Antoine, I guessed. I nodded.

"He wasn't bad; I persuaded him to do the postmistress and naughty delivery boy thing. It was okay, I suppose. He didn't get into being a spiteful postmistress quite as well as you do."

I wasn't sure how I felt about that compliment.

As a goodbye treat, we played out a stern headmaster discovering a thieving caretaker scene, one of Antoine's favourites. I played my part with more gusto than ever before, threatening him with detention and even giving him a few whip cracks with his belt. After we'd both cleaned up, we exchanged our first and probably last kiss, which, truth be told, was bloody awkward and an error on both of our parts. The hug that followed felt much more natural.

"The offer's still open, Guillaume, to stay on the island and become our football coach. You don't have to…what I mean is, I'm not part of the deal. I wouldn't expect…us…this."

He gave me a card with his contact details, which I stowed away carefully. "Thanks, Antoine, I appreciate it. Take care, mate, yeah? Hope things work out for you."

I felt strangely bereft after he'd left. One less person in my life, I supposed.

I suffered a restless night of very little sleep. The armed robber loudly snoring about four feet away from me didn't help. Three minutes after 7:00 a.m. on a cold November morning and not feeling totally in control, I walked out of the prison's discreet side entrance, holdall bag in hand. As arranged, Reuben was waiting for me, leaning against a lamp-post with a huge grin on his beautiful face. A taxi hovered nearby.

And the emotional floodgates burst wide open.

Nelson Mandela wrote that if he didn't leave all the anger, hatred, and bitterness behind when he left prison, then he'd still be in that prison. With my release date drawing ever closer, I'd pondered this a lot over the last year or so. And I'd concluded that as someone who'd been correctly imprisoned for a crime I did commit, I could have substituted his three chosen adjectives with shame, fear, and self-loathing. But fuck, it was damn hard to leave those faithful companions behind. It didn't take long for me to discover them packed in the holdall, alongside my meagre clothes and books.

The next few hours passed by in a blur. As we embraced next to the taxi, I might have clung on to Reuben for five minutes or five hours, breathing him in, losing myself in that mass of fresh chestnut-brown hair, that firm, familiar body. The journey through the island villages and across the bridge to the mainland had stunning views; I'd seen pictures of them, but on this trip, I saw nothing because my eyes were shut tight. Regardless, a few tears slipped out, and I clutched Reuben's hand like a drowning man. If the taxi driver thought I was weird, I didn't give a fuck.

In the tiny La Rochelle airport, I was peripherally aware of Reuben's quiet, calming words, his smooth negotiation of my luggage and our paperwork. Him locating our seats on the cramped, turbo-prop plane for the short flight to Bristol, an unfamiliar city in an unfamiliar country. If I ate or drank, I couldn't remember what, and Reuben's hand never left mine. In my head, on an endless loop, I reassured myself I would be all right. That the traffic, the people, and the cheerful, shiny cabin crew weren't at all overwhelming. That at any moment, I wasn't going to feel a tap on the shoulder. That no one knew I'd spent the previous night and more than five thousand nights before it in a soulless prison cell. That I was a convicted murderer.

Passport control at yet another tinpot airport brought with it a further sweaty panic attack. Despite looking and behaving as shifty as the shiftiest drug mule, the disinterested customs officer behind the glass screen obliviously waved us through, with only a cursory glance at our passports and a few taps of her keyboard. Throughout it all, Reuben eyed me anxiously, never far away, always touching—a quick hand squeeze, a steer in the small of my back, a brush of his lips at my temple.

I sort of came to myself when we arrived at the car, a small red Volkswagen, and Reuben buckled himself into the driving seat.

"Hey, you passed your test!"

He smiled shyly. "Yeah, only took me three attempts! Freddie bought me this as a present."

I nodded appreciatively.

"It's not brand new," he added hastily. "Although he wanted to buy me a new one, I insisted he didn't. But Rossingley is in the middle of nowhere, so it's kind of useful for getting to college and stuff."

I buckled up next to him. "It's okay. I'm glad he wants to spoil you. You deserve it. All of it."

Unlike me, who deserved nothing.

Turned out that Reuben was an extremely cautious driver, and for that, I was relieved. I'd had too many heady sensations and emotions already; reckless driving I could do without. As we headed out of the city, as the high-rises and dual carriage-ways turned into green fields and smaller roads, I found myself relaxing a little. As long as Reuben was with me, it would be okay. I could do this.

"We've got the house to ourselves for a couple of days," he informed me. "Freddie has a modelling shoot in London and…" He hesitated slightly. "He thought you might appreci-ate it being only two of us for a while. The earl and his husband are around, but they'll leave us alone until you feel like meeting them."

I felt choked again, my throat tight. These English strangers, all so kind and considerate. I didn't deserve it. And my precious Reuben, I could scarcely drag my eyes away from him. So confident and grown up, but still the same boy he was. How our roles had reversed.

"That's…that's very thoughtful of Freddie. Tell him I said thank you."

Even in the unflattering grey November light, Reuben's many cards and letters couldn't have prepared me for the gran-deur of Rossingley. As we swept up the drive, I hardly knew where to look—at the immaculate lawns, the lake, the pretty rows of cottages, or, of course, the enormous stately home looming directly ahead.

"Don't worry, it took me a lot of getting used to too." Reuben grinned, taking in my expression. "I still pinch myself sometimes that this is actually my life now."

He expertly steered the small car off the main driveway and down a narrower, shady one, weaving through overhanging oak trees. "Our house is down here. Try not to snort when you hear Freddie and Lucien referring to it as 'the cottage'."

I snorted in their absence as we rounded the bend. If Reuben's home hadn't been scaled next to Rossingley, I would have described it as a mansion. As it was, the long pale house, with its rows of elegant sash windows, was definitely a small manor. Reuben knowledgeably informed me that it was a dower house, historically home to the widow of the previous earl when she got chucked out of the big place to make way for her son and heir. The car came to a sweeping halt on a circle of pristine gravel, and I climbed out, surveying Reuben's new life.

And, overwhelmingly, I felt exhausted, bone-tired, as if I'd travelled for several days and nights instead of a quick hop across the Channel. Waking in my cell, only a few hours earlier, felt a lifetime away. Recognising it, Reuben hustled me inside and showed me to my room while he set about lighting a fire in the cosy snug adjacent to the cavernous kitchen.

Situated on the ground floor, my bedroom could not have been more different from my prison cell than if I'd deliberately tried to create it as such. The unlocked set of glass doors, opening into an elegant walled vegetable garden, screamed freedom more than any official paperwork ever could. Slumping on the palatial bed and surrounded by all this splendour, I felt lumpish and dirty. A fresh bout of panic threatened to engulf me and probably would have done if Reuben hadn't called me back to him and rescued me from my churning emotions.

I barely assimilated any of it, not the beautiful décor, the smart kitchen units, the range cooker, none of it. As the November afternoon drew to an early close, I let Reuben chatter and fuss until I found myself on a ridiculously luxurious sofa with him curled up next to me, tucked under my arm as we used to on the narrow beds at night in the cells.

"So, this is the famous Obélix," I surmised as a scraggy black-and-white cat jumped onto my lap. Looking surprised, Reuben laughed.

"Yeah. He generally avoids strangers, but he's obviously taken a shine to you. He and Freddie are arch enemies. They see each other as competitors for my affection."

It was soothing stroking the cat and sitting with Reuben, even if we actively avoided talking about anything that mattered. I almost felt sane. The low light emanating from the fireplace and side lamps streaked gold through Reuben's mad hair. He and the cat almost shared the same, contented expression.

He could have been mine, I thought. We could have planned a life together for after my release. Boyfriends, husbands maybe. I'd mulled this over endlessly in the last few years, painting pictures in my mind of our fantasy lives together. Thin on detail, but always content, quietly content. Prison was noisy and crowded, too many men rushing around, too many interruptions, too many rules. No, the simple fantasy life I'd mapped out with Reuben had none of those elements.

For all my endeavours to explain it to Marcel, I still didn't exactly understand the reasons I'd held back from making him mine all those years ago. Having him here with me now, in this amazing house, seeing his incredible new life, seeing how wonderfully he'd turned out, I discovered I was still proud I'd taken the path I had, even if a part of me was tempted to take his hand in mine, to lean down and kiss him properly, like lovers do.

Choosing him as a lover was no longer in my gift. From the light shining in his eyes whenever he mentioned Freddie, which was only about every two minutes or so, deep down, I knew Reuben was no longer mine to take. He loved me, and I would always have that, but in his heart, I'd been relegated to second place.

A football match played out on the widescreen television—for all that I was able to focus, we could have been watching back-to-back episodes of *Scooby-Doo*. At some point, Freddie phoned, and Reuben left the room for a while, his voice out in the hallway, anxious and muted, speaking rapidly in English. Not long after that, he produced dinner, my favourite stir-fry followed by ice cream. I was touched by his efforts. We drank a single bottle of lager each, the last of the heavy drinkers.

We hadn't talked much; I hadn't anything to say. Concern etched Reuben's face. He'd never seen me weakened like this and was unsure what to do. Eventually, he placed a hand on my arm.

"Bed, I think, don't you?"

I nodded, relieved to escape the awkward silences.

★

Sleep eluded me again, despite the heaviness behind my eyes. The bed was too big, the sheets too soft, the house too dark and quiet. The future too uncertain, the past too bleak to contemplate. Without anybody to see, tears ran unchecked down my cheeks.

I didn't know how many hours had passed, but a noise at the door was swiftly followed by a warm body sinking into the mattress next to me. Wordlessly, I curled myself around him, planting a soft kiss at the nape of his slender neck. He smelled of cut grass and wet earth.

"It gets better, Guillaume, I promise you," he whispered in the dark. "The first few weeks are the worst."

"Did I ever tell you how much I love you, Reuben?" I whispered back, pulling him closer still.

He chuckled softly. "No, but you never needed to because I always knew. You looked after me brilliantly, Guillaume. And now it's my turn to do the same for you."

Next morning, Reuben was scheduled to be at work, and he'd shrewdly decided that the best thing I could do would be to join him. And he was absolutely right. After sport, manual labour was a perfect antidote to excessive brooding.

From all of Reuben's funny stories in his precious letters, I felt like I already knew the gardening crew. If they were aware of my background, they didn't show it, and as I traipsed after Reuben, following his every instruction, some of the tension from the last few days began to fall away from me.

"You're quite bossy, aren't you, *mon ange*?" I observed about halfway through the morning when he'd delivered yet another set of instructions.

"No, Guillaume. I'm a perfectionist. There's a difference."

He said something to one of the others in English, and they all laughed.

"Okay, so, yes. Lee says I am bossy. He says that now I've become one of the landed gentry, I've started throwing my weight around."

"What do they think of your Viscount Freddie?"

Another conversation in English ensued, with much joking and hilarity. Seemed like they all wanted to share their opinions about Freddie. Reuben blushed.

"I can't possibly repeat any of Lee's comments. And Joe says he's going to take French lessons so he can explain to you exactly what he thinks of Freddie because he doesn't trust me to give his opinions full justice."

More chatting in English, clearly more banter and plenty of hard graft. I switched off and concentrated on the pruning task Reuben had delegated.

Breaking for lunch, it became immediately evident that the others took the piss out of Reuben almost constantly, even if I hadn't a clue what they were joking about. We sheltered together in their cosy hut, drinking sugared tea, which was disgusting, and eating chocolate biscuits, which were delicious. And for the next two days, even when Reuben went to college, I turned up and did some gardening. The tiredness in my muscles felt good, being in the open air felt good, and having Reuben asleep next to me felt even better.

Two things immediately struck me about Viscount Aloysius Frederick Lloyd Duchamps-Avery. One, he was wrapped around Reuben's finger so tightly it was laughable. His utter adoration of the pocket rocket that was my dearest friend, Reuben Costaud, was more than I could ever have hoped, even if my happiness for him was tinged with regret for what could have been.

And two, he was mind-blowingly handsome. Dazzling, stupidly, stop-and-stare, trip-over-your-own-feet handsome. Even when he was trying his hardest to extend the hand of friendship to me, while also warily pacing around as though I was plotting to steal his most treasured possession. Which I wasn't, but that was difficult to convey when neither of us spoke the same lingo. That he believed for a second an ex-con like me could compete with everything he had to offer was crazy. And equally crazy when, for a moment, cuddling up to Reuben on the sofa on my first night, that I briefly thought I should. The last few days had given me space to put my fantasies to one side.

Freddie had my sympathy, though, as Reuben had immediately divulged that we'd shared a bed for the last few nights. More than that, he continued to be as attentive to me as prior to Freddie's return, still clearly anxiously monitoring my mental state. Thus, Freddie and I politely circled each other for twenty-four hours, radiating toxic masculinity. Poor Reuben was stuck between us, trying to appease two tense alphas, unable to take sides. Obélix however, settled firmly in Camp Guillaume, which possibly wound Freddie up further. Eventually, Reuben had had enough.

"Guillaume? Freddie has something to say to you. It will be super awkward because I will have to translate for him, and it's about me."

"Okay." Freddie and I eyed each other suspiciously. "Fire away, *mon ange.*"

I added the *mon ange*—my angel—to piss Freddie off, which was admittedly childish of me. Reuben rolled his eyes. Standing at his shoulder, Freddie towered over him with an unnecessarily possessive hand at his lower back. I was disadvantaged by sitting at the kitchen table, and wished I could stand, too, without appearing confrontational. I did have the cat twisting himself under my legs, though, which was stupidly satisfying.

"Freddie has been thrilled to meet you at last. He's been looking forwards to having you here almost as much as I have."

I bet he has, I thought wryly and raised a sceptical eyebrow.

"*Putain*, Guillaume, it's true."

Running a hand through his unruly mass of hair, he carried on. "But now he's met you and can see how close we are, and how handsome you are…"

"Flattery will get you everywhere, Reuben!"

"Okay, so he didn't say that exactly, but I know he thinks you are because…because, well, you are. And even if Freddie acts like he can take on the world, deep down he's actually quite a sensitive flower."

It was my turn to roll my eyes. I hoped to goodness Freddie's French was as bad as he made out.

"*Mon Dieu*, Guillaume!" said Reuben, becoming increasingly frustrated. "What I'm trying to say is that he's jealous of you, okay? Of everything we've had together. You have to remember that when Freddie and I met, you were the centre of my world. My best friend, brother, and father all rolled into one. Everything! He needs you to reassure him that you're not interested in me that way, and then you two can kiss and make up, and we can all get along!"

Looking across at Freddie, as his blue eyes bored into me, challenging me, I detected something else there too. Unease and…fear maybe? I turned my gaze back to Reuben, still the most important person in my world, and then back to Freddie. It was time to let go. The boy had turned into an adult, and he'd found a man who loved him as much as I did. He'd moved on, and I had to do the same. With a heavy heart, I made it simpler for all of us.

"Reuben, you can tell Freddie that we are like brothers, you and me. We'll always have that. Tell him that when I leave

Rossingley, it will be with the knowledge that you are with a good, kind man. But that he should stop letting you have your own way all the time. You will turn into a spoiled brat, and that is not how I've brought you up to behave!"

Bless him, Reuben had tears in his eyes as he haltingly re-layed our conversation to Freddie. He walked over to me and hugged me, and I whispered in his ear.

"And tell him if he fucks up, I'll hunt him down and kill him."

"*Merde*, Guillaume," Reuben half laughed, half cried, "I think I'll keep that bit to myself. You have past form when it comes to murder, you know?"

We separated, and Freddie cleared his throat and spoke to Reuben. After listening carefully, Reuben turned to me.

"He says thank you for keeping me safe for all those years, and if it's okay, he'd like to give you a hug too. And maybe start again?"

It's not often one has the opportunity to hug a top inter-national model. Unless you are a stroppy little Frenchman named Reuben Costaud, obviously. I enjoyed the experience; Freddie gives good cuddle and smelled divine. Still a little stiff, if I was being super critical, but it was a détente at least. He said something over my shoulder to Reuben, who grinned with de-light.

"Freddie says that now you've met him, you are ready to meet Lucien. Brace yourself, Guillaume; he's quite peculiar."

Chapter Seven

Marcel

"So, Marcel, my darling. You mentioned a new man in your text. Pray tell."

I sat across from Lucien at his vast kitchen table, sipping a hot chocolate, having declined a Campari quite so early in the day. Because of the planned evening *soirée*, Lucien's delightful offspring were spending a couple of nights with his husband's doting parents, so I was the lucky recipient of the full glare of Lucien's scrutiny.

"No, Lucien, that's not strictly correct. You are the one who mentioned a new man, not me. I can assure you, I'm as contentedly celibate as ever, no thanks to my sister's efforts to find me a suitable partner."

"Actually, that's not strictly correct either, darling," he persisted. "You did say you had met somebody, but in an abstract sense, if I remember."

"Well, I'm not telling. And more to the point, there is nothing to tell."

He casually snaked a hand across the table, and then, quick as a flash, the *connard* snatched my inhaler from in front of me.

"I shan't give this back to you until you spill the beans."

I gave him a withering look. "Does Jay know how immature you can be, Lucien? And do I need to remind you that you're a doctor? For goodness' sake, you should know better than depriving a sick man of his medication. Isn't there some ethical code against that sort of thing?"

Twisting the inhaler around in his hand, Lucien pumped it into the air a couple of times.

"Oops. Shouldn't waste it."

"Lucien, you are behaving like a brattish thirteen-year-old."

More pumps in the air. "Gosh! Look, Marcel, it's nearly run out."

This wasn't the first time Lucien had played this game with me, and I doubted it would be the last.

"I do have others in my suitcase, you know. Fortunately for you, so you won't be tried and burned at the stake for deliberately killing your oldest friend."

He smiled impishly. "Yes, but I've allocated you the room furthest away on the second floor. You'll die from oxygen deprivation before you manage to crawl there."

Sighing, I shook my head. "Okay, you win. I'll continue to sit here, then, and wait until I perish."

"Or you could spill the beans, darling, and I'll consider returning your inhaler?"

I took another sip. I'd been outmanoeuvred.

"There really is nothing to tell. As per usual, you are making a ridiculous drama out of a complete non-event."

The pale blue gaze didn't budge. I sighed heavily.

"Do you remember those prison visits I told you about? Well, I met a fascinating man—he was imprisoned for murder, which is obviously dreadful, but…I, ah, I…well, I found myself kind of liking him. A lot actually."

"Gosh, is he very handsome? Let me guess, he's tall. Muscular, but not too chiselled. Dark hair, perhaps a touch of broodiness about him? A foreigner? A man with a mysterious past? Sexy deep voice? Sad, haunted brown eyes?"

Goodness, Lucien could be annoying. And he could read me like a book. To be fair, I did used to have a type before I gave up on men for good, and Guillaume fit that type to a tee.

"Ah…yes. Yes, he is very handsome. And…ah…yes, all of those things. But not foreign—French mixed with some Moroccan and Tunisian."

He smirked. "Not that you've been delving into his background or anything, darling."

I shrugged at him. "But it's immaterial, Lucien. He's been released by now, after serving fifteen years. He's likely halfway back home to Marseilles, which is a hell of a long trip from Ile de Ré. On top of that, more pertinently, is that he probably saw me as a slightly strange, nerdy man who behaved as though every breath would be his last. On one occasion, while he was giving me a tour, I had to hold on to his arm as I was so out of puff. Doesn't make me particularly attractive, does it?"

Lucien smiled warmly. "Gosh, I don't know, Marcel. Your breathy, damsel in distress act is quite a turn-on, darling.

Particularly when you start coughing your guts up and your lips turn blue."

"Lucien, *mon cher*? I shall get my own back on you before the weekend is out. And you know how I refuse to employ swear words? Well, this is me telling you to…ah, expletive off."

He laughed gleefully, and thankfully, our conversation moved onto less intrusive topics, mainly tonight's festivities. I was to be the guest speaker at his and Freddie's prison educational charity's inaugural dinner, which he was hosting here at Rossingley. No doubt, the great and the good, from whom he was hoping to extract money, would be so suitably bowled over by their lavish surroundings and charming hosts they would readily open their wallets and dig deep.

"Talking of prisoners, how is Rossingley's resident ex-convict? I thoroughly enjoyed his company when we met at your wedding."

"Our dear Reuben is marvellous; thank you for asking. Trust you to remember such a pretty young man. He'll be along later. He has an old friend staying with him, who is quite dashing himself. Freddie is paranoid he's about to seduce Reuben away from under his nose."

Finishing my drink, I automatically reached for my scarf, which I thought I'd left on the back of a chair when I walked in. Lucien and I had plans to take a stroll around the lake, and then I was going to head up to my room and catch my breath for a few hours prior to the evening's entertainment. For all Lucien's welcome light-hearted teasing, I needed a rest after the travelling, and he knew it as well as anyone.

"Now what have you lost?" he said with mock irritation, watching me fumble around. "If it's your passport, I've already put it somewhere safe out of your reach so you don't mislay it between now and tomorrow's flight."

Goodness, this man knew me far too well. "No, it's not my passport. It's my scarf, you know, my mad professor one. I like having it around…"

"Darling, I know you like having it around. You've been wearing it for aeons. It will turn up. You probably left it hanging in the hallway."

He stood and carried my empty mug over to the sink.

"Is this what you're looking for?" said a deep warm voice from somewhere in the region of the kitchen door behind me. Whoever it belonged to spoke French fluently and with a hint of a familiar sing-song southern accent that reminded me of… For a brief second, I could have sworn my heart stopped beating.

Oh, my goodness, it couldn't be, could it?

"Gui…Guillaume! Wha…what on earth are you doing here?" I'd jabbered in English; such was my level of confusion that I'd forgotten which language I was speaking.

He leaned casually against the doorframe, my blessed scarf in his hand. Guillaume Guilbaud, in all of his dark, devilishly handsome glory, was in Lucien's kitchen, standing not two metres away from me. I think I might have actually whimpered. My mouth probably did that unattractive goldfish thing as I gasped for breath, and I was aware of Lucien turning to look at him too. Unlike me, he was still in possession of his brain cells, and he switched to French.

"Oh, hello, Guillaume darling. Is everything all right? If you are looking for Reuben, he's popped up to the ballroom to oversee the flower arrangements for this evening. Not enough sprigs of yellow stuff, he says."

He switched from looking at Guillaume to looking at me. "Gosh, Marcel, are you okay? Do you need your inhaler? You've gone a dreadfully funny colour, you know."

Guillaume stepped properly into the kitchen and nodded to Lucien. He was looking at me with a mixture of shock and…was that delight? Which very quickly turned into concern.

"Um…thank you, Lucien, I'm fine. Yes, I was looking for Reuben, but…er…it can wait."

Crouching in front of me, he gently handed me back my scarf. The corners of the room were doing that sparkling thing that happens when my lungs decide to go on strike without giving me due warning. Desperately trying to keep a hold on reality, I focused on his soothing voice and grasped the familiar woollen material.

"Marcel."

Goodness, the way my name sounded on his lips. Not a command or an instruction, nor a question. Only…my name, spoken in his deliberate paced accent.

"Remember to breathe, Marcel. Relax, you're safe. Try to take a couple of slow, steady breaths."

And then I was aware of a few things happening at once. Lucien rushed over with my inhaler and forced it into my hand, then held my hand to my mouth. I gladly cooperated, sucking in the magical formula. Guillaume, still on his knees next to me, stroked my back in big warm circles.

"Shh. That's better. Marcel, you're calming. Sorry, I didn't mean to shock you quite so badly."

He was right; my breathing was coming under control once more, and the room had lost its glow of silvery fairy dust. A minute or so later, Lucien stepped back again, still hovering but obviously having concluded the crisis had been averted.

"Gosh, Marcel, you are such a drama queen, darling. I know Guillaume is a very sexy Frenchman, but they don't normally have such a profound effect on you."

"It's…it's Guillaume," I panted. "Not…any…sexy… Frenchman."

Thank goodness Guillaume didn't understand English, although his name and the word sexy in the same sentence was bound to have registered. By now, he'd stood up, too, clearly not sure what to do next, and an air of awkwardness settled about him.

"I know it's Guillaume, darling. He's been staying here for a fortnight. He's Reuben's friend that I was telling you about."

Pursing my lips, I managed to further regulate my breathing, blowing out air more steadily.

"Yes, but, but…Guillaume and I, we…ah, we know each other. He's the…ah, the extremely dull, not very interesting at all, and definitely unattractive prisoner who I might have briefly mentioned to you earlier?"

Lucien's mind went from A to Z in under a second. He regarded me with a perfectly arched and pencilled raised eyebrow. "Is he really? Gosh. How utterly, utterly extraordinary."

He smiled at Guillaume and switched to French. "Darling, I was going to accompany Marcel for a short walk around the lake, but I've suddenly remembered that the caterers need my attention urgently. Would you be an angel and take my place? I'm not sure he should be left on his own."

★

It would be an exaggeration to say that we went for a walk. It was more of a painfully slow shuffle. I had self-administered an impressive array of inhalers before we set off. Lucien had bundled me up in a long coat, found me some lambswool gloves, and adjusted my scarf so that it covered my mouth and nose in an attempt to humidify the cold wintry air on its route to my grumbling lungs. My gloved hand was tucked under Guillaume's arm. I felt a little like a toddler getting ready to play outside.

"How do you know the earl?" he asked as we headed across an immaculate expanse of lawn.

"He's my oldest friend," I replied. "We started Eton together and shared a dorm. I was this weird, sick French boy who couldn't partake in sport, and he was a beautiful, lanky blond creature who, for some reason, took a shine to me. And dragged me everywhere, including home to Rossingley for weekends and holidays when my parents were overseas. I know this place like the back of my hand."

I sighed. "He never anticipated it would all be his one day. No one ever saw that coming. I imagine Reuben has told you about his family tragedy?"

Guillaume nodded.

"When they died, it was probably the only time in my life I sincerely wished I wasn't me, that I didn't have this stupid illness. I was stuck in a French hospital recovering from pneumonia, so I was no use to Lucien at all, at a time when he needed me the most. I've…I've never forgiven myself. They were such wonderful, kind people, all of them."

I stopped for a moment. Simultaneously talking and walking in cold air was not compatible with breathing.

"Are you sure you shouldn't have stayed inside?" queried Guillaume anxiously. I waved away his concern.

"I'm fine. I'd never go anywhere if I let a little spot of wheeziness like this bother me."

"I think your idea and my idea of a little spot of wheeziness are two different things. You gave me a hell of a shock back there in the kitchen."

He smiled down at me, and I responded by giving his arm a little squeeze.

"Likewise, Guillaume! And thank you for your concern. You've probably deduced that I'm fairly disabled. I have what doctors call brittle asthma. By rights, I should have died years ago, but somehow, I keep on pulling through. Living by the sea, away from city pollution helps. The Ministry is very accommodating in that regard, although I do travel to Paris if I have to. The medicines are marvellous, of course."

Silence fell as we resumed walking again. The stillness and timelessness of Rossingley never failed to impress me.

"Can I apologise for something, Marcel?" Guillaume asked, halting once more. He sounded grave.

"When we first met," he began earnestly, "I congratulated you on having been dealt such a lucky hand. It wasn't a very nice thing to say, especially now that I know more about you. It's been preying on my mind, and I'd like to apologise."

"Well, I'm sorry that I responded by outlining your life history in such a callous fashion. I was probably very nervous about meeting a murderer and didn't want to appear weak. You were terribly fierce, you know."

I squeezed his arm again. "Let's call it even. And for your information, I do feel very lucky. I have a wonderful home, friends, and family. And…ah, you turning up today out of the blue has made things even nicer."

While I had been occupied doing my best impression of a beached trout in Lucien's kitchen, part of my brain had managed to put two and two together and make four. I tried to be as delicate as I could as I looked up at Guillaume, his dark face stern in profile.

"Your friend that you mentioned, the younger man you helped in prison. It was Reuben, wasn't it?"

Guillaume exhaled deeply and nodded.

"Don't worry," I reassured him. "I shan't tell anyone the things you told me about him."

"Freddie knows everything anyway, obviously, and I suspect Lucien and Jay do, too, or at least the gist of it."

"You were right when you said he was amazing," I answered, really meaning it. "And you are right to be proud of what he's achieved."

I paused. "Any…ah, any regrets now you have been released, that things weren't…ah, ever different between you?"

He shook his head and studied me carefully, with dark eyes that were almost black in the dim November light. He seemed on the verge of saying something important but then changed his mind. "Not now, Marcel, no."

Arriving back at the house, we reluctantly parted ways, me to have an afternoon nap and Guillaume to return to the dower house where he was staying with Reuben and Freddie. Slightly enigmatically, he said he had a few phone calls to make. I watched him go, with that easy, athletic stride, one that I would never be able to match. For the second time that afternoon, my breath caught in my throat. But on this occasion, it had nothing to do with my asthma.

Chapter Eight

Guillaume

I was still making phone calls when Reuben returned.

"Freddie said you took a stroll around the lake with Marcel. I'm glad you've met him—at least you'll be able to converse with somebody else apart from me all evening. He's a bit odd, but very nice, isn't he?"

I agreed. Odd and nice was one way of describing him. I would have embarrassed myself if I'd been asked to come up with some alternative adjectives.

I had walked at least five paces past the long, stripy scarf, looped over the banister, before it had fully registered in my brain. Probably because I was nervous—I'd spent quite some time by now with the sixteenth Earl of Rossingley, and despite his best efforts to put me at ease, he still had the same dazzling effect on me. Whether it was his extraordinary looks, the clothes, the palest of blue eyes, his fluttery way of speaking, or a combination of all of those things. His husband, Jay, seemed much more straightforward. Shame he didn't speak any French.

I'd stopped, backtracked, picked the scarf up, and surreptitiously held it to my nose, recalling immediately the scent of a man I'd deliberately put out of my mind. After inhaling that intoxicating smell, I hadn't needed to see his dark head bent to Lucien's blond one, as they conspired like naughty schoolboys together in the kitchen, nor hear him conversing easily in English. From the sound of it, they were bantering and giving each other as good as they got. I'd watched from the doorway for a second or two—even in the presence of the astonishing earl, I was mesmerised by the other man.

Obviously, in retrospect, I could have handled my entrance a little more carefully, but at least now I had a better insight into the full extent of Marcel's health issues. And strangely enough, I wasn't put off in the slightest. Seeing the scarf, then seeing him, I had suddenly made a decision.

"I'm leaving here tomorrow, Reuben. I've booked the flight from Bristol, and I'm going back to Ile de Ré. I'm taking Antoine up on his offer to work in the bar and to coach the Saint-Martin football team."

Reuben was startled. "Are you sure? That's a bit sudden, isn't it? You know you can stay here as long as you like. We always need extra help in the gardens and…"

I shook my head. "No. It's not that sudden actually. I…um…I met someone from back on the island who I thought I'd probably never see again. But things have changed, and, well, I want to give it a go. To see if we have something."

"*Merde*, it's not Antoine, is it? He's still married, and he's going to want you to pretend to be an evil sergeant major while you attach clothes pegs to his nipples or something."

I laughed. Reuben sure had an imagination. "No, *mon ange*, it's not Antoine."

"Is it a woman? Is it one of those nice ladies who work in the prison canteen? You've had girlfriends before. I bet you're great with women."

"No, Reuben, it's not a woman either. I'll tell you about him soon, but not yet. And my family don't want me in Marseilles, so at least going back to the island for a while gives me time to think about my future, even if the thing with this man doesn't work out."

"There will always be a home for you here, Guillaume. In the gay commune, as the gardening crew call it."

Laughing, I gave him a hug. Whatever happened, I'd always have Reuben, even if a suspicious blond viscount also came as part of the package. "I know, *mon ange*, but I need to strike out on my own."

"If that's the case, I will have to persuade Freddie that, from now on, we take all of our holidays on Ile de Ré so that I can see you as much as possible."

Good luck with that.

Marcel proved to be a fantastic public speaker. High praise from me, who barely understood a word. Although, I was totally biased, of course.

Being unable to speak English at the gala dinner was an asset; I'd dreaded being drawn into small talk and being quizzed about myself. Wealthy charitable donors might be willing to part with their dosh for a prisoner-related charity, but I'd bet an equal amount of dosh they didn't especially want to spend the evening with one of the recipients.

I had attended a few of these sorts of nights in my footballing days—award ceremonies mostly, though not as dazzling a show as Rossingley put on—so at least I knew what to expect. And crucially, it meant I didn't have to suffer the indignity of asking Freddie how to tie my bow tie.

As the guest of honour, Marcel was seated at the top table with Freddie and Lucien, so I didn't get a chance to speak to him before the dinner. I was sandwiched slightly farther down, between Reuben and Jay. And when I say sandwiched, I was practically in Reuben's lap because the earl's husband is a mighty big lad. As he quietly munched his way through the various food courses, I had the distinct impression that this sort of thing wasn't quite his scene. It was a shame we couldn't communicate more easily because I think we'd have got on well, and he was clearly very fond of Reuben.

I'd been anxious as I watched Marcel carefully make his way to the small dais, which was ridiculous because he'd no doubt done this sort of thing plenty of times. He was a senior figure in the French government, for goodness' sake!

The room quietened as he calmly looked around at the assembled guests before starting to speak, not a trace of nerves apparent on his delicate features. The reason for the lack of nerves became abundantly clear as Reuben quietly began translating for me. Marcel was a pro at this, and I relaxed back to enjoy the show.

"Ladies and gentlemen, you are probably wondering what on earth a senior pen-pusher in the French civil service could possibly have to say that was of any value regarding the British penal system. After all, I spend most of my days holed up in front of a desk performing—what a very dear friend of mine refers to as—tricky sums."

At this, he stared straight at me and winked, garnering a curious look from Reuben.

"Well, I shall begin by stating I have first-hand knowledge of British penitentiaries, having attended one of your most prestigious public schools from the tender age of thirteen."

There was a polite ripple of laughter, and Marcel waited until it had died down.

"I can't lie, my cellmate had a few hygiene issues, but judging from his appearance tonight, most of those have been ironed out. He scrubs up remarkably well, yet I'm reluctant to stand too close, even though I have been reliably informed he has since been introduced to soap and deodorant. I also hear he has finally conquered the verruca situation."

Jay, seated on my right, clearly enjoyed this one, and Marcel threw Lucien an extremely camp kiss. "I promised I'd get my own back, darling!"

Once the laughter had died down, he continued in a more serious vein, and after a minute or so, I told Reuben to not bother translating. I didn't need a translator, I was content to listen to the cadence of Marcel's slightly breathy voice as he delivered what was clearly an extremely well-received speech, sprinkling an important message with dashes of humour. And did I mention he looked bloody gorgeous in black tie? Suit porn wasn't really my thing, but I could easily be persuaded.

"*Mon Dieu*," whispered Reuben during a brief murmur of applause after Marcel had made a particular welcome comment. "He's quite a dish, isn't he, when he puts his mind to it?"

I stifled a smile. "Is he, *mon ange*? I hadn't really noticed."

"You should have a chat with him again afterwards, Guillaume. I think you'd quite like him if you got to know him."

I nodded, a pretence at seriousness. "I might do that, Reuben."

★

It was quite some time after the speech that I managed to get Marcel to myself. It seemed everyone had a question for him, and he answered them all with infinite charm and patience.

"You're good at this," I remarked as yet another woman fluttered her eyelashes and shook his hand before wandering away.

"Thank you," he replied with a hint of a smile. "It always surprises people."

I regarded him carefully as he pushed up his glasses. His face was pale.

"You look done in. Shall I pretend we are deeply engrossed in conversation so I can casually manoeuvre you away from everybody and find you somewhere quiet to sit?"

Laying a hand on my arm, he smiled up at me. "You can do better than that. Why don't you escort me up to my room? Lucien finds it hilarious to put me high up on the second floor. There are a lot of stairs."

By the time we reached the top of the first flight, Marcel had to pause to take a couple of quick puffs on his ever-present inhaler. Despite trying to hide his discomfort, he was clearly flagging. Another steep flight stretched ahead of us.

"Look, Marcel. Put your arm around my neck. I'll carry you."

"That's ridiculous, Guillaume, you don't need to...oh!"

I lifted him, cradling him in my arms.

"Christ, you're heavier than you look!"

I didn't know what I was doing—a romantic impulsive gesture or just the decent thing when he was clearly struggling. But if it had started with the intention of being vaguely romantic, then it ended with me staggering in an extremely ungainly fashion down a long corridor, with Marcel clinging tightly and giggling in my arms. It would appear that full-grown men, even slender ones like Marcel, are quite cumbersome. Fortunately, no one saw us.

"Put me down, you nitwit! You'll do yourself an injury!"

"Not…until…I've…fuck…delivered…you…safely… to…your…fuck, this was a mistake…room."

He held on tightly while I negotiated the door handle and then somehow staggered to the huge bed before virtually launching him onto it. I collapsed face down next to him with a heavy groan.

"The air must be thinner all the way up here. Christ, that was knackering!"

Marcel lay flat on his back, giggling breathlessly like a teenage girl. That made two of us.

"I can lend you an inhaler if you think it might help?" he offered with a smirk.

I groaned again and leaned up on my elbows. Despite loosening his bow tie and top button, and toeing off his shoes, he still looked uncomfortable.

"Come on; prop yourself up against the pillows. You can't breathe very well like that."

He scooted up the bed, and I eventually did the same, lying on my back next to him.

"Bloody hell, Marcel, I think you must have been burgled while you were downstairs," I observed deadpan, surveying the room. He giggled again.

It was a gorgeous guestroom (even though I was becoming accustomed to gorgeous rooms), all yellow silk draperies, delicate antique furniture, and rich Persian rugs. But it also looked like someone had tipped up a couple of suitcases and liberally thrown the contents around for the hell of it. Clothes and books were strewn across every available surface.

"And you're only here for one night!"

"Yes…I, ah, I'm not very tidy," Marcel confessed. "And…ah, I tend to overpack. I generally lose things too."

We both lay quietly, looking up at the huge crystal chandelier above our heads. It was a companionable silence; Marcel's breathing, while still raspy, didn't sound as laboured as before. I should have got up and left, but I kind of liked…being with him.

"Guillaume? Can I ask you something?"

Marcel had removed his glasses. He was even more boyish without them.

"Mmm," I murmured contentedly.

"Do you ever regret it, you know, killing that man?"

That was it. The question everyone skirted around was out on the table. It was inevitable, of course. We'd covered a multitude of topics during his prison interviews but had always skirted this one. Up until now, Reuben was the only other person who had ever broached the subject with me. I sighed heavily, and Marcel's fingers found their way across the eiderdown between us and laced with mine. Gratefully, I gave them a squeeze.

"I don't regret that he's dead," I answered eventually. "He was a monster, and I can't prove anything, but I don't think my poor sister was his first victim."

Marcel stayed quiet.

"But I do regret that it was me that did it. The person who killed him. Because I became a monster, too, and I'm ashamed of that."

I swallowed thickly, my throat suddenly very dry. Marcel's fingers tightened around mine. I deliberately didn't dwell on this subject much; I'd learned to park it somewhere in the distant past.

"No one has a right to take another life, Marcel. That's for the lawmakers to decide. So, if I could take back my actions, I would, even if it meant that bastard was still alive and free today. Which would be an injustice."

Reuben once confided in me that when he told Freddie about his years before prison and the crimes he'd committed, it had felt like he was describing someone else's life. It had seemed so far in the past, and he'd grown to be such a different person since then—a man, not a boy. I sort of felt the same. A man in his late thirties was not the same character he'd been at twenty-three, no matter how he'd spent the intervening fifteen years.

"I was an angry young guy back then. Cocky and overconfident, full of testosterone. My football career was going so well that I thought I could walk on water. That I could do anything, be anything. And yet inside, I was so very, bloody angry, as though the world still owed me something. I was angry that my father had left us without trace, left my mother to bring us all up without any help. That I'd had to be the man of the household and didn't want to be. I was angry that I fancied other blokes and couldn't ever admit it or act on it because of who I was. That I had to go on the pull with my teammates and have sex with girls and then brag about it, to fit in. Gay men aren't exactly welcome in the football dressing room. Things might have changed now, but back then, I'd have been out on my ear. Career over."

I gave a harsh laugh. "Then my career ended anyway, in an even more spectacular fashion."

Lifting my hand, I examined my fingers intertwined with Marcel's.

"And now I'm pushing forty, having lost what would probably have been the best fifteen years of my life. There's no anger left. Only a feeling of having to start all over again, and some days, I'm not sure if I can be bothered. Apart from a bit of cash, I've got nothing and no one, excepting Reuben, and I don't think Freddie would be overly enamoured if I kept turning up here like a bad penny."

That hand remained in mine for a good while longer. Not wanting to outstay my welcome, I began to gently and reluctantly extricate myself.

"I should go and let you rest."

Marcel stayed me with a hand on my arm.

"*On fait les bises* before you go? A kiss?"

I was grateful he hadn't commented or tried to offer platitudes or his opinion. There was really nothing to say. Those guileless, blue-grey eyes were so warm and inviting as he gently smiled up at me. And totally irresistible.

Leaning carefully across him, I brushed my lips first over one cheek, and then the other. His hot breath intermingled with mine as I eased away, the tip of his pink tongue just visible between his parted lips. On impulse, I moved in closer again, closing my eyes for the most tender of brief kisses on his mouth. God, it felt good.

"Is that how they *faire les bises* in Marseilles?" he whispered up at me.

"No," I shook my head. "But it's how I want to do it to you."

A second kiss, longer than the first, and my hand found its way into his silky hair as I parted the soft line of his lips with my tongue. As before, when we had said goodbye in the prison visitors' room, my head was filled with the sweet scent of vanilla and clean skin. For all of Antoine's expertise on his knees, nothing I'd ever known before compared to the burst of pleasure brought to bear by this most simple of kisses. Reluctantly, I pulled back again.

"Sorry, Marcel, I'm so sorry. I shouldn't have done that."

"Why not?" he replied.

"Because…because you are you, and I'm a slightly fucked-up ex-con. And you have that celibacy thing going on, which I'm pretty certain doesn't involve kissing men you hardly know."

I pulled away from him to give him space, stretching out again on my back. "I've been reading up on it, in fact."

"Is there any topic that you don't read up on, Guillaume?"

I grinned. "A few. Life in medieval China doesn't interest me, nor how to complete a Rubik's cube."

"Oh, that's so easy! You don't need a book to teach you how to do that."

Of course, Marcel would find a Rubik's cube easy. He studied maths for pleasure.

"So, this celibacy thing. It's quite interesting actually," I continued. "I read that some celibates abstain from everything, including masturbation. Yet at the other extreme, some people do everything apart from full penetration, which kind of doesn't fulfil the definition of celibacy in my eyes. But whatever floats your boat, I suppose."

Marcel shifted onto his side, facing me, resting his head on his hand. "Stop! You're making me blush. I'm not the sort of guy who ever introduces masturbation into a conversation. Not without prior warning anyhow."

"Can I say that you are extremely pretty when you blush?"

"Stop! Now I'm blushing even more!"

Taking his elegant hand in mine again, I brought his fingers to my lips. "So what I want to know is—at which end of the celibacy continuum are you, Marcel? The kidding yourself end? Or the boring, totally torturing yourself end?"

He laughed delightedly, still blushing. "At the boring, depriving myself end, I'm afraid."

"What, masturbation too?"

Slapping my cheek gently, he blushed again. "Guillaume! That is a very personal question!"

"Well, if we're going to become good friends and near neighbours, then I'm going to need to know some more about you."

His mouth hung open in mid-retort. "What do you mean, neighbours?"

I shrugged, feigning disinterest, when what I actually wanted to do was pin him underneath me and discover exactly how celibate he really was. My dick was uncomfortably hard in my dress trousers. Yet, I had a feeling that sort of approach wouldn't work with Marcel. If ever a man required slow seduction, it was Marcel Giresse. Problem was, I'd never seduced anybody. Relationships for me, up until this moment, had been platonic—with Reuben—or a purely sexual transaction, of which Antoine was an excellent and recent example.

"I'm coming to live on the island. I believe we're on the same flight back tomorrow."

I filled him in on my job plans, and he was clearly delighted.

"Oh, I'm so pleased. I don't think my poor heart would have stood saying goodbye again."

I raised an eyebrow. "I thought it was your lungs that were the problem? Don't tell me you've got a dicky ticker as well!"

"Only around you, you fool." Grabbing my lapels, he tugged me closer. "Kiss me again? And I…ah…I like the feel of your tongue stud, by the way. It's…ah, it's quite stimulating."

I kissed him until he was breathless, which wasn't much of a challenge, to be honest, and said more about his asthma than it probably did about my kissing prowess. It took all of my willpower for my hands to not stray south of his face and hair.

"Where are you going to live?" he asked suddenly, after recovering his breath.

"I don't know. A hotel for a night or two, and then I was going to rent an out-of-season holiday let. Antoine says it shouldn't be too difficult. He's got a few contacts."

"Come and stay in my annexe," he urged. "It's only a simple bedroom and bathroom, but it's clean and warm and empty.

And my sister is forever nagging me to get a lodger in there to keep an eye on me. It will get her off my back."

"I'm not sure I'm exactly what she'll have had in mind."

"That's ridiculous," he protested, waving away my concern. "You'll be perfect. She doesn't need to know your background. And if it makes you happier, I'll charge you some rent, but it won't be much."

"But you hardly know me. I've just come out of prison! You know what I've done in the past. You shouldn't be so trusting."

With his jaw jutting slightly, his face took on a stubborn expression I'd not seen before. "I know you enough. And I know what you've done for Reuben. I want to take a chance on you, Guillaume. I want to trust you."

Trust. Not something ex-cons like me heard very often. I thought of a soulless hotel room and an equally soulless holiday gîte. And then I looked at Marcel, with his relaxed, flushed face and tousled hair. I wasn't sure how to get it, but I wanted something more with this guy, whatever was on offer.

"Kiss me again, and I'll say yes."

I had no idea such tantalisingly soft kisses could convey such desire. They were almost better than fierce, horny, possessive ones. With every delicate brush of his tongue, I fell further and further into a morass of want and need and…

"There's an alarm going off, somewhere, Marcel. And… um…you seem to be vibrating."

He sighed, and I moved away so that he could sit up. He fumbled in his jacket inside pocket and retrieved his phone and silenced it, then gave me a slightly rueful smile.

"It's one of my many alarms. That one is to remind me to take my night-time medication, but I have others too. It's…ah, slightly embarrassing and a little pathetic."

He indicated the large washbag on my side of the bed, and after I'd passed it to him, he proceeded to methodically lay out rows of various inhalers and tablets across his lap.

"The last person I kissed, Guillaume, left me after six months. He said I didn't need a lover; I needed a caregiver. And it wasn't a role he was prepared to fill, I'm afraid. That was eight years ago."

Somehow, Marcel was managing to convey both anger and hurt in the way he sucked back his inhalers and downed the tablets, dry, without water.

"And the annoying thing is," he continued, "although he was being deliberately nasty and cruel, he was absolutely correct. I need a caregiver to make sure I don't stop breathing and fall down dead in the middle of the night. I need a caregiver to make sure I exercise and sleep properly. I need a caregiver to tidy up after me and find all the stuff I lose in the chaos that is my pitiful existence. Because—" He threw the inhalers forcefully back into the bag. "—the thing is, I'm never going to get better. Only worse. Gradually, but definitely worse."

After zipping up the bag, he then flung it carelessly onto a chair in the corner. "And then, of course, there is my work and my brain. Now, I'm perfectly content with my brain functioning exactly the way it does. I like to immerse myself completely in those tricky sums of yours. I like to sit at my desk for twelve hours straight without pause. And then I like to amuse myself by compiling crosswords and sudokus. Don't tell anyone, but I occasionally don't bother showering if I'm not going out. Or brushing my teeth. I don't care if my house is untidy or if I exist on a diet of stale bread and cheese for a whole weekend."

He shook his head sadly. "But it seems that, eventually, my preferred lifestyle becomes a problem for everyone else."

He leaned back against the headboard; his eyes closed.

"Hence the celibacy," he said softly. "I can offer you a place to stay and my friendship, with maybe the occasional kiss thrown in when I remember you're there and that I really like you. And that I've remembered to brush my teeth. But you need to know, Guillaume, that's all I have."

I considered the few relationships I'd experienced in my life so far and how the longest and most successful had been based entirely on a platonic friendship. I stood up, as if to go, then surprised him by bending down and planting a firm kiss on his forehead.

"I think, Marcel, that your friendship, with a few kisses thrown in, is exactly what I'm looking for."

Chapter Nine

Marcel

I didn't see much of Guillaume for the first few days. The annexe has its own separate entrance via the gate at the bottom of the garden. He must have been having meals out or eating cold food in his room because he hadn't made use of my kitchen, as far as I could tell. Although, there was a chance I might have been oblivious to his comings and goings as I'd immersed myself in my work, which was no hardship. He'd undoubtedly had his own stuff going on, the details of which I wasn't entirely sure. A part of me wondered if he was deliberately trying to stay out of my way to give me space; I had, after all, ardently responded to his kisses and then listed all the ways why becoming close to me was a really bad idea. If he had any sense, he was probably spending his time searching for alternative suitable accommodation.

We'd had fun at the airport though. And on the plane. Guillaume, at Lucien's firm behest, was in charge of passports, but apart from that, neither of us was in charge of anything. My general incompetence at modern living shone through, and

Guillaume not only didn't speak English but had missed the last fifteen years of technological advances, so automated check-in and passport control were mysteries to him. And the glamorous French woman seated on his right on the aeroplane flirted with him so much she was practically fondling his testicles by the time we landed at La Rochelle. Which was quite forwards, given that the flight only took an hour. The look of hatred on her face when I planted a loving kiss on his cheek as we disembarked will haunt me for the rest of my days. The look of pure pleasure on Guillaume's face will haunt me beyond the grave because it was directed at me and not at her.

My sister learned of his existence on day four.

"Who the hell is that man doing lengths in your pool?"

"What?"

She had come over in her lunch hour, ostensibly to spend some quality time with her brother without Clara being around, but more likely to check that I was still breathing in and out after my expedition abroad. Astonishingly, I had dressed, taken a short walk, *and* purchased a fresh baguette from the *boulangerie* that morning, thus we shared ham sandwiches and a simple salad.

"I said, who is that man swimming in your pool?"

"Oh, *him*," I responded airily, as though I struggled to keep track of the never-ending rota of hot men in and out of the pool every day of the week. I maintained it heated to the temperature of a warm bath all year round as I've been advised that swimming improves the performance of my respiratory muscles. "That's…ah, that's Guillaume. He's a friend of, ah… He's…he's…Lucien's cousin's boyfriend's best friend, and he's, ah…he's staying with me in the annexe for a while."

I gave myself a metaphorical pat on the back for managing to spontaneously tell one truth while completely avoiding another.

"Goodness, he's got quite a few tattoos, hasn't he?"

I turned to look at the rather divine sight of Guillaume, having evidently finished his daily fifty lengths (not that I had been watching or counting or anything), effortlessly pulling himself up out of the pool. The tattoos in question rippled across the smooth dark skin of his shoulder blades. From this distance, it was impossible to make out the designs. I'd caught sight of his tattoo sleeve in prison before and, of course, the one snaking up his neck. We both gawped, my sister as transfixed as me, as he stood, stretched, and then carelessly shook the water from his black hair before reaching for a towel. Unaware of his audience peeking from the kitchen window, he roughly towelled himself dry before wrapping it loosely around his hips and heading back to the annexe. We both admired his retreat.

"Er…and piercings…er…there too," she added warily, pointing in the vague direction of her own chest.

Yes, as well as the tattoos, we'd been alerted to the silvery glint of a nipple ring, thanks to the bright winter sunlight.

I felt the need to defend him. "The sixteenth Earl of Rossingley has his nipples pierced, too, but you've never felt the need to point that out. I hope you are not about to go all bourgeois on me, Sabine."

"No, no, Marcel," she responded hastily. "If he's er…a friend of Lucien's, then I'm sure he's a fine gentleman." She hesitated as if making a super effort to be polite. "And it's nice that you've taken a lodger."

"Yes, it is," I agreed firmly. "I'll introduce him to you soon. He's still settling in; I've hardly seen him myself since he arrived."

After the short taxi ride from La Rochelle airport to my house, during which I became ridiculously anxious and chattered non-stop, we'd not really spoken. As if escorting royalty, I'd nervily shown him the annexe, explained about the keys, the water, the electricity, and all that sort of tedious stuff. I then escaped before I did something really silly, like grab him around the waist and kiss him senseless. Which would have been totally inappropriate behaviour for a celibate landlord.

I finally caught up with Guillaume the following afternoon as I was taking a break after a long, tedious conference call, during which I'd had to refrain from pointing out that all the other members of the committee apart from myself were intellectual pygmies. Feeling rather worked up, I'd begun making a restorative soothing hot chocolate in the kitchen when Guillaume entered through the garden door. If his startled expression was anything to go by, it seemed he hadn't expected me to be up and about. If he'd been observing me at all, then he'd have known I generally didn't surface from the study until my 7:00 p.m. alarm.

I was stupidly pleased to see him and unthinkingly reached forwards to kiss both cheeks in welcome. Isn't being a Frenchman a marvellous thing? You can kiss people you fancy, both on greeting and departure, and no one thinks anything of it.

"Hello, stranger! I'm making a drink—can I make one for you too?"

He shyly accepted my offer, and we fell awkwardly silent as I heated up a pan of milk. It was as if our kissing on the bed at Rossingley had never happened. Dressed casually, in jeans and a light navy sweater over a white T-shirt, Guillaume was easily the most attractive man I'd entertained in my kitchen for ages, possibly ever. Fleetingly, I thought about the defined body under those clothes, which I'd ogled most mornings when supposedly knee-deep in paperwork, and pulled myself together.

"Tell me how you are getting on. I know I've been busy, but I've been thinking of you, you know."

So he began relating his new job behind the bar. Located on the other side of the port, the establishment was nothing special, more popular with locals than tourists. A place I'd never visited, which didn't narrow it down much. It seemed he'd made a good start; the patrons were friendly, the boss was helpful, nobody asked too many awkward questions, such as where he'd come from, and he had plenty of time to plan his coaching. He'd been to the football club, too, and met the fairly ragtag bunch of Sunday afternoon players, concluding they were keen but lacking discipline and tactical flair. I refrained from pointing out they were a bunch of waiters, plumbers, prison workers, and accountants trying to keep fit, not Olympique de Marseilles. Nonetheless, his ambition was admirable, and no doubt, they would be believing they were a topflight team by the time he'd finished with them. I hopefully nodded wisely as he went on to talk passionately about things like 4-4-2 formations, a flat back four, set pieces, holding play, and the like. Before I knew it, an hour or so had passed, and I was still enjoying his soft, melodic accent.

A low vibration in my cardigan pocket interrupted our cosy chat.

"Oh, sorry," I said, quickly cancelling it. I felt myself redden. "I'm trying to persuade my sister to mollycoddle me less, which she's agreed to as long as I make some…ah, lifestyle modifications. This is one of them. It's my alarm to remind me to go to the mini-market before it closes and buy myself some dinner."

If he thought this was odd, he didn't give any outward sign. I was enjoying myself so much I didn't want the evening to end. We'd talked as easily as this when I'd visited him in prison, and it felt as natural now as it did then.

"Do you…ah, I don't suppose you would like to join me for dinner? We can choose something together. I'm not much of a cook though."

"You'll be like a *MasterChef* contestant compared with me. I don't remember ever cooking anything before my sentence. I lived at home with my mother, and she did it all."

A look of sadness briefly crossed his handsome features. All of the confidence he'd previously shown when he'd talked about football and bar work had disappeared completely. And as I turned to reach for my wallet, it hit me. For a supposedly clever bloke, I'd been an absolute intellectual pygmy myself. For most of his adult life, he'd eaten prison canteen food. No wonder he'd not used my kitchen—he didn't know how to cook and was too polite to ask.

"Well, we can make a hash of things together." I smiled at him. "And perhaps if dinner is edible, we could do it most nights. I'm sure I can find a cookery book or something lying around here to assist us."

The winter light was fading as we walked the short distance across the port and up a side street towards the mini-market. He pre-empted me by tucking my arm under his as we headed up the minor incline. We probably looked a strange couple as I was wearing a dress shirt and a grey saggy cardigan over my most comfortable green chinos. I'd topped it off with my scarf and a woollen poncho Lucien had left behind years ago and had been gathering dust in the hallway. Guillaume, of course, looked like a handsome, fit, casually dressed guy who anyone would be proud to have on their arm.

It was fun in the mini-market. Words which I never expected to utter. We were both useless at meal planning and ended up with far more vegetables than we could ever get through before they perished. Guillaume, I discovered, had a penchant for the local specialty ice cream—*caramel fleur de sel* flavour, and I confessed my addiction to hot chocolate. We both bypassed the alcohol aisle. Guillaume had never had an opportunity to acquire a taste for it, and I was well acquainted with the significant body of research pertaining to alcohol triggering asthma attacks. By the time we were queuing to pay— he insisted we split the bill—the basket was full to overflowing. Thank goodness I had such a delicious hunk to help me carry it all back to the house.

We'd settled on salmon fillets, tiny island-grown new potatoes, and green beans. Not exactly *haute cuisine*, but we didn't do too badly, even though I said it myself. Maybe I'd cook the salmon for slightly fewer minutes next time, but Guillaume winked at me and insisted he preferred his fish dried up rather than tender and moist. And it was kind of cosy in the kitchen, with him peering over my shoulder to check on the state of the potatoes. Boldly, I slid my arm around his waist.

"It's really nice having you here, Guillaume. I wanted you to know that."

His lips found my temple and pressed against it as I momentarily rested my head on his shoulder. "I like being here."

"Is this enough though? You and me, close friends? I don't expect…exclusivity, you know. I can't expect that from you. I understand other people like yourself…have certain needs."

I was blushing as I gave this little speech, and he laughed, squeezing me closer.

"You're very funny; did anyone ever tell you that, Marcel? And I've noticed that you hum when you're happy. You hummed all the way around the supermarket and again while you've been cooking."

"Oh goodness, that must get on your nerves. I don't even know I'm doing it. Nudge me, or tell me to stop or something. It drives people mad."

"No, I like it; it's sweet."

Dinner continued in the same happy vein, nothing fancy, merely two men sharing a simple meal across from each other at the kitchen table. We followed it up with a small chunk of brie each and some of the ice cream we'd bought earlier. I'd almost forgotten about the spreadsheet I'd been looking forwards to completing later that evening. At some point, during the ice cream course, our hands found each other across the table. All that was missing was a rose-scented candle and a mariachi band.

The sound of a key turning in a lock at the front door spoiled everything.

Simon. Blast. He shouted to me in greeting.

"You appear to have a visitor," observed Guillaume, visibly shrinking. He pushed away from the table, withdrawing his hand from mine. "I'll leave you to it. Leave the mess. I'll come back and clear up later."

I stood with him. "Don't go. It's…he's a friend. Sort of. He helps me with things, but somewhere along the way, he has forgotten that this is my house, not his. I really should get my key back from him. He won't stay long."

Simon appeared at the doorway, all Lycra'd up after his cycle over from La Couarde to mine. He did a double take when he saw I wasn't alone.

"Oh, hi, Simon. This is…ah…this is my friend, Guillaume Guilbaud. He's staying with me in the annexe for a while."

"Pleased to meet you," responded Simon, his voice conveying the message he wasn't pleased at all. "I'm Simon. Marcel and I are *very good* friends. Old friends."

Not that it was a competition or anything.

Stepping forwards, Simon briefly shook Guillaume's hand before ignoring him completely and turning back to me.

"Marcel, darling. I had a nightmare getting the car serviced for you. Something wrong with the carburettor. It cost another two hundred and fifty euros; can you believe it? Do you mind transferring me the funds? Sorry to be a pain."

Darling? That was clearly for Guillaume's benefit. Men who chose to dress head-to-toe in red-and-blue Lycra, as if they were auditioning for the role of Spiderman, never get to call me darling. I raised my eyebrows in surprise. "Goodness, the car's not even two years old! The garage haven't contacted me to discuss it."

"I told them not disturb you. I know what you're like when you're busy."

I reached for my phone and transferred the money online. I seemed to be doing that an awful lot lately. "Do you have the invoice?"

Simon made a pantomime of searching the pockets of his jacket. "Oh, bugger, I must have been wearing my other coat. I'll bring it in later during the week."

Guillaume had started transferring our dinner plates over to the sink, his back to us.

"Have you written out a shopping list, Marcel? I'm off to Intermarché tomorrow."

"Thank you, Simon, but there's no need to go on my behalf. Guillaume and I have been shopping already this evening and have all we need for the week. Going forwards, I think we'll be doing that a lot from now on. Which will save you the bother."

"But thank you anyway," I added hastily, seeing his face take on a curious look. He was eyeing Guillaume's rear view appraisingly. And a very attractive rear view it was; I'd been surreptitiously doing the same myself.

"No bother," he said coolly. "I hope you are not overdoing it, Marcel." His tone, intended to be soothing, irritated the hell out of me. "You know how tired you get sometimes, darling."

Dropping his voice almost to a whisper, he leaned forwards. "Especially when you are trying to make a good impression on a new friend."

The patronising…expletive.

Simon wasn't a bad-looking man. Possibly a few years older than me, but he kept himself in shape doing the middle-aged-man-in-Lycra thing and had a naturally angular frame. Spiky was how I always thought of him, both in looks and personality. He had a sharp nose and thin lips, and his calculating eyes missed nothing, including the cosy scene he'd intruded upon. Somehow, over the last year, he'd insinuated himself far too deeply into my life without me noticing, and I wasn't sure how to politely extract him. He certainly hadn't looked pleased when I mentioned the shopping.

"I didn't catch where you came from, Guillaume," he said suddenly.

"I didn't say," Guillaume replied, reaching for a tea towel.

"How did you two meet each other? You've never mentioned Guillaume before, Marcel."

I wavered, not wanting to meet either Guillaume's eye or Simon's. "You don't know everything about me, Simon," I began weakly.

"We have mutual friends," interrupted Guillaume smoothly. "In the UK."

"Yes," I added, relieved. "You've heard me mention Lucien, haven't you?"

"But that's not a local accent, is it?" persisted Simon. "Nor a British one."

"No," said Guillaume placidly, passing me the now dry plates to put away in the cupboard. "It's not."

He turned back to hang up the tea towel, conversation over. Thankfully, Simon backed off. While Guillaume wasn't exactly intimidating, there was a certain firmness about his manner, and the tattoos and tongue piercing certainly helped in that regard.

"Well," said Simon briskly. "Here are your car keys. You and your new friend seem to have everything under control. Nothing to worry Sabine about this week. I'll be back in a couple of days. And you know where I am if you need me."

There was an unmistakable sneer about the way he said 'new friend', and I was mightily relieved when the door closed behind him.

"Sorry about that, Guillaume. My sister's rotten attempt at matchmaking. He can be okay some of the time, and the last episode when I was very ill, he was quite helpful. A fact of which he constantly likes to remind me."

Guillaume shrugged. "It's fine. I don't expect you to explain me to your friends if you don't want to. He obviously feels like he's had his nose pushed out slightly, that's all."

"Yes, well, he'll have to get used to it. He likes to be useful. Odd business about my car though," I pondered. "I don't know much about cars, but new Audis don't generally have problems like that, do they?"

Guillaume picked up his jacket from the back of the chair.

"I don't know anything about cars, I'm afraid. Sorry."

Simon had broken the mood, and now I felt out of sorts and wanted to escape back to my study. "*On fait les bises*, Guillaume?"

He grinned at me. "I thought you'd never ask. Goodnight, *mon coeur.*"

Chapter Ten

Guillaume

I met another of Marcel's friends the following night, and he was infinitely preferable to that Simon jerk, who clearly resented my existence. I never thought of myself as someone who made snap judgements, but there was something about Simon that left me cold. The familiar rumblings of anxiety I'd experienced since my release, which had disappeared during my evening with Marcel, had resurfaced.

To put it bluntly, this new guy had a face only a mother could love. Short and stocky, he held himself awkwardly, as if he was concentrating on following a set of rules about how to behave with a new acquaintance. Marcel introduced him as Dominic, his good friend and regular chess partner. From the minute he arrived, it was plain Dominic was besotted with Marcel. It was equally obvious that Marcel knew and was kind to him anyway. Unlike Simon, Dominic greeted me with genuine warmth, although he stared at his own feet as he shook my hand, and he accepted our vague cover story at face value. After some forced chit-chat in the kitchen, I left them to it and headed back to the annexe to change for football training.

The blokes at the football club were as disinterested as Dominic in my background. As long as I elevated the team from the bottom spot in the local league table, which they had ignominiously occupied for four years, I could have descended from Venus, then massacred an entire city, and they would still have been pleased to have me on board. A couple of the guys, as well as Antoine, worked at the prison—it was the biggest employer on the island—so I guessed everyone knew who I was anyway. Maybe that accounted for the distinct lack of dissent in the ranks. Every order I gave, even the tedious squat thrusts during warm-up, was obediently followed.

I'd sort of avoided Antoine since my release. Well, not avoided exactly, but deliberately not found myself alone with him. The thing we'd had between us was over, for me anyhow. He managed to corner me, however, after the warm-down.

"You seem to be settling in okay," he observed cautiously as we sat side by side, unlacing our boots.

"Yeah," I agreed because he really wasn't interested in hearing about the night sweats and four-in-the-morning conviction that I was a worthless piece of shit. "It's a bit odd after all that time, takes some adjusting, but, yeah, I'm okay. Thanks for setting me up in the bar—your cousin, Stefan, is a nice guy."

He accepted my thanks with a nod of his head. I had the distinct impression he had more to say, so I waited patiently.

"Stefan says you're living with that posh bloke who did the prison visits."

A statement, not a question.

"Yeah, I am. At least, I'm lodging in the annexe attached to his house," I clarified. "Until I get myself a bit more sorted. It was nice of him to offer."

Antoine raised his eyebrows knowingly at the last remark. "It was. Very nice. I bet he wouldn't extend that offer to all the inmates."

"It's not like that, Antoine. We're friends, that's all. He's been very kind."

Friends who cooked together, and kissed, and held hands like innocent teenagers. Exclusive, to use Marcel's phrase, even if this particular brand of exclusivity left me horny and frustrated.

"As I said, I bet he wouldn't be so kind to all of the inmates."

"I didn't make you any promises when I took the job, Antoine, you know that. We were perfectly clear about that when I agreed to come back here. And you are married, in case you forgot."

"I can't bloody forget, can I?" Antoine exploded. "She's in my bed every bloody night. And she's suspicious; she thinks I've got another woman. I know she does."

I stood and slipped on my tracksuit bottoms. "Well, she's reasonably safe on that front, at least. How's it going with the bloke in 33M?"

"Annoyingly," he grumbled. "Seems like he wants to be the one on his knees as well, so we have to take it in turns. I'm not very good at being the disciplinarian. I find it a real turn-off actually."

"Oh." I reached for my sports bag. "That doesn't sound like a recipe for a beautiful friendship."

Antoine stood, too, sighing. "I've fucked up, haven't I? My life, I mean. I never wanted to get married anyway, but when I got her up the duff, it seemed the right thing to do. And

I don't think she likes me much anymore anyway. But putting all of that aside, how the hell, after thirteen years of marriage, two kids, and a mortgage, do you turn to your wife and say, 'Oh, by the way, babe, I'm bi and have been sucking prisoner's cocks for the last four years?' While pretending to be a caretaker, or a vicar, or a dental nurse? How the hell do I explain that to my kids?"

He'd raised his voice, and I hastily looked round. Thankfully, no one had heard. The dental nurse one was unfamiliar—he must have been exploring that scene with the prisoner in 33M. I'd have definitely remembered posing as a dentist wielding his big drill.

"Listen, Antoine, calm down. People will wonder what the hell we're talking about if you carry on shouting. Don't do anything hasty."

I paused, desperately thinking. He was on the verge of tears. In uniform at work, he had seemed so in control, happily compartmentalising the two halves of his life, joking about it even, relishing the role play, always wanting more than I could offer. I now had the impression this outburst had been building for a while.

"Could you get some professional counselling and support?" I asked, clutching at straws. "You need to offload this onto somebody with better advice than me. Or your brother or your cousin, maybe? I mean, I'm here for you, mate, but I haven't got a clue how to help."

"You're possibly the only person I know who does understand," he answered, brushing at his eyes. "There's no way I can tell my family. My wife would take the kids, and that would be that."

Stepping back, he took a couple of deep breaths, attempting to get himself under control. We were starting to receive a few curious looks.

"I can't carry on like this, Guillaume. I mean, I know you and me are over, but there will be others, won't there? I can't stop myself; it's who I am. I'm not sure I can hold it all together any longer."

We had begun walking towards the gates leading back onto the street. Antoine stopped at his car; I was jogging home. After glancing round, I put my hand on his arm.

"Listen, Antoine, you can always call me, okay? You've got my number. Take it one day at a time. See you for the match on Sunday, yeah?"

If I'd thought Simon's reaction to my presence was bad, he was nothing compared to Marcel's big sister, Sabine.

It was a couple of days later. Having rained solidly all morning, the bar was so quiet for my lunchtime shift that, knocking off early, I had decided to surprise Marcel at his desk with a gift of a mug of hot chocolate. Knowing him, he wouldn't have moved from his study all morning. Letting myself in quietly through the garden entrance to the kitchen, I could hear raised voices coming from the direction of the study. One was female and shrieking loudly.

"Tell me Simon's wrong, Marcel. Please, for goodness' sake. I knew there was something fishy about him when I saw all those tattoos."

"What is there about him, Sabine? Tell me what it is about tattoos that you suddenly find so appalling?"

Marcel sounded calmer than his sister, his warm voice pleasant but with a hint of firmness.

"His bloody tattoos aren't the problem! Simon's been to that bar he works at, asked a couple of questions. Searched around online. Amazing what you can find out these days about people, isn't it, with merely a click of a mouse? Especially when you're a journalist."

"I know what you are about to say," replied Marcel, "and I don't care."

Angrier this time, Marcel's voice now came from a different angle, as if he'd left his desk and moved over to the windows. The room he referred to as the study, and which housed Marcel's bank of computers, desks, and bookshelves, was actually the main sitting room of the house. Which made perfect sense to me because if the room housing your work was the one where you were happy to spend most of your days, then why not have it as the nicest one in the house? Light and airy, it was big enough to accommodate a comfy sofa and armchairs, too, with an excellent view over the walled garden.

He coughed and cleared his throat. My heart hammered in my chest, my skin suddenly hot and clammy, despite recent exposure to the full blast of cold December air. Those 4:00 a.m. instincts were bang on the money; deep inside, I'd known this couldn't last. There were no prizes for guessing what was coming next, and I mentally calculated how long it would take me to pack my bags.

"He's a bloody murderer! You've invited a man, who's killed another man in cold blood with his bare hands, to waltz into your home! Are you mad?"

What started as a small cough and a throat clearing from Marcel turned into a full-blown spasm of coughing. Someone paced the polished wooden floorboards. I guessed it was Sabine.

"The key"—cough—"words here, are my"—cough—"home. My home. Not yours or Simon's. I am a solvent, thirty-six-year-old man who holds down a high-level government position! I can have whoever I please here to stay. I don't have to answer to you or anyone else."

Another wheezy spasm of coughing followed. Sabine spoke over it.

"Which is perfectly well and good, Marcel, if you were capable of managing your home by yourself, but you're not, are you? Half the time, you're not healthy enough, and the rest of the time you're so engrossed in your precious work that you wouldn't notice if this *man*"—she spat out the word 'man' as if it tasted of arsenic—"if this *man* dragged his next victim, covered in blood, across the floor in front of you!"

Silence, except for the sound of laboured breathing, which, frankly, caused a sharp ache in the pit of my stomach. Over the last few days, I had come to understand why, if he could help it, Marcel rarely left the vicinity of his home and garden, and I didn't blame him one bit. Because when he was at his desk, or pottering in the garden, or preparing a simple meal in the kitchen, or even planting a soft kiss on my cheek, his asthma scarcely bothered him. And for all of that time, I imagined he could forget he was different to anybody else. He could temporarily forget he suffered an illness that threatened his existence on an almost daily basis. When he sat behind his desk and communicated with his colleagues, five hundred kilometres away in the Paris office, they didn't see a man crippled by his own lungs. They only saw the incisive decision maker, the extraordinary intellect, an articulate and generous boss.

"I need…" Pause. "Sabine, pass me…"

Some rustling of papers.

"The blue one's not here, Marcel. God knows where you've left it. Which proves my point exactly."

"I…think…I…"

More rustling and lifting up of objects. "For Christ's sake, sit down. I'll go and get one from upstairs. And I'll bring the oximeter too."

I couldn't stop myself. The thought of Marcel suffering for even a few minutes longer than necessary was unbearable. To hell with the consequences.

"There's one here," I announced, pushing through the half-open kitchen door. "One of your blue ones. Here, Marcel, take this."

He was back at his desk, hunched forwards in his chair with his elbows on his knees and gasping for breath. Putting the inhaler in his left hand, I knelt in front of him and rubbed his back in big slow circles as I had done that time at Rossingley. It was probably of no help whatsoever, but it was all the comfort I could offer. His right hand squeezed mine.

"I've got you, *mon coeur*. Breathe. Everything will be fine."

I became acutely aware of Sabine standing, watching us, arms folded across her chest as his breathing rate gradually settled, the rise and fall of his chest less profound as the inhaler performed its magic. The siblings were strikingly similar in looks, although her blue-grey eyes, locked onto mine, didn't convey anywhere near the kindness in Marcel's.

"You heard everything, didn't you?" she said accusingly. "So you listen at doors as well? Honestly, Marcel, this man is not the sort of person you should be sheltering. I've a good mind to call the police."

I stood, releasing Marcel's hand. "I didn't know Marcel had a visitor. When I came into the kitchen, I couldn't help overhearing. But it's okay; I'll go. I don't want to cause any trouble. Give me half an hour or so to pack my stuff."

Marcel vigorously shook his head and grabbed at my hand again to prevent me from leaving.

"No, Guillaume," he wheezed out between gulps of air. "I don't want you to go."

Sabine remained motionless, her lips set in an angry thin line. The asthma attack didn't have the same gut-wrenching effect on her emotions as it did mine. No doubt, she'd witnessed them countless times before. I wasn't certain I could ever become used to them, not that I had a hope of ever finding out now anyway.

"Marcel, I think I should leave. I don't want to be the cause of a rift between you and your family. Or your friends, for that matter. You need them."

"I know I need them, Guillaume, but that's not the point."

Those blue-grey eyes looked up at me beseechingly as he hitched up his glasses. "I…ah, I…think I could, ah…possibly need you too?"

A harrumphing noise from Sabine, and he turned to her. "I know Guillaume has only been here for a few days, but I've known him longer than that. I trust him. And since he's been here, I've had more independence. We've cooked; I've even shopped! I feel safer knowing there is someone available in the annex if I have a bad attack."

"Yes, I've been nagging you to get someone in for ages. But it didn't have to be *him*! I bet there are lots of perfectly decent, law-abiding folk who'd be happy to lodge in the lap of luxury."

"I don't want anybody else," Marcel replied stubbornly. "I want Guillaume. And stop shouting at me. You're upsetting me."

There's something about siblings that brings out the worst in each other. Sabine was clearly doing the bossy big sister thing, and Marcel was starting to sound a tad petulant. Despite how hurtful it was, I accepted Sabine's anger was coming from the best of places—concern for her vulnerable brother. Both of them appeared to have forgotten I was there. Facing Sabine, I held out my hand.

"Sorry, we haven't actually met. I'm Guillaume. And I'm sorry that I've caused you both to fall out. If you prefer me to leave, I will, because the last thing I want is for Marcel to get upset."

Stiffly, she returned my handshake.

"Sabine," offered Marcel, "I didn't tell you about Guillaume because I knew you would worry and we'd have exactly this conversation. But I think you should be prepared to give him a chance. Please. He's my, ah, friend, and we've grown quite close. At least stay and have lunch with us."

Chapter Eleven

Marcel

Possibly the most awkward meal I've endured. Ever. Which is saying something, considering I joined Sabine and her ex-husband for Clara's birthday dinner last month, which ended in tears and tantrums. And they weren't from the birthday girl.

Guillaume put together a basic salad, produced a baguette, and the remainder of the brie, and we attempted to make small talk. It was one of those meals where every clink of cutlery against china resonated around the room as if we were the only diners in an edgy, modern restaurant that was all hard surfaces and shiny floors. Hardly ever lost for words—apart from when I literally didn't have the breath to form them—for once in my life, I could think of nothing to say.

Guillaume sat miserably across from me, shuffling lettuce around on his plate. I would have liked to reach over and hold his hand as we sometimes did at the end of dinner, but that would have only inflamed Sabine even more.

My overwhelming feeling, however, while I scrambled around for conversation, was one of relief that Guillaume hadn't gone back to the annexe and packed his bags. He might still decide to do it anyway. After all, my sister had been phenomenally rude to him. And annoyingly, she was mostly a good person, kind and caring. I probably wouldn't even be alive today if it wasn't for all of her love and support. Thus, it was even more upsetting that he'd only seen her at her worst. And then I remembered.

"Guillaume used to be a professional footballer before he went…before he…"

Okay, not a great opening sentence. Don't mention the war, Marcel, you idiot. I tried again.

"Guillaume used to be a professional footballer in his teens and early twenties."

Much better. I smiled at him encouragingly. "Which is that team you used to play for, Guillaume?"

"Nîmes Olympique," he replied. "In the second division. It's based in a town about one hundred kilometres outside Marseilles."

My sister nibbled a corner of baguette and deliberately looked at her watch. "I'm fully aware of the location of Nîmes," she replied coldly.

"And what position did you play?" I doggedly persisted.

"Midfield—left or centre," he replied.

That meant absolutely nothing to me whatsoever, but I nodded knowingly. Sabine stared out of the window.

"My niece, Clara—Sabine's daughter—is football-mad, isn't she, Sabine?" I ploughed on without waiting for her to reply. "Goodness knows where she got that from. She has those sticker books, you know? The ones where you buy a few mystery players every week in the *tabac*, and trade them with other kids? How many books has she filled now, Sabine? Four, five?"

Mention of Clara usually had my sister smiling, even when she was trying her hardest to remain cross with me. But not today.

"Five," she agreed. "Costs us a fortune doesn't it, Marcel?"

"I have a few of those sticker books in storage somewhere," added Guillaume. "From when France won the World Cup back in '98. And the Euros in '84 and 2000."

"Goodness, they sound fascinating, don't they Sabine?"

From the expression on Sabine's face, it was clear she found them about as fascinating as the history of Norwegian thrash metal bands and nowhere near as fascinating as the branch of a bay tree knocking against the kitchen window.

"I could get hold of them if she'd like to see them," Guillaume added gamely. "They're all completed. The '84 one is probably a collector's item by now."

"I bet she would," I responded enthusiastically. "I would too."

Okay, so Sabine and Guillaume probably saw this for the blatant lie it was, and it suddenly occurred to me that, sadly, there was no way my sister would let Clara anywhere near an ex-criminal such as Guillaume. Even though, knowing Clara, she'd have him eating out of her hand in minutes. But at least the meal ended on a vaguely harmonious note—in football parlance I would have called it a no-score draw.

After I'd seen Sabine to the door and she'd promised to call me in a couple of days (which was about as much as I could wish for), I found Guillaume tidying up in the kitchen.

"Thank you for staying," I said simply, slipping my arm around his waist.

"It's not going to be easy, Marcel, having me here." He kissed the top of my head, and I felt him inhaling the scent of my hair, which I'd fortunately remembered to wash that morning. I couldn't help but snuggle closer. He responded with another kiss. "For either of us, especially when you hug me like this."

"Mmm," I agreed. Because there was nothing much else to say.

Holding him felt marvellous; there was no denying it. On the one hand, I was thrilled because I had a feeling I was on an exorable slide down that celibacy continuum thingy. My resolve was slipping, and there was nothing I could do about it. But on the other hand, how fair was it to foist myself upon this man? Hadn't he had enough trouble in his life without being burdened with me and all my daily dramas? Rubbing my back when my chest unexpectedly became tight was one thing, one very lovely, thoughtful thing, actually, but he had yet to experience the full drudgery of it all, week in and week out.

And the other truth? The top-secret, toe-curling, embarrassing truth I hadn't ever confessed to anyone, the one he'd rapidly discover if we ever got that far? Something to which no red-blooded (youngish) male should ever, ever admit, even at knifepoint, possibly? And which will be a 100 per cent guaranteed turn-off to my prospective, gorgeous lover, and send him running for the hills, or at least back to Marseilles?

Here goes.

I found sex knackering. Absolutely…expletive knacker-ing. And asthma-inducing. In fact, so knackering and asthma-inducing I frequently had to abandon halfway through and take a nebuliser. Or sometimes two. Which generally killed the mood.

★

Christmas was rapidly approaching, and as Clara would be spending a few days with her father, Sabine planned to jet off with a friend for some winter sun and a well-earned rest. A bit of time apart would be good for both of us. She'd popped over a couple of times since our debacle and had been reasonably civil to Guillaume, so that was something. Guillaume trod a fine line with her between trying to ingratiate himself without seeming to pander. He'd bought a few packs of football trading cards for Clara, which struck the right tone.

Although invited to spend Christmas over at Rossingley, I had graciously declined as I tried to avoid travel as much as possible during the winter months. Amusingly, Guillaume had separately been invited, too, by Reuben. Lucien had obviously kept his thoughts about the pair of us to himself as, from the one-sided conversation I overheard Guillaume having with Reuben, he was very concerned Guillaume would be spending the festive season all on his lonesome. Which was super sweet, and Guillaume gently reassured Reuben he would be perfectly all right and had plenty of work at the bar to keep him busy. Oh, and that the guy who was letting him lodge in his annexe didn't mind him hanging around during the festive period.

My private daydreams for keeping Guillaume busy over Christmas were massively highjacked by Dominic's forlorn face when, over an evening game of chess, he described his own holiday arrangements, which basically amounted to a microwave dinner for one.

"Unless," he began, earnestly addressing one of my white pawns, "you…I mean…we could…we could spend it…er… together?"

He wriggled around uncomfortably in his chair. Pretending I hadn't noticed his black queen begging to be castled, I made a pointless forwards step with the pawn that held his gaze. Being mean to Dominic was akin to drowning newborn puppies. Groaning inwardly, I plastered on a smile.

"I would love it if you would join Guillaume and me for Christmas lunch, Dominic. Why don't you provide the cheese?"

"I like Guillaume, Marcel."

"I like Guillaume, too, Dominic."

"Do you really want to invite me, or are you being polite because you feel sorry for me? Like when you let me win at chess, like you are doing now?"

Most people were ill-equipped to deal with Dominic's conversational style. I was most people.

"I really want to invite you, Dominic."

His relief was palpable. When he wasn't frowning with worry, or fidgeting, or looking anywhere but at me, he almost had a sweet smile.

"Thank you, Marcel, for inviting me."

"Thank you for wanting to come, Dominic."

"Thank you for letting me provide the cheese, Marcel."

"Thank you for… Goodness, Dominic, have your turn."

★

Having Dominic's gentle company over Christmas, and the accompanying fuzzy glow from doing a good deed, was one thing; having to endure Simon for the day was another. He usually visited his elderly mother in Paris for the festivities, followed by an extended stay at his brother's, also in Paris, thereby cleverly avoiding shouldering any entertaining costs himself. It appeared his family had finally wised up to him as, this year, his brother was spending the holidays at his mother-in-law's house, and his own mother was going on a cruise on the far side of the world with a bunch of other old ladies.

I heard this tale of woe over a hot chocolate in my kitchen. Simon was on the *pastis*—my *pastis*, naturally. Encroaching on my personal space, he breathed unpleasant aniseed fumes down my neck as he watched me preparing Guillaume's and my chicken Caesar salad supper. Guillaume was due back from work imminently.

"Watching you putting that together is making me hungry," Simon hinted, slightly slurring his words.

"Goodness, I'm so sorry; it looks like I've only bought enough chicken for two."

Another swig of *pastis*. More fire down my neck.

"This will be our first Christmas together, Marcel. The first of many, I hope."

Eh, what?

Momentarily taken aback, I let the paring knife slip in my hand, nicking the end of my index finger.

"Ouch! Pass me a paper towel. Quickly, before I drip blood onto the chicken."

As I held my hand under the cold tap, Simon came up behind me and leaned over my shoulder to assess the damage. More hot aniseed breath mixed with last night's garlic. Yuck. As his hand accidentally brushed against my hip, I moved to one side to give him some space. His hand followed. Oh…bother. Not accidental, then.

"Look," I said breezily, holding up my finger for him to see. "Only a tiny cut, thank goodness. Nothing to worry about. My hopes of becoming an international concert pianist still abound. You can stand down, Simon."

Instead of budging, he remained ridiculously close behind me, and thus I found myself effectively stuck between Simon's body and the sink. If I turned around, we would be face to face, and that pastis breath would be in my face and…

"Simon, for goodness' sake, stop doing that!"

The hand that had been resting at my hip had moved. As if pawing me in a dodgy nightclub, his fingers goosed between my buttocks. I shivered with revulsion.

"Come on, Marcel," he breathed into my neck, his lips wet on my skin. "You know you want it."

With effort, I pushed him aside before picking up the knife again, my finger wrapped in kitchen towel. We'd performed this dance several times before, and it was usually when he'd had a few too many drinks, like now, so I should have been on my guard. I didn't feel threatened in any way; I knew he wouldn't actually try to force himself upon me, but still, unrequited advances were unpleasant, all the same.

"Simon, trust me on this. As I made it clear last time, and the time before that, I really don't."

I always thought Dominic was the one completely lacking in emotional intelligence, but Simon either didn't pick up the vibe or deliberately refused to see it.

"Yes, you do, baby. It's written all over you. You're making me wait, that's all."

"Look." I turned to face him. "I'm really not. You are a good friend, and I really appreciate all that you have done for me, but…"

A dark shadow appeared at the kitchen window. Thank goodness, Guillaume had returned. A second later, he joined us in the kitchen. Simon's expression changed from hopeful lust to one of disdain as he registered my relieved smile.

"I'll leave you to your salad," he said, ignoring Guillaume completely. "What time are we sitting down to our Christmas lunch?"

Chapter Twelve

Guillaume

Two days before Christmas and we fancied our first win, an early Christmas present that would lift us off the bottom of the table. Combined with our home advantage, gastroenteritis had unfortunately struck down several members of the usually strong opposition, so we faced a depleted team made up of teenagers and oldies. I'd take the wins however we found them.

Following a heavy frost overnight, it was bloody freezing, which the teenagers expended a lot of energy moaning about. Capitalizing on their grumpiness and the sharp breeze against them in the first forty-five minutes, we were two–nil up at half time, one of the goals a scorcher into the top left scored by yours truly. My predecessor had used the fifteen-minute interval at half-time for a fag break and a shot of *pastis* in a plastic cup. But my team had learned the hard way—fifty press-ups hard—that this wasn't tolerated. Thus, they endured a motivational talk, glugged some overpriced hypertonic sports drinks, and performed three sets of leg stretches to keep their muscles loose. Before the whistle signalling the start of the second half, Antoine gave me a nudge.

"Look over there! Your lover boy's come to watch. *Putain*! Who's the cute guy with him?"

I looked up immediately and tried to prevent a huge grin from spreading across my face at the sight of Marcel bundled up in his stripy scarf and about fifteen layers of clothing under his overcoat. Reluctantly dragging my gaze from him, I cast about for a cute guy. The only other person standing with Marcel was Dominic. Er…Dominic?

"Antoine, do you mean the man to his left with dark hair, in the blue anorak?" I tried and evidently failed to keep the astonishment out of my voice.

"Yeah, um, obviously?" replied Antoine, giving me a look that said I was clearly unhinged. Belatedly, I remembered his description of the 'cute Neanderthal' in cell 33M.

"Oh, right. That's…ooh…that's Marcel's friend, Dominic. So…er, you go for that sort of look, do you?"

"Fuck, yeah! Sorry to burst your bubble, mate. Don't get me wrong. You're not bad-looking, Guillaume. You've got a good body and everything, but you know, you're a bit too smooth for my liking. Not rugged enough. I like my men a bit more…earthier. Hairier."

Bloody hell, Dominic had found himself an admirer. Now all I needed to do was investigate where he stood regarding role play, and I could set myself up in the matchmaking business. And Antoine was a decent bloke, easy on the eye too. Married, obviously, but a small detail like that shouldn't get in the way of cupid's arrow. It sounded as if the marriage was on its last legs anyhow. And on a baser level, Antoine gave great head; the man was not in possession of a gag reflex as far as I'd been able to tell. Although, the idea of receiving a blow job was not something I wanted to dwell on at the moment, especially while fifty spectators watched me running around in a pair of clingy shorts.

Fuck, I was in a permanent state of horniness these days. My final sexual encounter with Antoine had been weeks ago, and the closeness I was developing with Marcel, all those tantalising kisses and cuddles, was gradually killing me. I felt like I'd been walking around with a half-hard cock for days.

And that was the state of affairs *before* I witnessed Marcel's bloody morning yoga session. My God, that yoga session.

Up earlier than usual, I'd wandered bleary-eyed into the kitchen for a brew, planning on taking it back to bed with me. I knew he practised yoga; I'd seen the padded pink mat lying about, and it made perfect sense. Yoga was the easiest way for him to attempt to keep fit; he informed me he'd been contorting his body into a pretzel to a background hum of whale music for the best part of the last fifteen years. But to actually witness him in action? Bloody hell.

He'd been wearing pyjamas. Not sexy, hanging-low-off-the-hips 'lounge pants', suitably paired with a tight white T-shirt to ward off a chill while simultaneously demonstrating a perfect set of abs. No, no, no. Marcel had sported an old-fashioned pair of winceyette, stripy blue jim-jams, a bit baggy round the arse, a bit worn over the knees. There was no way on God's earth anyone dressed in that outfit should have made me horny, but *mon Dieu*, that bloke was limber. It didn't feel right surreptitiously ogling from the open kitchen doorway, and it certainly didn't feel right hiding a boner at the same time under my towelling robe.

"I know you're there, Guillaume," he'd said, his voice coming from somewhere between his thighs. "I'm happy for you to watch, or you can join in if you like."

He had gracefully relaxed his limbs, and his face reappeared. Smiling at me disarmingly, he'd then rearranged himself into some sort of upside-down elbow stand. His pyjama top had ridden up, affording me a marvellously unimpeded view of his taut, white belly, and the dark trail of hair disappearing under the elastic waistband of his pyjama bottoms.

"Scorpion pose," he'd continued. "Very good for strengthening your core."

My core was already very strong, hard as concrete actually. I'd shifted it into a more comfortable position, using the old hand-in-the-dressing-gown-pocket ruse, and then tightened the knot of my towelling robe as an extra precaution.

"And this one is the garland pose. A favourite of mine towards the end of a session. It stretches the thighs, hips, and groin. Probably a good football wind-down, I'd imagine."

I really hadn't needed Marcel doing a downward dog right after he'd murmured the words thighs, hips, and groin. His pert little arse had wiggled in the air as he stretched out his upper body along the mat and exhaled deeply and contentedly. Fuck, I'd had to escape.

"I'll…um…I'll make you a hot chocolate, yeah?"

A whistling sound jerked me out of my happy place, and I deliberately stared at Dominic's warty thing for a few seconds to get myself back under control before stepping out onto the pitch for the second half. The tactic worked like a dream.

Our opposition had rallied at half-time, and the cold wind was in their favour, but they were no match for a bunch of men who could almost taste moving off the bottom of the table. They clawed one goal back—a messy header from a corner which had no right to hit the back of the net—but we retaliated three minutes later with an absolute spanker from the edge of the box, and the game was over.

After much handshaking, back-patting and a quick shower, I headed out to find Marcel. Winning and the camaraderie felt good, but having Marcel waiting for me felt even better. He was chatting to Dominic, and not for the first time did I thank the Lord for being a Frenchman. A gentle peck in greeting on both smooth cheeks, inhaling vanilla and…the bloody essence of Marcel. Of course, I had to repeat it with Dominic, too, because he was becoming a friend as well. But, you take the rough with the smooth.

"That was fantastic!" cried Marcel, patting me on the back and leaving his hand there as though he couldn't quite bring himself to lose contact. "Three assists, four shots on goal, and one goal yourself—man of the match in my opinion!"

Trust Marcel and Dominic to have collected the stats. Marcel grinned happily, the tip of his nose and ears red from the cold air. Dominic seemed pleased, too, although he was fussing a little.

"Are you going to be okay walking back, Marcel? It is turning colder; the temperatures are set to plummet this evening. I'm happy to give you a lift home."

"Oh, no, Dominic. Thank you for the kind offer, but we're fine, aren't we Guillaume?" Marcel was as desperate for us to be alone as I was, and I threw him a conspiratorial look.

"Perfectly fine, thanks, Dom. It's not far."

We should have taken him up on the offer of a lift; he'd been right to be worried. Which showed how much I still had to learn about Marcel's health. It was only a twenty-minute stroll, but we were walking into a headwind, and even holding onto my arm, Marcel was struggling. By the time we made it into the house, he was shivering like a jelly and wheezing like an accordion. More familiar now with the drill, I momentarily left him slumped in the usual pose, leaning forwards with his elbows on his knees, while I ran upstairs to retrieve his bag of tricks.

"The problem with winter sports is that they take place in the winter," he joked through chattering teeth. I marvelled, not for the first time, how he managed to stay so upbeat when even walking a short distance on the flat could leave him so utterly helpless.

We waited for the inhalers to do their thing. "Bloody hell, Marcel, these hands are like ice blocks. Stick them up my hoodie to warm them up."

I moved closer and tried not to wince as he jammed his bloody freezing mitts in my armpits. It made him giggle, though, and I reached forwards to kiss the tip of his cold nose.

"Thanks for coming today; it was a lovely surprise."

"It was Dominic's idea. A perfect excuse for him to ogle twenty-two young men wearing skimpy shorts."

His breathing was almost back to normal, and the hands were definitely improving. I packed him off, still shivering, for a steaming shower while I made a hot chocolate and cranked up the wood burner. By the time he returned, clad in my favourite blue stripy pyjamas and a threadbare paisley dressing gown, I was sitting on the sofa waiting for him, with his drink and a couple of woollen throws.

"Seeing as we're entertaining on Christmas day, I thought I'd have a flick through some recipes, see what's…er…achievable for a pair of amateurs like us."

As I packed a blanket round him, he leaned his head on my shoulder, hands wrapped around the mug.

"Maybe not the stuffed goose, Guille. I'm not sure our culinary expertise is quite there yet."

"Mmm, I agree. But I'm not sure we can serve a *croque-monsieur* either. Mind you, Simon will be critical whatever we do."

Marcel turned a page of the recipe book. "Remind me why we invited him again?"

"I think you'll find that he invited himself."

While Marcel drank his chocolate, we happily wandered through the recipe book together, occasionally commenting on potential Christmas menu items.

"Thanks for looking after me," he said, placing the empty mug on the coffee table. "You don't have to, you know. It's not a condition for staying in the annexe."

I gave him a sideways look. "I know. But I don't mind. Are you warm enough now?"

"Yes, doctor, but you may need to check your patient thoroughly, to be on the safe side."

I was growing quite fond of flirty Marcel. He didn't come out to play very often, so I decided to make the most of it and reached for his hand. I kissed his fingertips.

"These are much warmer."

Brushing my lips over his cheek, I nodded with satisfaction. "Warm." Forehead. "Warm." The end of his nose. "Warm." The other cheek. "Warm." His lips. "Marvellous."

Without another word, his arms slid around my neck, and he was kissing me. Not the teasing, chaste stuff I'd come to expect, but full-on, demanding kisses, his tongue probing, his lips pressed hard against mine. It wasn't the smoothest of unions; our teeth clashed and we both tilted our heads to the same side as we delved deeper, our noses bumping. But none of that mattered when he tasted of sweet chocolate and promises of more. A soft moan escaped my throat. As we readjusted and he breathily devoured my mouth, I shoved my hands through his silky damp hair, pulling his face closer still.

"I'm steaming up," he panted, and a smile tugged at his lips as he lifted off his glasses, allowing them to clatter to the floor. We were no longer side by side; somehow, we'd shifted so he was half straddling me, and I scooted up the sofa, bringing my legs up so I was now fully reclining with him on top, his hips in between my opened legs and his elbows positioned either side of my head. The repositioning had involved him accidentally kneeing me in the balls while we freed up his dressing gown cord, which had somehow become wedged under a sofa cushion. As I said, not the smoothest of unions, but hell, Marcel was lying on top of me, so I didn't have much to complain about.

"This is an unexpected surprise," I murmured between kisses, and he nodded his agreement.

"It wasn't planned. I…had the notion that I needed to kiss you properly."

"You should come and watch me play football more often if this is the effect it has on you."

"Maybe I should."

Dipping down, he thoroughly kissed me again, licking, nibbling, sucking, and I let my head fall back with a groan of pleasure as his tongue traced a line across my jaw. For a celibate of the last eight years, he certainly hadn't forgotten how to kiss, and sliding my hands down to his arse, I canted my hips upwards, pressing us together. Separated by layers of paisley dressing gown, stripy pyjamas, and tracksuit bottoms, our dicks ground against each other, eliciting a delicious whimper from Marcel. Puffs of air came hot and quick against my mouth as we settled into an unhurried pace. The edge of something hard and knobbly dug right between my shoulder blades, causing sharp discomfort, and the sofa creaked distractingly on an uneven floorboard, but hell, I wasn't going to stop. Coming up for breath, I looked up at his flushed face.

"You're kind of dry-humping me here, Marcel."

"I know," he panted a little wheezily. "I'm also reciting reverse Fibonacci sequences in my head to prevent myself from ejaculating into my pyjama bottoms."

"Me too."

He paused mid hump. "Crumbs! Really?"

I grinned. "No, but I am mentally listing all the players in the Manchester United 1999 Champions League winning team."

He groaned as he pressed down against my throbbing dick. "It's not working. I can't think properly. My goodness, this feels good. You feel good, Guillaume. I might…goodness…oh goodness…"

"I shan't tell anybody if you do," I whispered, and he groaned again, circling his hips over mine and, yeah, wheezily dry-humping the stuffing out of me. I could have reached down, grabbed hold of him, and yanked off my trousers, his pyjamas, and pushed aside the dressing gown. But fuck, the whole innocence and simplicity of it felt so perfect that I didn't want to stop.

He came—sorry, *ejaculated*—into his pyjamas with his face buried in my neck and a sweet moan of pleasure before flumping down on top of me, out of breath and gasping. And giggling.

"I've kind of blown the whole celibacy thing out the water, haven't I?" he said eventually, snuggling onto my chest.

"Oh, I don't know," I teased. "From my perusal of the available literature, some of your lot consider what we've enjoyed as 'outercourse' and completely within the rules."

"What? So I'm still a voluntary celibate?" He grinned.

"Totally," I nodded gravely. "One hundred per cent."

Lifting my head, I pointedly flicked my eyes in the direction of my still-hard dick, the outline clearly visible against the material of my tracksuit bottoms. I arched my hips up to give him a reminder. "Me, too, although this is totally involuntary."

He blushed prettily. "Would you…ah…goodness. Would you…ah, like me to do something about that?"

He was still wheezy, his lungs playing a fine old tune against my chest.

"Only if you want to."

For a moment, as he hesitated, I thought he would decline, which would have been, well, disappointing. Instead, he completely blew my mind by doing the most un-Marcel-like thing ever. After sitting up and straddling me, he firmly gripped my leaking dick in one hand and, with the other, reached into the slit of his damp pyjamas and used his own spunk as lube. I nearly came from watching.

"I'm, ah, I'm a little out of practice," he murmured as he took me in hand.

"It's fine, keep going," I grunted, pushing up into his fist. It was more than fine; I hadn't seen any action for way too long, and this man had done the most fucking erotic thing ever. This hand job was going to be over before it had properly started.

"I mean, I…ah…masturbate, obviously, only now and then. Rarely, in fact, these days, but, you know, ah…"

"Just…just keep going, Marcel. You're doing great." Fuck, he was different.

"Yes, but, ah, I'm…actually… Guillaume, I'm a bit short of breath. I…ah…you're… I think you're possibly lying on my inhaler."

Jesus. Despite the ferreting around for the inhaler and protestations that his technique was lacking, somehow my dick stayed rock-hard. Fuck. From the second he'd coated me in his own spunk, the outcome was always going to be positive.

For those doubters who think it is impossible to laugh and come at the same time? Think again.

After we cleaned up, Marcel sat on the chair at his desk. "Do you mind if I, ah, do some work?" he pleaded. "I, ah, I think I need to, ah, process for a while. This…um…this is kind of a big deal for me."

"As long as you don't mind if I lie here and watch you?"

So I sprawled on the sofa, half perusing recipes and half watching Marcel as he worked, hunched over at his desk. Sometimes, he hummed to himself, and occasionally, he did a funny rocking thing I've caught him doing before, but only when he was really happy. It was cute beyond words. When I slipped away a couple of hours later, he barely noticed.

Chapter Thirteen

Marcel

Guillaume's last fifteen Christmases were spent locked up behind bars, so I guess Christmas day spent with Simon, Dominic, and me was always going to be better than that. Marginally. Mine, of course, was sublime because this wonderful guy, covered in tattoos and with a pierced tongue (that I secretly fantasised about licking along the length of my penis), somehow wanted to spend his days hanging around with weird old me.

I suppose that after our unanticipated but terribly sophisticated lovemaking session on the sofa, the next step would have been bed and the rude stuff. But Guillaume didn't push it. Which suited me perfectly. As much as he was making me contemplate those sorts of things for the first time in years, the longer he remained ignorant of what an anti-climax—literally—sex with me would be, the longer he'd stick around. And he still hadn't experienced my asthma at its worst, a bout of which was long overdue as the weather had been dreadful for a few weeks now. It was only a matter of time before I picked up some bug, and the whole circus came to town. Who knew if he would still want me after that?

In the end, we'd settled upon roasting a couple of big chickens. It was easy to bung them in the oven and then spend our time concentrating on dauphinoise potatoes, which felt like a high-risk venture, but Guillaume was confident we could pull off.

Our first guest to arrive was Dominic, knocking at the door while Guillaume had popped out to the *boulangerie* before it closed. Sweetly, he'd made an effort and was dressed in a very smart sweater I hadn't seen before. I complimented him, which was enough encouragement for him to boldly confess he'd been giving our relationship some serious thought. Until this moment, I hadn't actually appreciated we had a relationship beyond chess and the occasional coffee. Addressing me, but embroiled in a staring match with one of the kitchen cupboards about six inches to the right of my head, he made an announcement.

"I still want to play chess with you, Marcel, and I still want to be your friend, but I'm going to make a conscious effort not to ask you out for a drink anymore."

Okay, so this was slightly awkward. Should I express dismay or punch the air with relief?

"Well, that's…ah…thank you for telling me. And your friendship means a lot to me, so I'm glad we can still be friends."

"I'm glad that you're glad that we can still be friends. And I'm glad we can still play chess together."

"I'm glad that we can still play chess together too, Dominic."

"Good, I'm glad."

"So that's settled, then."

I busied myself opening a bottle of wine. Dominic enjoyed an occasional glass, and Simon never turned down an opportunity to imbibe something he hadn't purchased himself. I handed the wine to Dominic.

"So I'm going to ask Guillaume out for a drink instead," he blurted, transferring his attention from the cupboard to the wine glass.

"You can't!" I responded, slightly panicked. "I mean, sorry. I mean, certainly, of course, you can. It's only that…"

"Is he a homosexual like us?"

Goodness. In between preparing the dauphinoise potatoes and negotiating an apéritif, starter, and dessert, I really wasn't ready for this conversation.

"Er…ah, yes. I mean…I think he likes women too. But, yes, I do know he likes men. We…ah, he…"

Say it Marcel. I steeled myself. *Spit it out!* Better he finds out now than put himself through the torture of plucking up the courage to ask Guillaume out.

"What I'm trying to say is…ah, I also like Guillaume. I like him a lot, in fact. He's…well, he's already going out for drinks with me."

Crushing the hopes of a decent man is a very hard thing to do. Especially one as sweetly hopeless as Dominic. He blinked a few times, then took a longer drink of his wine. I'd never asked him about his previous relationships, but he hadn't had one for as long as I'd known him.

"I'm lonely, Marcel."

"I know, Dominic."

"I want a boyfriend."

"I know, Dominic. Can I hug you?"

"I'd like that, Marcel."

Not for the first time, I wished I knew someone who would fall head over heels in love with this funny, sweet man because he had so much love to give. We embraced stiffly; I'd hugged lampposts that yielded more. I'd found myself a true friend, even if he was an oddity, and I felt a pang of guilt that I'd not ever been able to give him the sort of love he was searching for and deserved. One day, hopefully, somebody would. As I let go, he clutched my arm urgently.

"Stay with Guillaume. Don't choose Simon. He's not right for you. He'll make you sad. He's…he's a little bit mean."

I'd never heard Dominic say a bad word about anybody. His face was full of concern, his long furry eyebrow creased into a deep frown.

"Dominic," I began gently. "You can rest assured I have no intention of ever being anything more than casual friends with Simon."

He breathed out a sigh of relief as though it had been bothering him for a while.

"But you should be with Guillaume. You will be good together," he urged. "I've watched you with him. You're different when he's around. You relax more."

He was right. Since Guillaume had moved here, I felt safe, even when my asthma woke me up in the middle of the night, and my sleep-addled, oxygen-deprived brain vaguely wondered if this was it, if this was the attack that would bring my life to a premature conclusion. In my darkest hours, knowing he was sleeping next to the house helped me breathe easier. Literally.

Dominic gave his glass that earnest gaze. "I really like him. But I understand if you do too. So I'm going to like him as your friend, not mine."

"I'm glad about that, Dominic."

"I'm glad that you're glad."

Crumbs, I was going to have another cycle of the glads again.

"Good, now do you want to help me to set the table?"

Simon and Guillaume arrived together, Guillaume wielding two baguettes and Simon swinging his cycle helmet from one hand, dressed head to toe in Lycra. Eww! Even though he was in quite good shape—in fact, he could have been displaying the physique of one of Guillaume's Ligue 1 footballers—I'd still have attempted to avert my eyes. No man should ever be able to ascertain if another man has been circumcised from their choice of clothing. While he disappeared into the bathroom to change into something hopefully less frightening, I took the opportunity to exchange a quick snog in the kitchen with Guillaume because it was Christmas, and he was there, and, well, I hadn't seen him for almost twenty minutes.

"How long are our guests staying?" I whispered, making a face as I reluctantly pulled away. In the other room, Simon was giving Dominic an unsolicited and boastful account of yesterday's cycle ride. From the figures he was spouting, it sounded like he'd broken the land-speed record.

"He's a bloody tool. 'I love me; who do you love?'" Guillaume whispered back, rolling his eyes. He picked up a tray of canapés I'd ordered from a deli in town. We'd prepared our own dauphinoise potatoes, so a little cheating was excusable. "Come on; let's put Dominic out of his misery."

As predicted, Simon helped himself to more than his fair share of my booze, and the more he drank, the more he became determined to paint Guillaume in a poor light and himself in a very bright one. The only good thing about it was that it gave Dominic a rest from being his usual target, and Guillaume proved much more adept at handling Simon's barbs.

"Do you remember, Marcel, that wonderful day we spent in Rochefort visiting *L'Hermione*? I was only telling somebody the other day how we must go again, now that the boat is back in the shipyard permanently. Fascinating part of French history, it really is. Did you ever get to see it, Guillaume? The display was the summer of, ooh, let me see, 2015, wasn't it, darling?"

"I think that was the summer I had my parole request turned down, Simon, so no. But do tell me more."

If Guillaume felt like punching him squarely on his smug, weak chin, he gave no indication. Not only was Simon endeavouring, not too subtly, to remind us all of Guillaume's chequered past, he was also being a hideous intellectual snob.

"Oh, Marcel, we've had so many wonderful trips together. We should organise another one soon. Do you remember that Christmas when Sabine and I took you to hear the Bordeaux Symphony, a few days after your hospital discharge? I think it was the Christmas before last, wasn't it?"

"I believe it was," I agreed sourly. "And I also remember coughing throughout the second half and eventually having to leave early as I was spoiling it for the other three hundred people who'd paid good money to hear it too."

Dominic sniggered, earning himself a filthy look from Simon.

"I don't suppose," Simon continued, "you ever had a chance to see them perform, did you, Guillaume? It was Bruckner's Symphony Number Seven, quite special indeed."

"I believe I was on toilet block cleaning duty that Christmas, so no, Simon. Not quite my thing, to be honest with you though."

Okay, so if Guillaume didn't feel like punching him, then I was going to do it on his behalf.

"Right," I announced briskly, checking my watch. "The chickens should have had long enough in the oven. Simon, come and give me a hand carving the meat, why don't you?"

Turning to Dominic, I gave him a wink. "My dear, I promised Guillaume last week I'd demonstrate to him the advantages of the Ruy Lopez versus the King's opening gambit, but I ran out of time. Perhaps you could make a start for me. The chessboard is on the coffee table next to my desk."

Guillaume was no more interested in chess openings than he was Bruckner's symphonies. I knew it, and Dominic knew it, too, but at least my suggestion will have given Simon something to chew on. Guillaume might not have had the benefits of Simon's and my expensive overeducation, but he was as smart as anyone else I knew, and I'd be damned if Simon was going to belittle him all afternoon. Dominic and Guillaume's chuckling floated down the hallway as they made a pretence of setting up for a game of chess. Simon wittered behind me.

"Before I forget, Marcel, the pool company phoned me yesterday. That cartridge filter we bought last year is on its last legs already. I've ordered another one on your behalf—I didn't want to bother you with it. I don't suppose you could transfer me the money, could you? Seventy-four euros. Should be fitted in the first week of the New Year, when you are working in Paris."

I nodded absentmindedly as he followed me into the kitchen. Everything I owned seemed to be packing up these days—car problems, pool problems. Until recently, I had felt grateful that Simon was always eager to intervene on my behalf; mundane household matters made my head spin. But Guillaume had offered several times to liaise with the gardener and the pool company, and it would be so much more convenient as he was always here. And with the added benefit of Simon becoming less of an irritating presence in my life. Taking as deep a breath as my pathetic lungs allowed, I turned and faced him.

"Yes, will do, Simon. I'll transfer it today. But so you know for the future, I think Guillaume will be able to deal with the pool company from now on. You've been so helpful, and I'm eternally grateful, as you know, but him living here makes it easier to manage and will free you up. I'm sure there are so many more important things you could be doing with your time. Like writing, for instance?"

Crumbs, I'd dared to mention The Writing. As if doing him out of yet another reason to loiter in my house, eating all of my food, wasn't enough, I had the temerity to bring up the most taboo subject of all.

Simon's excuse for his rather stalled journalism career was that all his energies were focused on France's Next Great Novel. From listening to him drone on about it, ad nauseam, he'd give Proust and Victor Hugo a run for their money. But it had been four years now, and as far as I was aware, zero progress had been made.

"Fine," he hissed. "Let that thug take over supervising the pool. But it's not that simple a task, you know! Don't expect me to come running with a packet of pH strips when the water turns green!"

"I think Guillaume is perfectly capable of arranging regular pool cleaning and keeping an eye on the chemicals," I stated calmly, handing him the carving knife.

"Oh, yes, I suspect he'll be *very* good at keeping an eye on the chemicals," Simon responded waspishly.

"And what's that supposed to mean?"

He gave me a dark look. "I don't need to tell you all about prisons, Marcel. Rife with hard drugs! And they use pool chemicals to make bombs, you know. Terrorists do; I've read all about it. And French prisons are a hotbed for terrorist activities. Oh, yes." He nodded with satisfaction. "I suspect our Guillaume Guilbaud is an expert with chemicals."

I counted to ten in my head. And then to twenty. And then did the same but backwards. Nope, I was still cross.

"Simon?" I said carefully. "Be thankful that, at the moment, it is you holding that carving knife and not me."

The dauphinoise potatoes were a rip-roaring success. A teensy bit mushy, if I were to be supercritical, but Guillaume and I gave ourselves a metaphorical pat on the back anyway. By now, Simon was on his second bottle of red; the potatoes could have been soaked in white emulsion paint, and he wouldn't have noticed. He ate enough of them to sustain him for several days, and not for the first time, I wondered how he made ends meet. Thankfully, he was sulking, which meant he had stopped baiting Guillaume.

It turned out that Dominic had a surprising amount of football knowledge. His father had been a season ticket holder for a team called Paris Saint-Germain, which was apparently very famous. So he and Guillaume rattled on quite happily about some Brazilian chap called Neymar, while I admired the way his jaw moved when he swallowed, and the flex of his upper arms as he cleared away afterwards, effortlessly balancing several plates. Guillaume's jaw and upper arms obviously, not Dominic's.

Dominic's generous cheese course, followed by dessert (crème brûlée from the delicatessen), proved both delicious and uneventful. While Simon made serious inroads into a bottle of Sauternes, the three of us took advantage of his ensuing somnolence by playing a few rounds of whist and making our way through some rather delicious La Maison du Chocolat pralines, which I'd successfully hidden from him. We all agreed the empty box should linger next to his armchair for when he woke. A lively debate followed regarding the relative merits of ice cream macaroons over normal macaroons, and before we knew it, Dominic had thanked us profusely, given us both stiff, but heartfelt hugs, then headed off into the night. All that remained was to crowbar Simon out of my house.

Chapter Fourteen

Guillaume

Marcel generously insisted that Simon was an irritating buffoon yet essentially harmless. The idiot part I wholeheartedly agreed with, but the harmless bit? I had my suspicions. He was certainly accomplished at freeloading off Marcel—even Marcel had cottoned on to that. But on more than one occasion, I'd had my doubts regarding a couple of financial transactions Simon had conducted in the name of easing Marcel's busy lifestyle.

While an apparent genius at juggling the nation's finances, the daily humdrum of Marcel running his own household accounts had somehow slipped from his grasp and into Simon's. To be blunt, I wasn't convinced that all of the money transferred to Simon's bank account was strictly used to cover the bills. However, not having had a squeaky-clean past myself, I didn't feel it was something I could raise with Marcel, not until I had evidence anyway.

Once we'd sent Simon off on his wobbly bike ride home, Marcel and I decided to stretch our legs. We wandered around the port, his arm, as ever, tucked cosily into mine.

Marcel declared that Ile de Ré at Christmas, and the port of Saint-Martin in particular, had the atmosphere of a ski resort minus the snow. I had to accept his word for it, but it was certainly festive. It was hard to believe my former prison home was literally less than three hundred yards down the road, shrouded in darkness. Twinkling lights festooned lampposts and boats; on all sides of the cobbled port, restaurants and pop-up stalls plied steaming *vin chaud* and roast chestnuts to merry locals and tourists. At one point, when Marcel stopped to examine some woollen gloves at a little wooden cabin, he leaned over and planted a warm kiss on my cheek.

"Thank you for making today so bearable," he said. "Last year, it was only Sabine, Dominic, and me, and incredibly dreary. I vowed never again—I would have joined Lucien at Rossingley if you hadn't been here. Or faked an asthma attack and cancelled the whole thing."

"I wouldn't have wanted to be anywhere else." I smiled and took his arm again as we continued our snail's pace. Marcel hummed tunelessly. As we turned up a side street, he spoke again.

"I…I know the…ah, the slowness of the development of our, ah, sexual relationship is probably frustrating for you." He twisted away from me to peer intently into a shop window. He was either hiding something fairly important about himself or deliberately avoiding my gaze because the window displayed some quite racy ladies' underwear.

Bringing us to a halt with my hands at his shoulders, I turned him back to face me. The tip of his nose shone red from the cold, his cheeks flushed a delicate pink, and little puffs of air escaped his mouth. Absolutely adorable. Unable to help myself, I leaned in to gently brush his lips against mine, not caring if anyone saw us. I meant every word of what I was about to say.

"Believe it or not, Marcel, I don't mind. Simply being with you is enough right now. And the…um…the other stuff, well, it's only sex, isn't it? Don't get me wrong; I like sex as much as the next man, but if it's meant to be, then we'll get there."

"What if…ah…what if the next man…doesn't like sex very much at all?"

Marcel's eyes slid away from mine, his cheeks a little redder.

Kissing him again, I was rewarded with a curious stare from a passing middle-aged couple.

"Then, I'd say the next man hasn't found the right person to have sex with yet."

That drew a small smile out of him, and then he sighed, briefly chewing on his bottom lip.

"Sometimes, I wonder if I've wasted valuable time avoiding sexual intercourse over the last eight years. I may find I'm too ill, a few years from now, to have an intimate relationship with anybody. That I'll have left it too late."

Conversations like this with Marcel were sweet and odd. Despite all the stammering and hedging, his raw honesty floored me. He pondered his mortality much more than most men of our age—understandably, as he endured frequent and sobering reminders of it. And his preference for correct terminology like 'intercourse' over coarser language was impossibly sweet. However, his message was no less emotional for it and, tonight, tinged with an edge of vulnerability I hadn't heard before.

"Marcel. Listen to me. The most intense, meaningful relationship of my life, up until now, was a platonic one. Ten years of no more than cuddles and an occasional peck on the cheek. And I wouldn't change any of it."

"Your Reuben was a very lucky boy."

"I think it was the other way around, actually, but thank you anyway."

"But you did…ah…seek relief from other sources, didn't you? I…ah…I wonder whether in the future I'll regret all the years I've spent not engaging in sexual intercourse. And on that note, I…I need to confess something. Although, I suspect you've probably guessed already."

He hesitated, biting his lip again, and then his words came out in a rush. "I…just…goodness this is awkward. I…erm… well, the thing is…I don't enjoy sex very much. Or rather, I haven't on previous occasions. Particularly when I'm required to be…energetic. Mostly, I find it extremely tiring. It leaves me breathless, and sometimes, I don't, or my partner doesn't, successfully reach completion as I'm too out of puff. And then it is horribly unsatisfactory for both of us. Particularly if I'm busy teeing up a nebuliser while he's lying there with a rapidly wilting erection. And…I am too fond of you, Guillaume, to put you in that terribly awkward position as, believe me, it is terribly awkward for all parties concerned."

I wasn't sure how to reply at first. I almost retorted that if he really wanted to experience an awkward sexual encounter, he should try pretending to be a sexy seamstress, fake-chastising a junior, naughty seamstress while simultaneously having his knob sucked. But that would have been glib, and he didn't deserve that.

It was an odd place to make such a confession, out on the street in front of a ladies' lingerie shop, but Marcel was most wonderfully odd all round. Hitching his glasses up his nose, he glanced up and down the street, clearly uncomfortable with his outburst. I thought back to the astonishing dry-humping episode a few days earlier on the sofa. Despite being basic, clumsy, and interrupted by having to dig out an inhaler from underneath my shoulder blades, it'd been one of the most pleasurable erotic encounters I could remember. And, certainly, the funniest.

"Marcel, my sweetheart. Swinging from the chandeliers is overrated. Did no one ever tell you that?"

He smiled weakly, and I opened my arms wide before wrapping him up in them. "I've already had sex with you in my mind," I confessed into his ear. "Countless times. And each time was better than the last. The details vary, but the only thing that doesn't is you and me. And it is perfect every time."

"Then I'm afraid the reality will be truly disappointing." He shook his head slightly against my chest, and I squeezed him a little tighter still.

"No, it won't. Because the Marcel making love in my mind is the same Marcel who can't climb two flights of stairs at Rossingley. He's the Marcel who takes my arm every time we leave the house. The one who has to swallow rows and rows of pills that I can't even pronounce. The one who breathlessly walked into that dreary visitors' room that first time and lit up my world. There's not a swinging chandelier in sight, *mon coeur.*"

After a moment, he pulled back a little and gripped the lapels of my coat in both hands. Those blue-grey eyes crinkled at the corners as I adjusted his stripy scarf higher onto his face, covering the tips of his pink ears. It wasn't only the bitterly cold wind making his skin flush.

"I have to drive up to the Paris office for a few days next week. But when I return, can we…can we…I mean, only if you want to… Goodness, this is awkward… What I'm trying, and failing miserably, to say is can we, ah, work towards possibly consummating our relationship on my return?"

I considered that question for about the length of time it would take for one of Neymar's powerful strikes from the edge of the penalty area to hit the back of the net. I nearly grabbed him then and there up against the window display of fancy lingerie.

Best. Christmas. Ever.

"What do you think?"

Marcel left for Paris a week later in a whirl of inhalers, medicines, hugs, kisses, and paperwork. And several trips up and down the stairs on his behalf, for the various items he forgot each time he concluded he was completely packed and ready and then decided he wasn't. We also vainly searched high and low for an amethyst signet ring I'd noticed him wearing occasionally, a beautiful gift from Lucien for his twenty-first birthday. Last seen in the vicinity of the kitchen sink on Christmas Day, when he'd removed it to do some washing-up, it was nowhere to be found. As I carried his belongings to the car, I promised to continue the search in his absence.

Truth be told, I was anxious about this trip. Naturally, I recognised he'd done it hundreds of times before I ever appeared on the scene, and, yeah, he was an accomplished man in his midthirties in charge of a huge governmental department, blah, blah, blah. But still, he was scatty as hell and had an illness that could unexpectedly poleaxe him. The thought of him being alone in his Paris apartment and fighting for breath filled me with horror.

Balancing a suitcase in one hand and a huge box of books and papers in the other, I opened the garage door, still insisting he phoned me when he arrived, and immediately felt better about the travelling part of the trip at least.

"Bloody hell, Marcel! This is…blimey…not what I was expecting."

I knew he had an Audi because Simon had mentioned a mechanical problem with it a few weeks earlier. But there was no way on earth this one had sprung mechanical problems. All Audis are nice, of course, *Vorsprung durch Technik* and all that, but the lump of metal idling in Marcel's garage was much more than nice. A low-slung, silver beast of a car, it was a new model A8 saloon with all the trimmings that even I knew cost the best part of one hundred thousand euros.

Marcel observed my bewilderment with a smile. "I like cars?" He shrugged, slightly apologetically. "And I, ah, I like to travel in comfort."

"I can see that." I patted the roof carefully. "Do you use the main Audi dealership in La Rochelle?"

It was a spur of the moment question, casually asked, and he answered in the affirmative, hopefully not giving it a second thought. A few ideas had been forming in my mind since Christmas Day, and Marcel's absence, as much as I was going to miss him, was going to allow me to do something about them.

★

The house without Marcel was unsettling. It felt wrong for him not to be there, either working, quietly pottering, or practicing his sublime yoga. Marcel *was* the house—his presence filled it; his illness almost confined him to it. All of the rooms, but especially the study, smelled of him, and it felt strange to be in there without him, amongst his haphazardly strewn papers and heaps of books. Thus, apart from cooking a few simple meals in the kitchen, I mostly stayed in the annexe.

Simon had no such qualms.

I'd had a few more fruitless hunts for the signet ring. The day after Marcel left, I'd even taken the kitchen sink waste pipe apart to check it hadn't fallen down the plughole, but no joy. On returning from the garden shed to locate a wrench to re-tighten the plumbing, I startled Simon mooching through the freezer.

"What are you doing here?" I asked with surprise. Marcel hadn't mentioned that Simon was coming over.

"I could ask the same of you?" he responded sniffily, continuing his rummaging.

I raised my eyebrows questioningly. "Er…I live here?"

He pulled out a frozen pizza. "Exactly," he snapped. "What are you doing here? Are you playing Marcel for a fool, trying to wheedle your way into his favours? Because I imagine it's rather pleasant for you living here, isn't it, in this big posh house? Especially considering your accommodation for the last fifteen years."

Hah! That was rich coming from Simon. He was the one scrounging for a free dinner, not me. My first instinct was to tell him to get the fuck out of the house, but seeing as it wasn't actually my house, I didn't feel I had the right. Ignoring his barb, I slid under the sink again to finish the job. Calming my anger, I tried a different tack.

"Marcel said to ask, if I saw you, whether you had that invoice from the Audi garage?"

A complete lie, the invoice had slipped Marcel's mind, but I hadn't forgotten. It was only fair to give Simon another chance before I started skulking around. I hadn't forgotten the pricy dry-cleaning bill, either, or the new pool filter. As far as I knew, nobody from the pool company had been to change it, and the current one appeared to be working perfectly.

"Damn, I knew there was something," he muttered. Dissembling if ever I heard it. No offer to bring it with him next time though.

"So why are you here, Simon, apart from to help yourself to a pizza?"

I peered out from under the sink in time to catch Simon throwing me a disdainful look.

"I often pop in to check over the house when Marcel is away."

I bet you do.

"There's no need, not now I live here."

"But he appreciates it," Simon added. "He trusts me. And there are all the other bits and pieces I do for him."

I saw an opening. "Talking of other things, I have some dry-cleaning to drop off for him. Which dry-cleaner does he use?"

After protesting that he was happy to drop it off on his way home, and me insisting I was equally happy to take it there myself, Simon reluctantly gave me the name of the dry-cleaner.

"He'll see through you, Guillaume. One of these days. I know he currently worships the ground you walk on, but it's only a matter of time before he becomes properly ill, and then he'll turn to his real friends for support. You wait and see. You're merely a passing fancy. A bit of rough."

Another minute in this man's company, and I would find myself doing something I might regret. The sink plumbing finished, I stood up, rolling my shoulders back and drawing up to my full height. I'd removed my sweater earlier to keep it clean while I was delving under the sink, and now in a white vest top, my extensive tattoos were on display in all their full glory. Schooling my features into a threatening leer, I stepped up and into Simon's personal space, so close I could smell last night's garlic on his breath.

"You're starting to piss me off, Simon, you know that?" I murmured, keeping my voice low.

He had been very pleased to inform anyone who cared to listen about my past. Yet the full implications of it had probably never completely sunk in until the precise moment when he found himself face to face with a convicted murderer and utterly alone in this big, quiet house. As the precariousness of his situation dawned on Simon, his expression altered from one of superior, middle-class smugness to one of pure fear. God, this was fun. I still held the wrench tightly and deliberately flexed my fingers around it for good measure.

"And you know what happened to the last bloke who pissed me off, don't you, Simon?"

★

Extremely confident Simon wouldn't be dropping by unexpectedly again any time soon, I had several hours of privacy to indulge in some detective work. Firstly online, perusing the website of the local dry-cleaner and checking out their price list. Finding out whether someone had added a couple of euros here and there to a dry-cleaning bill might have sounded petty, but my gut instinct told me I was right, and a few quid here and there added up to quite a tidy sum over several years. I wasn't entirely sure what I was going to do with the information, but it might come in useful one day as I had made myself an enemy. Feeling like a low-end private eye, I noted down the dry-cleaning costs of three suits, a tuxedo, and two cashmere sweaters. My kind, generous Marcel might have deep pockets, but I'd be damned if he was going to be swindled.

Next came a phone call to the Audi dealership in La Rochelle. Pretending to be Marcel, I confessed that I'd mislaid my most recent invoice, and three minutes later, an email pinged into my inbox, confirming that Simon was a snivelling, conniving bastard. As expected, the car had passed its forty-thousand-kilometre service with flying colours.

"Are you going to introduce me to your friend?"

As Antoine and I jogged back to the centre circle, I jerked my head around to follow the direction in which he was pointing. The lone figure of Dominic, dressed in his usual blue anorak, stood shivering on the touchline, and I gave him a small wave. Our pretend chess lesson on Christmas Day had turned into a real one, and we were heading into town for a coffee and then back to his place for tutorial number two. The plan was to surprise Marcel by being vaguely competent; I was under no illusion I would conceivably ever beat him.

"I can do better than that, Antoine. Why don't you join us for a coffee? Unless, of course, you have something planned with your *wife*," I added pointedly.

He pulled a face. "Thanks for the regular reminders that I have a wife," he replied sarcastically. "Although probably not for much longer. In an attempt to get my marriage back on track, I broached the subject of a little 'naughty prison officer needs disciplining by hot, scary prisoner' role play in bed with her a few nights ago. Needless to say, it didn't go down particularly well. I'm now well acquainted with the mattress in the spare room."

"Oh dear," I responded, trying to keep a straight face. I didn't know much about marriage guidance counselling, but I assumed it went more along the lines of setting time aside for each other, arranging romantic date nights, maybe making the effort to listen to your partner's worries.

"That's…er…that's a very specific scenario, Antoine. Do you think…do you think she may have guessed it had some basis in…er…like, your real life?"

Antoine reddened. "Quite possibly. But I can't confirm that as we're currently not on speaking terms. So, in answer to your first question, yes, I'd love to join you for a coffee."

Observing Antoine attempting to flirt with Dominic, and Dominic not picking up either the non-verbal clues or the not-so-subtle verbal ones, was kind of hilarious. Spotting Antoine's wedding ring, he had correctly assumed Antoine was married and then politely asked him about his wife and children, oblivious to the fact that Antoine was doing his level best to steer the conversation away from them. The pair of them were like the north ends of two magnets, orbiting each other but determinedly remaining at arm's length. When Antoine excused himself to visit the gents, I gave Dominic a gentle nudge, or probably more of a firm poke.

"Dom, I think Antoine really likes you."

"He's handsome," he responded dreamily. "I bet he looks good in his uniform."

This I could affirm. He also looked good with the uniform pooled around his ankles and a cock in his mouth, although I thought it best not to share this insider knowledge just yet.

"If Simon were here, he'd tell me that Antoine was way out of my league," he continued, shaking his head sadly.

Simon was a bloody menace.

"And anyway, he's married."

"Dom, Antoine isn't the first married bloke to fancy a bit of the other, and he won't be the last. And if you really want to know, his marriage is not a particularly happy one. From what Antoine says, it's on its last legs."

Despite having spelled it out to him, Dominic in flirting mode was not a huge improvement. After outlining his day job as a computer programmer, he launched into great detail regarding a malware something-something-complicated-something that sounded incredibly tedious, yet Antoine appeared to be lapping it up. Turned out Antoine was a techno geek in his spare time. My eyes glazed over as I left them to it, my thoughts drifting inevitably towards Marcel.

To tell the truth, I was both excited and terrified. Excited about what lay ahead—I'd watched him practice yoga; I'd glimpsed that taut lithe body. Sex was going to be great, whatever his concerns, mostly because I fancied the pants off him. So what if we weren't going to be medalling in the sex Olympics? I was pushing forty, after all. Not old, but certainly old enough that I no longer felt the need to prove my stamina by having sex thrice daily. Or to try out every sexual position conceivable. Having rarely had the luxury of it, and certainly not for the last fifteen years, loving and consensual vanilla sex in a big, comfy bed was a more than satisfactory goal. I couldn't bloody wait.

What terrified me was the depth of my feelings for a man so far above me in every way. Clever, articulate, wealthy, and classy, I was punching above my weight with Marcel and had totally fallen for him. Although my night-time hot sweats had thankfully become the exception, not the norm, my sense of not being good enough for him had not entirely left me. I still had to pinch myself that this was actually my life, that he was part of my life.

The conversation at the table had drawn to a natural close. Antoine stood and put a few coins down next to the empty coffee cups. We said our goodbyes, slightly reluctantly, I felt, on Antoine's part.

"It's nice to meet someone interested in remote administrative software," Dom happily commented as we drove away. "He's also very interested in religion—we talked in quite some detail about relationships between senior clergy and junior vergers, for some reason, which was…different. He lost me a bit, to be honest, especially the part about self-flagellation. I liked him though."

"Dom," I began cautiously, "How to you feel about role play? You know, just asking for a friend."

Dominic's eyes lit up, giving me a modicum of hope on Antoine's behalf. "Ooh, you mean like battle re-enactments? All those horses and men dressing up and doing pretend jousting? I love those! I went to one with Marcel at Fouras last year, in the grounds of the old fort. Why, do you and your friend want to get tickets sometime? We could all go together!"

Bloody hell, this matchmaking malarkey was difficult.

If ever a day came when I once again owned a home, I hoped to be reminded never to give a key to helpful friends and family. Feeling a little chilly in the annexe, I decided to light the wood burner in Marcel's study and spend an evening sprawled in front of the television. I had been settled all of five minutes, with a glass of sparkling water, a slice of delicatessen quiche, and an old Clint Eastwood western, when Sabine let herself in, her daughter Clara traipsing behind, football sticker book in hand.

Sabine's pleasure at seeing me on a scale of one to ten? I reckoned it was about a two. If I hadn't lit the wood burner and had the room toasty, I'd have downgraded that score back to a one. Clara, however, clearly hadn't received the memo and smiled at me with delight.

"Hello, Uncle Marcel's friend! Did he leave any sticker packs for me before he went to Paris? He promised he would."

I smiled at her. She was cute, swinging blonde pig tails and a gap where a front tooth should have been. "Here, on the coffee table."

"Oh, goodie! Three packs, wow! I hope there is a Portuguese player in one. I've only got two team members so far. Getting Ronaldo would be ace!"

She plumped down happily on the sofa next to me and opened her book.

"Clara," ordered Sabine. "Take your sticker book into the kitchen, and do it in there, please. Don't argue."

I could have predicted that response. Killing a grown man fifteen years ago for abusing my underage, handicapped sister also made me a potential paedophile. After Clara had flounced off, Sabine turned to me.

"I didn't know you had carte blanche to roam the house when Marcel's away."

"I don't roam the house," I replied, immediately annoyed. "This is the first time I've spent an evening in here and not in the annexe, and that's only because it's so cold tonight."

That I had to justify my actions was crazy, and a waste of breath, anyway, as I could tell she didn't believe me.

"Look, Sabine," I tried. "I know you and I have got off on a rather bad footing. I'm sorry for that, and I'd like to…"

She butted in. "Are you sleeping with him?"

"I'm currently sitting here having a conversation with you," I replied pointedly. "Those two actions are probably mutually exclusive."

"Don't be facetious," she snapped. "You know what I mean."

Bloody hell, this was tiresome. Especially as I sensed Sabine was quite a nice lady if only she could see beyond her antipathy towards me. Marcel had promised she could be hilarious company when the mood took her. I'd have to take his word for it.

"Yes, I do know what you mean, but I'm failing to see what it has to do with you."

Sabine exhaled loudly and folded her arms. "It has everything to do with me because I have no intention of allowing a vulnerable person like my brother be taken advantage of by the likes of you. Simon said he dropped in here earlier in the week, and your behaviour was very threatening."

I had no desire to give Sabine any ammunition to dislike me even further, and I was determined my presence wouldn't drive a wedge between Marcel and his sister. They were obviously very close—too close perhaps—but I understood they had relied very heavily on each other in the past. The vulnerability thing pissed me off though. Especially as the only person I knew who had taken advantage of Marcel so far was the man Sabine had introduced into his house. But with my background, the chances of her taking my word for it were slim to approaching zero.

"Sabine, I don't know how I can reassure you, but I'm not taking advantage of your brother. And even though it is none of your business, no, I'm not sleeping with him."

I'd like to, though, Sabine. I dream about having his lean thighs wrapped around me pretty much every night.

Chapter Fifteen

Marcel

It wasn't quite the homecoming I had envisaged. Guillaume was likely disappointed, too, although he endeavoured not to show it. Me being me, a hysterically passionate reunion and divestment of each other's clothes before we'd left the hallway was never on the cards anyway. Nevertheless, thrusting my suitcase at him before collapsing breathlessly onto the sofa wasn't exactly what either of us had anticipated or hoped for. And…expletive…but I'd spent the first half of the week actually feeling positively libidinous, dreamily imagining our careful, considerate coming together. Which, in itself, was a cause for celebration.

Showing nothing but concern, Guillaume swiftly produced my medicine bag from the depths of my case, and eventually, my chest felt less tight, my respiratory rate slowed, and I was able to give him a watery smile, albeit followed by a coughing fit. The three-hour drive, and too much salbutamol during it, had left me jittery and irritable. And frustrated, horribly frustrated because, for the first time in years, I had been looking forwards to being touched by another man, being held by another man, spending a night in bed with another man. Knowing my failing body better than anybody, I had a hideous premonition that my current shortness of breath heralded worse to come. Confirmed when I surreptitiously pegged the oximeter onto my finger and read the value nearer to ninety than one hundred.

"Stay for a while, Guillaume? Please?"

Having picked up on my bad mood after ensuring my comfort and fixing me a hot drink, he was keen to give me some space. Something in my pleading tone must have stopped him, though, and instead, he retrieved a book from the annexe and settled on the sofa next to me.

"Sorry for being such a grump," I muttered, stretching out. "I think I may have a cold brewing. The person across from me at a meeting on Wednesday never stopped sneezing and snorting. I was virtually cowering behind my jacket by the end of the session. He's not up for promotion this year; that's for sure."

Guillaume laughed softly. "Do you want me to kill him for you?"

"Depends on how bad this cold gets."

Somehow, my head found itself on his broad chest and his arm around my shoulders. He had a sixth sense about when I needed him, something Simon had never mastered. Guillaume was a quiet companion. We could spend hours together without exchanging words, particularly if I was working. And if I was wheezy when I worked, he never suggested I take a break, like Sabine always did, as if he understood it was the only part of my life I could fully control. And now, as my coughing fits increased in frequency and I availed myself of my mini-nebulisers, he continued to sit with me, anxiety clear in his eyes, offering occasional observations about his book and planting soft kisses in my hair. All in all, he was perfect.

At some point, I must have fallen asleep because I woke a few hours later, semi-reclining on the sofa with a blanket tucked around me. Guillaume slept in the armchair opposite; I could make him out in the gloom and hear his gentle snores. I'd woken from a recurring dream, where someone nearby was playing a harmonica or an accordion exceedingly badly. Even in my dream, I was aware the sound radiated from me, my lungs playing a tuneless melody as air squeezed along narrowing tubes. I listened for a while in a semi-doze, too fatigued to rise and reach for one of my ever-present inhalers, as if putting off the inevitable. Because as sure as the sun rose and the sun set, this episode was only heading in one direction.

"Guillaume."

I wasn't sure how long had passed; long enough for me to realise I had to stop ignoring my increasing shortness of breath, and for fuzzy stars to appear around the edges of my vision. He woke with a start, blinking rapidly before focusing on me.

"Guillaume, I'm…I'm not feeling so well."

He was up in an instant. "Tell me what to do. Do you want me to get Sabine? Or Simon?"

I shook my head. Definitely not Simon. I wanted the fuzziness to go away and to rest my head on Guillaume's broad chest once more. My internal orchestra of squeaks and whines had diminished, despite the fact that my respiratory rate was climbing. Which was not a good sign. Wheezing indicated air was still squeezing through my narrowed bronchioles. Silence meant it was not.

"Phone 112. And Guillaume, stay with me. Please?"

And then I closed my eyes, not wanting to see the horror on his face.

Chapter Sixteen

Guillaume

Marcel had warned me this could happen. Dominic had warned me. Bloody Simon had warned me, in his nasty, threatening sort of way. Even so, nothing could have prepared me for the sheer terror of watching Marcel desperately fighting for air and finding myself entirely, hopelessly useless.

On autopilot, I made the phone call to the emergency services before racing upstairs to throw a few of his things into a bag. Even this made me feel inadequate—we weren't a couple; it wasn't my bedroom; I didn't know which drawers housed his pyjamas and underwear. Would he need shaving stuff? Shampoo? Would this be an overnight stay or a month? Which bag? Would he still be alive when I ran downstairs again? Fuck, I was lost.

A hammering at the door signalled the arrival of the ambulance crew. By now, Marcel wasn't speaking, slumped forwards on the sofa, chin on his chest. The wheezing, which was part of the soundtrack of his daily life and used to make me anxious, was now terrifyingly absent. The paramedics bundled through the door and calmly did their thing, cheerfully even, as they clamped an oxygen mask to his face and some monitoring to his chest and arm. All the while, they spoke to him reassuringly, and I knew it should have been me doing that, me who should have been holding his hand, not some highly competent woman in a high viz jacket. But, instead, I hovered on the periphery, clutching his leather bag of belongings in my sweaty hand, trying desperately not to let all the panic burst out.

As he efficiently manoeuvred Marcel into a wheelchair, the other paramedic asked me if I was coming with them in the ambulance. It was the only time Marcel gave a response; he nodded forcefully and reached for my hand.

"Are you his partner?" asked the woman kindly.

I didn't know. Was I? We'd spent hours together, laughing and drinking hot chocolate, reading side by side on the sofa in front of the wood burner. We'd kissed, breathy innocent kisses; I'd stroked his hair and tried not to push for more. I thought of him as my sweetheart. Did that make me his partner?

Marcel's weak hand squeeze gave me the answer.

"Yes, yes. I am Guillaume. Marcel is my partner."

A blur across the bridge to the mainland, flashing lights and screeching sirens. And nausea as we hurtled around corners. Marcel's monitor bleeped a fast heart rate, and every time the jolting of the ambulance caused the signal to stutter was a jolt to my own heart. The oxygen mask hid Marcel's waxen face, though he still had insufficient breath to speak or cough; the silence inside the ambulance was deafening.

And then the bright lights and bustle of the emergency department, a rush of people in theatre scrubs and frenetic activity. I felt increasingly more in the way every time I was reassured that I wasn't. I held Marcel's hand as much as I was able as he was jabbed with needles. Drips were set up around us, then a brief pause in activity as X-rays were taken. Blood results were shouted across the room from someone manning the phone; a huddle of older doctors made decisions about the next level of care, my sweet, sweet man a thin, frightened, motionless figure in the centre of it all.

One of the older doctors pulled me aside for a conversation, her words a jumble of terms I could scarcely compute: viral pneumonia, infective exacerbation, beta agonist, bronchodilator, theophylline. It was like learning a new language with a knife held at my throat, or being forced to take a test I was already set up to fail. Then two firm hands guided me to a chair. I'd reportedly turned white and clammy, my head now between my knees, a plastic beaker of water thrust into my hand. The corridor outside of the emergency room was cooler. My higher functions returned, and with them the certain knowledge that I couldn't face this alone. Taking some huge lungfuls of air, I came to my senses and made a phone call.

Later, much later, Reuben told me how Lucien had moved hell and earth to board a dawn flight on a private charter out of Bristol airport. All I knew at the time was that Marcel had been in intensive care not quite four hours when both Lucien and Reuben made their presence known through the window. The calm bubble of an individual room had replaced the chaotic pace of the emergency department; the only objects which weren't high-tech, white, and shiny, were me and Marcel. Even the nursing staff, efficiently padding in and out, wore dazzling white uniforms.

The monitors were thankfully alarming less frequently. It was difficult to discern if Marcel was sleeping or too exhausted to do anything except fight for breath. His usually shiny dark hair plastered his forehead, his face deathly pale. Black and blue bruises covered the almost translucent skin of his delicate wrists where he had been repeatedly stabbed, to check his blood oxygen levels. In my sleep-deprived, panicking mind, that damaged skin upset me as much as anything.

My hand had scarcely left his. Publicly displaying my affection for another man felt odd; I was vaguely attuned to curious but not unfriendly glances. It wasn't odd enough to make me remove my hand, though, or refrain from occasionally leaning across to kiss his damp brow and murmur quiet words of encouragement.

Lucien swept serenely into the room, looking as if he'd spent the last eight hours blissfully asleep, not commandeering an aeroplane and travelling through the night skies. He plonked himself onto the bed and gathered Marcel up into a crushing embrace, and I felt even more inadequate. Lucien paid no heed whatsoever to the monitoring, the oxygen, the drips, the frowns of the nurse, doing exactly what I wished I'd had the balls to do. As he whispered in Marcel's ear, Marcel gave him a tiny smile.

"Why don't you go and take a break, Guillaume? I'll stay with Marcel."

That fluttery voice, a command wrapped up as a gentle suggestion, his arms still firmly supporting his oldest friend.

"I can't leave him."

Even to my own ears, I sounded almost hysterical, the strain and fear in my voice clear. My overtired, overwrought brain had, during the small hours of the night, convinced itself that if I let go of Marcel's hand, he would die.

"Guillaume," Lucien persisted calmly. "I've spoken to the doctors. Marcel's condition is stable at the moment. I'm not asking you; I'm telling you."

★

An old hand at this game, Lucien had already booked a couple of rooms at the hotel next door. Dragging me with him out of the hospital, Reuben eyed me anxiously as I breathed in lungfuls of the cool night air. I guessed he had a dozen questions vying to be the first, but sensibly asked none of them. After checking in, I took a much-needed shower, while he ordered room service and laid out some fresh clothes for me. The jeans and shirt neatly folded on the bed were considerably swankier than I usually wore.

"They belong to Freddie," explained Reuben as I wearily dressed. "He's probably closer to your size than me. Lucien suggested I bring you something as he guessed you wouldn't have anything."

"That's thoughtful of him."

"This isn't the first time he's done this; I think he knows the drill."

Of course he knew the drill. I bet Simon and Sabine knew it too. Dominic even. There was only me who hadn't yet got with the programme. I sank heavily onto the bed, wanting to curl up in it with a pillow over my head but knowing I couldn't, not until I knew Marcel was safe. Reuben sat in the chair opposite.

"I didn't know you and Marcel had become so close," he ventured, gauging my response. "One minute, I'm telling

Freddie how I'm worried you've spent Christmas on your own and, the next, I receive a frantic phone call at midnight, telling me a bloke I thought you hardly knew was trying to die. What's going on, Guillaume?"

"Fuck, I don't know." I yawned, rubbing my face with my hand. "I…we…well, we sort of kept it to ourselves."

"Evidently."

I reached for one of the sandwiches and took a bite. It felt dry and tasteless, and I dropped it back onto the plate as a surge of emotion closed my throat. Closing my eyes, I sank into the pillows and proceeded to give him an outline of our prison meetings and what had happened at Rossingley.

"I need to get back to him," I declared urgently and sat bolt upright.

"No, you need to eat something first," Reuben replied firmly. "He's safe. Lucien won't move from his side."

"I'm so scared. I love him, and I don't want him to die."

"He's not going to die. Why the hell didn't you tell me what was going on, Guillaume?"

"God knows. It just…it just happened. Well, nothing has happened really. We've, as you said, become extremely close."

Christ, I was tired. My words had come jumbling out, sounding thick on my tongue. Did I…did I…?

"Reuben, did I just tell you that I love him?"

Reuben grinned; his green eyes gleaming. "Yeah. Yeah, you did. It was kind of cute."

"It's not cute. I don't want to love him. Nor him to love me. I'm fucking useless for him."

A puzzled expression crossed Reuben's face. "I'm getting the impression it's too late for that."

"You saw Lucien in there! He knew exactly what to do. Whereas I've stood around like a lemon all night, getting under everyone's feet, petrified Marcel's going to stop breathing."

Reuben frowned. "I haven't much experience of hospital visiting, but isn't that, like, a normal response when someone you love is really ill?"

"Lucien didn't respond like that."

"*Putain*, Guillaume, you can't compare yourself to Lucien! He's a bloody intensive care doctor; he spends his life caring for patients like Marcel."

He looked at me naughtily. "But imagine Lucien corralling ten testosterone-fuelled prisoners into a five-a-side soccer match without them pulling a knife on one another—he wouldn't look quite so clever doing that, would he?"

I almost smiled at that image, picked up the sandwich again, and forced down a few bites.

"So, does Marcel love you back?" Reuben asked slyly. "Were you too busy up to your nuts in guts to spend time visiting your oldest mate at Christmas? Have you been doing the no pants dance?"

Sometimes I forgot that Reuben was ten years my junior, that he'd seen a lot of bad stuff; he had wise old eyes. Those childish comments, however, served as a quick reminder.

"No, *connard*. We…we're taking it super slowly. Marcel isn't exactly into the physical side of things. Don't look at me like that!"

"I wasn't looking at you like anything! But it must be love if you are as upset as this and you haven't even, you know, bumped uglies."

I rolled my eyes at him, then looked at my watch. "I must get back. I shouldn't have left him this long. What if something has happened?"

"Calm down. Nothing has happened; Lucien would have phoned. Drink your coffee and have another sandwich. It's going to be a long day."

"I want you to get to know Marcel like I do. You'll see I don't deserve him. He's amazing. And I don't care about the physical stuff… He's clever and kind and funny. You should see his life, how he copes with this asthma. Because he lives with it every fucking day, and it doesn't get him down. Even when he's having a bad day, he still does his work and his yoga and his crosswords. He has hardly any privacy. His sister and his friends monitor his every move, in case he has an attack and no one is there to help. And he manages to behave as though he hasn't got a care in the world, but all the time, he's got this bloody awful illness hanging over him that might kill him at any moment. He's on borrowed time, Reuben; it should have killed him years ago."

That lump in my throat appeared at all the wrong bloody moments. And Reuben's arm around my shoulder didn't help.

"*Merde*, Guille, don't talk like that. Lucien says Marcel is as tough as old boots. And don't say you don't deserve him. I don't want to hear it; we've heard it too much. The haters can hate all they like. But people like you and me? We do deserve happiness. We've done our time; we're not the men we were."

God, I needed to remember these wise words when all this was over. I'd got myself tied up in knots, lost in my own twisted thoughts. I'd been strong for Reuben, always, and now I needed to find that strength for Marcel. There was no room for self-doubt here. Fifteen years of prison brought with it a pile of shame I had to cast off if I was going to be half the man Marcel needed me to be.

"You are a decent person, Guillaume. And if that man lying in that bed is what you want, then you go and get him. Because you are as good as anybody. You used to drill that into me all the time. It's time you listened to your own advice."

As he rested his head on my shoulder, I closed my eyes, breathing in the fresh outdoorsy scent of that thick wavy hair.

"I know better than anyone how much love you have to give," Reuben said softly, and then my tears did start to fall for the first time since Marcel woke me, asking me to call the ambulance. "You have fifteen years of patience and love, all stored up. Everything is telling me you've found someone worthy of it."

Chapter Seventeen

Marcel

"Gosh, darling, you've finally re-entered the land of the living. I'm pleased to see it because I'm struggling dreadfully with eleven down. If you'd slept much longer, I would have been forced to cheat and google the answer."

I hadn't needed to hear him speak to know which hand rested loosely in mine. Over the last three days, Lucien and Guillaume had come and gone, and each of them had a very different presence, even when my eyes were shut and the fuzzy sparkly thing happened around the edges. When Lucien was in the room, my muddled thoughts drifted to the past, and this episode of illness became jumbled with some of the ones that had gone before. In particular, memories of my teenage years and recuperating one summer at Rossingley. I could almost smell the apple blossom and the pungent stink of manure on the fields. Or maybe the last one was Lucien's aftershave—I'd have to tell him that sometime. The drugs always messed up my sense of smell for a while.

Guillaume taking over always brought me back to the present. The firm grip of his fingers around mine and the occasional whisper of his lips in my hair brought waves of peacefulness washing over me. When I slept, while the drugs did their work, I allowed dreams of a future together, where we were back at my island home, cuddling on the sofa or snug in my giant bed upstairs. Not performing sexual gymnastics, of the like I could only imagine, but merely…being.

Overnight, my bronchoconstriction had improved sufficiently that nasal prongs had replaced the claustrophobic oxygen mask. Infinitely preferable, and even though they made my nose sore and crusty, they were a step forwards along the winding road that led to returning home. I hadn't required a nebuliser for a few hours either. Apart from the coughing fits, which wrenched my rib cage, and the ever-present, bone-numbing weariness, things were gradually settling back to normal. Normal for me anyhow.

"I've survived another one, then." My voice was dry and hoarse. Lucien lifted a plastic beaker of water up to my chapped lips.

"Yes," he observed. "It would appear that way, darling. Although you gave your gorgeous Guillaume a bit of a fright. His brittle asthma cherry has been well and truly popped."

I didn't speak for a while. Lucien helped me drink some more, and I endeavoured to keep my eyes from closing. The drugs left me jittery and sore, my whole body aching from top to toe as if I'd run back-to-back marathons, not spent a few days lounging around in bed.

"Do you think I've scared him off?" I asked, watching my oldest friend carefully. If there was one person guaranteed to tell me the truth, it was Lucien.

"I thought so when I arrived, but not now. It was the shock, I imagine. It is rather frightening the first time, especially when you go all weak and floppy, darling. Honestly, you should really try to hold it together a bit more, for all of our sakes. I'm glad he called us; he needed Reuben's support."

And I needed yours, I thought, but I didn't have to say it. And I also needed this gentle teasing, the brushing off of my near-death experience. Lucien didn't come running every time I had one of my episodes, but the bad times he never missed.

"I think he's the one, Lucien," I whispered in my hoarse voice. My pulse beat faster, and it wasn't down to the drugs. "He doesn't ask anything of me; he lets me be myself. He doesn't mind if I sit at my desk all day and hardly speak to him. He doesn't even care if I don't bother to dress."

"What? He's seen you parading around in those ghastly pyjamas?" Lucien laughed out loud. "Gosh, he's definitely a keeper, darling. Propose to him at once."

A nurse bustled in and fiddled with the IV line. A familiar team of doctors followed—old friends by now—and I was poked and prodded for a while. My tired brain switched off when Lucien was by my bedside; he asked all the right questions and ascertained the plan. All I had to do was pretend I wasn't totally exhausted, then attempt to demonstrate my finest peak flow so I could be discharged as soon as possible. This evening, if I behaved myself.

After they had gone, Lucien helped me shuffle to the shower, and I stood unmoving under the thin jets of water like a small child as he briskly washed my hair and soaped me down. It wasn't the first time he'd done this, either, or the first time he'd helped me into my pyjamas afterwards. An attack such as this one could leave me weak for days. After he'd towelled me dry, tutting over my bony ribs and jutting hip bones, I sank back onto the bed, hungry for my oxygen prongs and absolutely drained, desperate for a nap. But we weren't finished.

"And now for a shave. That stubble will make you itchy. And your gorgeous man will be along in a minute—we need to have you looking your ravishing best for him, darling."

Which was pretty ridiculous really, considering how Guillaume had seen me at my absolute worst. A terrifying vision that a fresh shave, shower, and clean pyjamas wouldn't eradicate in a hurry.

With a bowl of soapy water and a towel balanced on my lap, Lucien carefully folded back the sleeves of his crisp white shirt. There was a light tap at the door, and Guillaume appeared. As our eyes locked, I was at a loss to figure out what was running through his handsome dark head. Apprehension? Dread? One thing for sure, he looked bone weary; it hadn't been only me having a rough few days. He, Lucien, and Reuben had alternated between catching a few hours' sleep and sitting by my bedside. Even Lucien didn't look his best, although he'd never have admitted it.

"Gosh, the cavalry has arrived, darling," he announced, dropping the razor back into the bowl. "You've had a reprieve—Guillaume can take over. Last time I shaved him, Guillaume, we had to send for a row of butterfly strips and some surgical glue. I'm sure you'll do a much better job."

He was exaggerating; Lucien performed a very competent shave, but I let it pass as he'd broken the awkward silence, at least.

"And now, my darlings, this is my cue to leave. I have a very impatient husband and two children waiting for me at home. Not to mention a grumpy cousin, who has texted and accused me of kidnapping his favourite French gardener."

He gave me a quick hug. "Always a pleasure, Marcel, especially the dash through the night for that bit at the start when you do the dying swan thingy."

He turned to Guillaume who received the same treatment. "Look after him for me, Guillaume; he's very precious."

I wasn't wearing my glasses, but I could have sworn Lucien's eyes were wet. Not that he would ever have admitted to that either.

After Lucien had gone, Guillaume seemed unsure how to proceed, awkwardly hovering rather than taking up his usual seat at my bedside.

"You don't have to give me a shave," I said. "It can wait a couple of days, until I've summoned up the energy to do it myself and am not so breathless."

Guillaume sat on the bed. "I'd like to do it, but I can't promise I'll be any good."

There was something indescribably intimate about being shaved by another man. Not at the barbers, of course, where it is a financial transaction during which one chats about the weather. Nor by Lucien, who turns it into such a ridiculous piece of fun I somehow forget I'm too poorly to do it myself. But in a quiet hospital room, when the other man is sitting on your bed, and so close you can see every fleck of hazel in his dark brown eyes and count every criminally long eyelash, then, yes, very intimate.

With the fingertips of his right hand lightly resting underneath my jaw, Guillaume tilted my head up and back, assessing me. With his other hand, he carefully massaged soap over my chin and cheek before picking up the razor. He began scraping upwards, hesitantly at first, and then growing in confidence as he continued along the line of my jaw, frequently rewetting the razor between strokes. His eyes narrowed in concentration as he shaved the tender skin above my upper lip, avoiding dislodging the nasal prongs, frowning and chewing his lip even as his shoulders relaxed into the task. Soothing, tender, and, yes, wonderfully intimate. Astonishingly, his gentle touch even managed to induce my knackered body to conjure up the beginnings of an erection.

When he'd finished and cleared away the water, he returned and sat back down on the bed, not on the chair as he'd always done previously.

"I'm sorry for putting you through this, Guillaume." I took his hand, enjoying the damp warmth of it and the fresh scent of soap.

"It's not your fault."

"I know, but it's still not very nice for you anyway."

I hesitated. Even though the shave had brought us in close proximity, he still felt further away than before I'd become ill. We'd lost the easy ebb and flow of conversation, the easy silence. Goodness, I was so rubbish at this sort of thing, especially right now, when I was achingly tired, yet it felt so desperately important.

"I…I'd understand if you didn't want me anymore, Guillaume. Because these episodes, the acute attacks, well, they are…unfortunately, not too infrequent. Worse in the winter, but I have been known to have them in the summer, too, which is peculiar but due to… Well, it's complicated; you probably don't want to know the medical ins and outs. But what I mean to say is that it's not for everyone. I totally understand that. Being my, ah, my partner. I mean, you could carry on staying in the annexe for as long as you wished and we…we could continue to be friends? So, yes, yes, I…as I said, I would totally understand if you didn't want me in that way anymore."

I'd become increasingly short of breath with each sentence. But I couldn't bring myself to stop because then it would be his turn to speak, and I daresay he'd be polite and all that, but the awkwardness would remain. And, yes, he'd stay in the annexe for a while, perhaps until the spring, but then he'd move on, probably off the island, maybe go back to Marseilles or Bordeaux perhaps. He'd mentioned Bordeaux before, and it was a very nice city, and he'd find a job, and then an equally handsome, healthy young man, and then…

"Marcel."

His deep, firm voice, soft in my ear. His face so close I could feel his gentle, slow breaths against my newly shaved cheek, and he would definitely have been able to feel my quick, hot ones against his. The pad of his thumb found my lips, quietening me.

"Marcel," he repeated in that low melodic southern accent, that dark, chocolatey rasp that matched his eyes and his skin, in a way that no one else had ever said my name. I brought my eyes up to his, my heart beating violently in my chest, once more, the wild thrumming not attributable to the vast swathes of bronchodilator drugs coursing through my veins.

He closed the distance between us, and his full, soft lips found my parted, dry, chapped ones and swept across them in the lightest of brushes.

"*Mon coeur.* How could anybody not want you?"

Eight simple words, murmured so tenderly that my breathlessness temporarily increased, and behind my ribcage my heart threw itself around crazily, causing the bank of monitors surrounding me to ping madly and a worried nurse to come rushing in to see what all the fuss was about. I could list a thousand reasons why somebody wouldn't want me, but it would seem Guillaume had none.

Chapter Eighteen

Guillaume

In the end, Dominic picked us up from the hospital and dropped us back home. Sabine had wanted to, but it was late in the evening, and Clara had school the next day. She'd visited earlier that afternoon and fussed around the bedside for an hour, producing some of Marcel's preferred throat sweets to combat the dryness of the oxygen therapy. Yet another person familiar with the routine.

Dominic also unwittingly exposed my inadequacies as he efficiently organised a wheelchair and settled Marcel in the car, adjusted the heated seat and air blower, ensured the blue inhaler was in easy reach, and provided a cushion for his back. But it was good to see him anyhow; he was his usual, peculiar sweet self and attentive to Marcel without swamping him. As he drove across the bridge back to the island, hunched over the steering wheel at an extremely cautious thirty kilometres per hour, he informed us that Simon had been keeping a close eye on the house. *How predictable*, I thought gloomily; the fridge would need restocking.

Back home, I had planned to settle Marcel on the sofa with a bundle of cushions, soft throws, and a blazing fire. But from the way he was longingly eyeing the staircase, I guessed he had other ideas. Not sexy ones; he'd fallen asleep on the journey back from the hospital and struggled to stay awake now. After all the drama, he desired nothing more than to collapse into his own familiar bed.

"If this becomes a regular thing, I'm going to have to join a gym," I panted, hefting him into my arms.

He had one hand curled around my neck and planted a breathless kiss on my cheek as I staggered under his weight. Being Marcel, with his rather lackadaisical attitude towards dressing, he'd left the hospital with only a sweater and coat thrown over his pyjamas. So, getting him into bed, propped up against a mound of plumped pillows, was relatively straightforward. As he began laying out the usual array of medicines across his lap, plus a few new ones, he looked up at me anxiously.

"Stay with me, please, Guillaume? I still feel quite awful."

I didn't need asking twice. Of course, by the time I'd closed up the house downstairs and performed some hurried ablutions, he was out for the count, gently snoring with a faster respiratory rate than I would have liked, one hand loosely cradling an inhaler. After stripping to my T-shirt and boxers, I snuck in under the duvet next to him and anxiously monitored the rise and fall of his chest for a while.

Apart from a mad dash to grab some essentials while we waited for the ambulance, it was the first time I'd properly been in Marcel's bedroom. Dragging my gaze away from his sleeping form, I had a look around. The room was spacious—he owned a big house—and the ceiling was high. Amusingly, a rather ornate crystal chandelier hung directly above my head, well out of reach in every sense. Jewellery, socks, photos, pens, and papers cluttered every surface. Clothes liberally covered every chair, books stacked on the bedside and dressing tables, even piled carelessly in the corners. As with the study, he inhabited every inch of the room, and the scent of the enormous bed in which I now found myself was pure Marcel. Inhaling deeply of the pillow, my last thought before joining him in an exhausted, dreamless sleep was that I hoped to lie here next to him every night from now on.

Reuben had pointed out, during those anxious hours sitting by Marcel's hospital bedside, that instead of moaning about my perceived inadequacies regarding Marcel's health issues, I could consider opening a book and finding out a bit more about brittle asthma. He also kindly observed as he ordered me to eat yet more sandwiches in that depressing hotel room, that I'd read up on every other subject during my fifteen years incarcerated, so why was I avoiding the one topic that actually might be of assistance in my everyday life?

Thus, when Marcel woke up gasping at 4:00 a.m., although my default mode was instant panic, I repeated to myself that early morning wakening was expected in poorly controlled asthmatics. If I propped him upright again and administered one of his nebulisers, everything would be fine. The little machine was already plugged in and primed to go, and when Marcel's sleepy face disappeared behind billows of steam, I held his hand and watched nervously because there was bugger all else I could do.

"Feeling better?" I asked twenty minutes later. I knew the answer because his wheezing had quietened (not in the scary bad way) enough for him to fractionally lower the pillow mountain from behind his head and snuggle down onto his side. I curled up behind him, resting my arm across his torso, and wormed my fingers between the buttons of his pyjama top to gently caress the smooth skin of his thin chest. This position was not only rather lovely—it had been many years since I'd lain like this with a man who wasn't Reuben—but it also enabled me to keep subtle tabs on the rise and fall of his rib cage.

"Yes, much, thank you."

I wiggled closer and closed my eyes, intermittently succumbing to temptation and softly kissing the warm skin at the back of his neck. His heart thrummed briskly under my fingers; my new knowledge reassured me it was merely a temporary side effect of the bronchodilators in the nebuliser. Nonetheless, I was happy for it to slow down because, combined with a noticeable increase in his respiratory rate, I was rapidly developing a sinking feeling in my stomach. The nebuliser should have worked, dammit. Why the hell wasn't it working?

"Are you sure you're all right?" I whispered, trying to stay calm. "You're not getting short of breath again, are you?"

Once more, I pressed my lips to the back of his neck, transmitting my concern.

"Yes, I am a bit," he admitted. A pause as he took my wrist and gently removed my hand from under his pyjama top. "But it's the good sort of shortness of breath."

With his hand over mine, he guided it lower, down across his flat belly until it rested on the thin cotton overlaying his groin.

"See, Guillaume? The good sort of breathlessness."

Putain, his dick was hard. Properly hard, able to scratch diamonds hard. The front of his pyjamas was damp under my palm. He took a sharp intake of breath as my hand automatically closed around his shaft. For a few seconds, I forgot to breathe myself, utterly lost for words.

"Christ, Marcel. I mean, *merde*, you feel so good. Are you…are…are you sure about this? Fuck… Fuck!"

"Ah…yes…please," he stammered. "I mean…I'd have probably framed it a little more prettily, but, yes. I want you to…ah…yes. Just…do that…yes."

"Have you got anything we can use?"

He writhed with pleasure as I gave his dick a gentle squeeze. "What? Oh, yes, yes. Here, in this drawer."

Disappointingly, I had to briefly let go of him to reach across, but it did mean I could plant a smacker on his lips on the way. The words 'I love you' almost burst out of me; it took a monumental effort to hold them back. Predictably, all sorts of crap filled the drawer, ranging from receipts, lottery tickets, old keys, and random cufflinks, to a pair of hiking socks, still with the price tag attached. I grinned to myself as I riffled through it; no way was Marcel ever going hiking. And underneath all the crap, a crinkled blue condom packet and a dented tube of lube that had definitely seen better days.

"Probably wise not to check the use-by dates," murmured Marcel, wriggling into me as I settled behind him again. If an out-of-date condom was the difference between me fucking the man I'd been craving for months or not, then no, I wouldn't look very closely at all. I'd been tested on my release from prison, and I guessed the risk with Marcel was miniscule.

Stripped of my boxers and with my eager cock sheathed, I resumed caressing Marcel, checking he was still hard. *Mon*

Dieu, yes. As I eased down his pyjama bottoms, I gave him a few firm strokes, my own dick pushing into the crease of his arse.

"Probably better if you didn't do that with your hand too vigorously," he panted. "I'm already rather…well, rather…"

Swivelling his head around, his tongue found mine, and for an all too brief few seconds, we kissed deeply before his asthma forced him to break away. I opened the crusted, ancient lube and moved my greased fingers from his dick to massage one of his bony arse cheeks. He whimpered softly as I brushed over his hole.

"Fuck, you're beautiful," I blurted, the words falling out of my mouth unfiltered as I breached his sensitive ring of muscle. *Putain*, the words kept coming, whether it was the emotional roller coaster of the last few days, sheer amazement that Marcel was so turned on and we were actually doing this, or the overwhelming tsunami of feelings I had for this brave, ill man.

"I've fallen in love with you, Marcel," I whispered as I added a second finger, opening him up carefully, unhurriedly, attuned to every hitch in his breath and every beat of his heart. "I hope you don't mind, but I'm in love with every last drop of you, *mon coeur*."

I didn't expect an answer. I didn't expect him to have the breath to say anything, but in response, he pushed against me, silently asking for more. I gave it to him, my fingers searching for that all too wonderful hidden place inside. I knew the moment I'd found it because another soft moan escaped his throat, and his breath came faster in hurried puffs. But there was no indication he wanted me to stop, not from the way he bore down on my hand nor the shudder of pleasure that followed.

Keeping him on his side and my arm encircling him from behind, my cock took the place of my fingers as I gently sought entry. Remaining in this sideways, awkward position, with the man I so desperately wanted opening up to me, was an almost impossible task. It took everything I had not to push him onto his belly so I could take him hard. After fifteen years behind bars, I'd mastered a wham-bam-thank-you-ma'am approach. That of hurried encounters pushed against the walls of dirty shower stalls and on the floor of unlocked cells, not loving seduction in a king-sized bed.

"Tell me it's okay, Marcel. Please let me know you're okay," I panted. "I need that, *mon coeur*, my love."

He nodded. "I think…ah…that okay would be…goodness… That is…very…inadequate at this exact moment." He extended his arm back and tugged at my hip, urging me forwards.

Somehow, although unable to find purchase with my heels or my hands, I found a gentle rhythm, the position not allowing me any forceful thrusts, only a determined steady glide. He was hot and tight around my dick, with his back slick against my front, and I crushed his body against mine, licking and nipping at his neck and shoulder. Adjusting my angle, I drove deeper and was rewarded with his soft low moans, which grew more frantic as I hit his sweet spot over and over. Desperately close, a hot, urgent rush enveloped me, beginning in my toes and surging up to my balls. I grunted with need and the effort of holding back. With Marcel's wet shaft in the tunnel of my palm, we moved together.

"Coming," he ground out. As a splash of hot seed spilled over my hand, his arse spasmed around me, and my own release pulsed into the condom, every last drop milked out of my soul.

"*Mon Dieu*, we did it, Marcel; we did it!" I was almost sobbing into his neck as I held him close, my softening cock still buried inside him.

"Yeah," he panted and wriggled frantically out of my hold. "Gui…Gui…I…need to sit up. Can't breathe."

So much for a lazy untangling of arms and legs followed by a postcoital snooze. But Jesus, I did not need to find myself explaining to a bunch of friendly paramedics how my lover had come to be, once again, in extremis, having left the hospital in a perfectly stable condition a few hours earlier. Having flung the soggy used condom goodness knew where, I had him sitting over the side of the bed in a trice with the inhaler at his lips as I scrambled to set up another nebuliser. Scooting behind him, I spread my legs to embrace him from behind, and his head fell back onto my shoulder.

The drug did its thing, and I held my lover close as he did his.

"Yeah, Guillaume," he managed eventually and laughed softly. "We did it. And it was perfect."

Chapter Nineteen

Marcel

I was bone-tired. Even my fingernails ached with weariness. And when I'd ejaculated, more powerfully than I could ever remember having done before, my vision had blurred and my chest felt as if a thousand tiny needles were pressing their way in. If we hadn't had that second nebuliser ready to go, I would have passed out from lack of oxygen to my brain and lack of blood flow to my poor, useless lungs because it had all pooled in my penis. Afterwards, when I'd felt safe to get off the bed, on exceedingly noodly legs, Guillaume had helped me to the bathroom to clean up, grinning at the sight of us in the mirror, both wearing clothing on the top half but bare from the waist down. He said we resembled overgrown toddlers learning to potty train. He'd wiped me down so carefully with a face cloth, not minding that I didn't have the energy for a shower and that I probably smelled a bit whiffy. Nor minding that he had to hold me up over the toilet bowl while I emptied my bladder, laughing as we crossed swords, him with one arm securely around my waist and my embarrassed face buried in his neck.

"Did you mean it?" I had asked him after he'd helped me into my pyjamas again, and we were back in bed. I found it easier to breathe propped up on several pillows, so he had his head on my shoulder with his arm draped across my belly, his hand resting at my hip. He knew to what I was referring, of course.

"Yes, *mon coeur*, I meant it," he replied gravely. "Every single word."

And I fell asleep with his whispered words soothing my weary soul.

I woke some time around noon to an empty bed and a note informing me Guillaume had gone to work and that I was to spend the day in bed recovering. Recovering from my bout of asthma, I guessed, not the sex, although I needed to recover from that too. Not physically—despite a lingering pleasant ache—but mentally. I was overwhelmed. Obviously, my celibacy status had been comprehensively blown out of the water; even the memory of having him inside me had me sporting a partial erection under the duvet. No one had ever loved me so tenderly, either during intercourse or afterwards, especially afterwards. Yes, it had wrung out every last drop of energy I had, but I'd been an idiot to have sex when I was still coming out of one of my bad attacks. It hadn't put me off wanting it again, though, notwithstanding my bone-weary exhaustion.

He loved me. Wow.

I pondered that for a while, vaguely fondling myself. I'd like to have returned the sentiment because I was confident that I loved him too. But something held me back; he'd only had this one episode of being both my caregiver and my lover—the novelty had worn thin pretty quickly with my previous partners.

But, older for a start, Guillaume wasn't like my previous partners. For one thing, he wasn't forging an ambitious professional career, which didn't generally find room for the caring aspect of being with me. Yet he'd only been released from prison three months ago, and I didn't know him well enough to understand if part-time bar work and running a football team was sufficient to keep him fulfilled. And on the subject of him being newly released from prison, I'd read up on the psychological consequences of long periods of incarceration. Guillaume appeared extremely stable mentally, but would it all come crashing down? Would an unforeseen event trigger the anger, depression, shame, and feelings of loss and anxiety that came with his situation? Should I be looking out for them? Should I discuss this with him?

Perhaps being here on Ile de Ré was merely a temporary pitstop on the way to establishing a proper career—he was smart and had gained a few distance learning qualifications while behind bars. He could become a professional sports coach, or a personal trainer, or even run his own bar. He had some savings set aside, although I didn't know how much, and while he wasn't flash, I didn't think he had money worries. The income from his bar work and his house rental seemed ample for his modest needs. Would being with me hold him back from what he really wanted out of life? He might not have reached that conclusion yet, but would resentment creep in? A few more months of the ups and downs of my day-to-day existence and he might find he'd developed itchy feet.

My head hurt. Thoughts like these exemplified why I preferred maths to people.

Next to Guillaume's short note were two fresh croissants, butter and jam, and a flask of hot chocolate. Even more thoughtfully, he'd delivered my laptop to the bedroom too. I obediently ate one of the croissants, then flipped open the computer. Sabine and Simon would have insisted it was too soon for me to return to work, even if it was merely lying in bed and catching up on emails, but Guillaume had recognised the need in me without ever discussing it. I wouldn't manage much today, but the Ministry were sufficiently familiar with me going AWOL for a few days to be confident I'd rapidly be back on top of things after my return. I'd been headhunted for this government post, and I'd be damned if my asthma stood in the way of my career.

Two hours passed in dreamy post-coital, nerdy bliss, with me wrapped up cosily in my duvet and my spreadsheets. Usually, this immersed me totally, but I'd surprised myself by half listening for Guillaume's return. Even more surprisingly, I wanted some more of that man's naked body next to mine. Time to hang out the bunting and light some fireworks because there was no denying it. Marcel Giresse was officially randy.

My concupiscence had just surged hopefully when a key rattled in the door downstairs, only to be rudely quashed when my sister's voice called my name. I listened as she padded into the kitchen and then, from the sounds of her receding footsteps, most likely to the annexe and back to the study before she started up the stairs.

"I can't believe he's left you on your own," she grumbled as way of greeting. "Anything could have happened to you! Simon would never have done that."

"Hello, Sabine. Nice to see you too. Yes, I'm feeling much better; thank you for asking."

"Whatever. You may scoff, but it's true!" She came farther into the room and, frowning at my usual mess, absently started to pick up some of the discarded clothes from the floor. "It's too soon after your discharge for you to be home alone. It's irresponsible of him not to stay with you!"

I sighed. Guillaume wasn't my keeper, and neither, for that matter, was Sabine. Nor Simon, definitely not teacher's pet, Simon. I held up my mobile phone. "Look—I have a modern means of communication right here next to the bed. And a plate of food, so I don't even have to get out of my pit if I don't want to. *And,* he only works fifty meters away should he have to come back in a hurry. I can virtually see the bar from my bedroom window!"

She tutted as she folded a sweater and put it neatly on the back of a chair. I wished she wouldn't fuss like this. In fact, I wished she didn't think it was okay to wander into her thirty-six-year-old brother's bedroom without knocking at all. But there had been a time when I'd been alone and needed checking on, so I appreciated that it was difficult for her to let go now I had Guillaume here with me. Surely, she could see how much his presence made her life easier.

It could be worse, I suppose. At least we weren't having an inquisition regarding the status of my relationship with him. That would predictably come later when she'd deduced that I looked at him as though he were my next meal. I tried to refocus on the email in front of me as she continued to tidy up, tutting as she went.

"Shit, Marcel, what the hell have I trodden on? This room…ugh… It's something squidgy and, oh, oh my God. Aaagh! Oh my God, oh my God. How long has that been living there? That is repulsive!"

Seems like she'd discovered last night's condom, then. It was tempting to ask her to pass it to me so I could frame it as commemorative proof that I'd succeeded in having an enjoyable, fulfilling sexual interaction. In the frantic rush to get my medication, Guillaume had no doubt thrown it overboard and promptly forgotten about it. And this morning, he'd probably crept around in the dark to let me sleep. Okay, so we were going to have the relationship conversation after all. I placed a bet with myself which way it would start.

"He's taking advantage of you."

I owed myself ten euros.

"Remind me in what way he's taking advantage of me?"

She folded her arms, preparing for a fight. "He's been living here for a start, in your lovely big house."

"He's been living in the annexe, Sabine. He's had use of the kitchen; we've shared the cooking. Next?"

"He's freeloading off you."

I shook my head. "He pays me rent. I've never bought him anything. We split the grocery bills."

"Well…well…he…" Her eyes flashed angrily at me. I knew what was coming and exhaled deeply.

"Go on, Sabine, say it. Tell me the other way in which you think Guillaume is taking advantage of me. The one you are hinting at but think is too vulgar to spell out."

Her head whipped around as she reached for the laundry bag. "Christ, you're being absurd. You know exactly what I'm getting at. He's intent on worming his way into your life so he can get his hands on your money. He's been to prison, which makes him untrustworthy. And he lied to me that he wasn't sleeping with you! I asked him straight up when you were in Paris because I need to protect you, and he lied!"

"I refuse to let you accuse him of lying, Sabine! He's not a liar! Goodness, I can't believe we're even discussing this, but if you must know, when he answered your question, he was not lying. Last night was the first time we've slept together."

She harrumphed, hands on hips. "And now he's got you lying to me too! As if someone in your sorry state could have…initiated a sexual relationship last night. You could barely breathe when I saw you yesterday afternoon!"

I seethed with fury. With my chest tightening, I angrily took a puff of my inhaler. If I'd been smart, I'd have stalked out of the room so we wouldn't take this row any further than it had already gone, to avoid saying something which might damage our relationship irreparably. But my body was weak; I was still knackered and, frankly, didn't trust my legs to stomp off anywhere. Reclining in bed in pyjamas was not exactly a position of strength, but it was a lot stronger than having to be helped up off the floor.

"Can I conclude, Sabine, that the only way you believe your pathetic, disabled brother can get a lover is for it to be someone who is after his money? Is it too far a stretch that I may have actually found a man who likes me, despite all my baggage?"

"Don't be ridiculous. I don't think that at all."

I was on a roll. "Well, that's exactly how it sounds. All you see, and all the doctors see, for that matter, is a man with a life-threatening illness. Is it so unbelievable that Guillaume might see a guy he fancies?"

We were both shouting by now; if I got myself into such a rage that my asthma killed me on the spot, it would have been worth it because no way was I going to lie here and take this utter garbage.

"It's not all about him," she screamed, kicking angrily at a shirt minding its own business on the floor. "It's bad enough he's staying with you, and now you're having sex with him! What are you thinking?"

"I'm thinking that my sex life is no business of yours."

My breathing had become erratic, and I should have paused the argument, had a nebuliser, and then picked up again in a much more mature fashion when we'd both calmed down. But I'd gone beyond that.

"It is my business when you choose to have sex with a murderer!"

I threw up my hands in disgust. "So you don't think someone like me should be able to choose with whom they have sex? Should it be someone more suitable? Someone like Simon. Someone vetted by you?"

Anyone overhearing our blazing row would be astonished to learn that sex was actually a topic we avoided discussing in our family. Like breaking wind, or menstruation, or any other normal bodily function, for that matter. Basically, anything that took place below the waist. I had a childish urge to repeat the word over and over, just to make her even more mad.

"Well, let me tell you something, Sabine. Being virtually housebound doesn't mean I'm not entitled to make my own decisions, even if they turn out to be bad ones. I seem to remember someone else made a bad decision about a life partner not too many years ago, and look where that left you. Bringing up Clara on your own. But no one suggested you weren't competent enough to make that mistake, did they?"

That was a low blow, and we both knew it. A real charmer, Clara's dad had fooled everyone until he suddenly didn't anymore, and by then it was too late. A quick divorce followed, and he walked out of the marriage with a decent chunk of Sabine's inheritance from our parents and a rather nice house to go with it. Essentially, we bought him off when we discovered his multiple dalliances and slippery financial dealings; the alternative would have been lengthy legal battles and half custody of Clara.

"You bitch, Marcel. You complete bitch," Sabine bit out, tears of anger in her eyes. "Don't come running to me when he stabs you to death in your sleep."

"I won't be able to, will I? Not if I've been stabbed to death."

Exceedingly immature, *moi*? Bringing up her marriage had been a cheap shot and totally unacceptable. No way was I ready to apologise though. She flounced out of the room and thumped down the stairs. A second later, I heard the front door slam.

I sighed heavily, slumping farther into the bed and wishing I could erase the last few minutes. Later, when we'd both had a chance to calm down, I'd phone and apologise. I always did.

★

My next bedroom visitor was far more soothing. After the drama with Sabine, I must have nodded off. I woke to a gentle hand brushing the hair from my forehead and soft lips grazing mine. Guillaume had slipped off his shoes and straddled my knees, grinning down at me.

"Hi, sleeping beauty."

Goodness, in a pair of thigh-hugging jeans, his spread legs were divine. Flushed from the cold air, his face was pretty good too. The wind had whipped his silky black hair into a shaggy mess. He'd undressed down to his white T-shirt, and his toned, tattooed arms bracketed my belly as he leaned over me. The irony that my new man was an ex-professional athlete and a poster boy for health and fitness had not escaped me. As he reached down for another kiss, I became acutely aware I hadn't washed, dressed, or brushed my teeth since last night.

"I'm probably a bit grubby, Guillaume," I murmured.

He laughed and burrowed his face into my armpit, wrinkling his nose. "So was Sleeping Beauty, I should imagine, after one hundred years."

He ran his tongue across the line of my jaw, a gentle reminder of the delicious scrape of that silver stud. "Remember, for fifteen years I lived in close proximity to four hundred other blokes—you, *mon coeur*, are positively fragrant by comparison."

While he was talking, I'd trailed my hand down his abdomen. I pushed up his T-shirt, drew a line across the top of his waistband, and tugged gently on the soft hairs disappearing south. He briefly closed his eyes, sighing deeply.

"Mmm, that's nice. I think you're beginning to feel much better, Marcel."

I unfastened the buttons of his jeans and started stroking him. Rocking gently into my fist, he claimed another kiss, fully hardening in my hand.

"I'd feel even better if you helped me into the shower. To make sure I'm perfectly safe, perhaps you had better join me."

"Try stopping me," he said, grinning.

Reclining back on his heels, he pulled his T-shirt off over his head and tossed it onto the floor. With his tousled hair, toned tattooed body, and half undone jeans, he could have passed for a cocky twenty-five. And, as a bonus, judging from the way he'd carelessly abandoned his T-shirt, he wasn't a neat freak. Goodness, I was a lucky boy. I flicked his nipple ring mischievously, and he yelped in shock.

"You, Marcel Giresse, are going to pay for that."

Which is how I found myself scooped up out of bed, then squealing under a cold shower, still fully clad, while feasting my eyes on Guillaume performing a leisurely strip tease out of his denim. After adjusting the temperature, he joined me, hands in my hair and pushing me up against the shower wall. As his eager tongue found mine, I groaned into the kiss, helplessly caged against him, relishing the feel of his naked erection against mine.

"These need to be on the floor," he panted, pausing only to rip off my soaking pyjamas and kick them aside.

The kissing was filthy and magnificent, even if I did have to stop frequently to catch my breath. Somehow, the wetness and the breathiness enhanced my pleasure. And Guillaume certainly wasn't complaining.

"Are you okay doing this standing up?" he asked around my mouth, and it was all I could do to nod because, what with the kissing and the imminent explosion in my nether regions, there wasn't enough space in my brain for coherent conversation.

His mouth left mine, giving me pause to catch my breath, but only to tease its way down my body, licking and sucking en route. His hand slipped between my legs, cupping my balls as he sank to his knees. When his soft mouth engulfed my throbbing penis, my leg trembling began in earnest, my knees buckling under the hot, velvet caress.

That tongue stud grazing my shaft was every bit as fabulous as I'd imagined—an indescribable pleasure pain that had me throwing my head back against the tiled wall and my hips pistoning up to his mouth as I grasped at his hair for support. He had me safely covered, both hands at my waist, pinning me upright against the wall tiles as he voraciously sucked me. With a cry and no time to give him a warning, I erupted down his throat, pumping into his mouth, before he pressed his face against my thigh, holding me tight.

"Goodness, Guillaume, you're…very good at that," I exhaled eventually.

An understatement if ever there was one.

He stood and supported me against the wall again. Flicking his gaze at me almost coyly under his lashes, he stroked himself with one hand. "Fancy a turn?"

Dropping to my knees was certainly an appealing prospect. If Guillaume's hands hadn't been supporting me, it was likely I'd already have found myself rolling around the bottom of the shower tray in a very ungainly fashion. But returning the gift of fellatio? Um…possibly.

"Ah…yes, yes, but…I'm a little out of practice, and that is to say, ah, years out of practice, to be honest. And…and you have …given a masterclass in how to do it beautifully, which you certainly did, no hands, in fact, which was very impressive. And that tongue stud was, well…ahem, yes, I liked that, too, so…if, ah…I get a bit breathless, we may have to…ah…"

"Marcel."

That musical low tone, firm and sweet. And patient. This man had lashings and lashings of patience.

"Shh, Marcel. Do it. It will be brilliant because it's you."

Chapter Twenty

Guillaume

Somewhere in his past, somebody had robbed Marcel of his sexual confidence, so much so that he felt he had to apologise in advance almost every time he touched me. And apologies really weren't necessary when a man you'd gradually come to adore had his mouth around your cock. Even if his action was a little stop-start and he had to break off for gulps of air, technique was totally irrelevant. Because, well, he's got his mouth around your cock. And what bloke was going to complain about that? Especially when his finger up your arse, hitting exactly the right note, supplemented his mouth.

There was an explanation for why he'd lost his confidence, of course. He'd warned me that his physical limitations had repeatedly disappointed previous partners, including his frequent requirement for sleep instead of sex. However much I hated the faceless bastards who had been mean to him before he gave up and chose celibacy, I sort of understood them. Sex was pretty much at the forefront of your mind morning, noon, and night when one was young and single. I only had to listen to

Reuben's rather too detailed exploits to be reminded of that. By all accounts, young Viscount Freddie was quite the gymnast.

So the shower blowjob did not disappoint—far from it. Afterwards, I left Marcel to his own devices for a while, so he could do his post-sex processing and dorky, humming thing in peace. I had dinner prepared for when he felt ready to wander downstairs and had used the intervening time for some dorky stuff of my own.

"Right, Marcel, I've been doing some reading," I announced as we cuddled on the sofa after a perfectly acceptable spaghetti bolognese. Dressed in another pair of grandad pyjamas, he looked clean and fluffy and unbelievably sweet. I tucked a woollen throw around him to make him even cuter. If any of my fellow inmates could have seen me fussing, they'd have pissed themselves laughing.

"And I've made you a list."

That caught his attention. He raised his eyebrows with interest. Marcel's analytical brain enjoyed nothing more than working its way through a list, which was why I'd targeted this approach. This list, however, was possibly a little different to the work-related ones he was used to.

"I've decided the only way to get you back into wanting sex, without becoming all anxious and flustered on me, is to have lots of it. And if you don't feel well enough for that, we'll practise saying the word a lot until you do. Sex, sex, sex. Flooding therapy, if you like."

He laughed. "Are you going to be my therapist?"

"Well, I'm sure as hell not going to let anyone else do it. So, yeah, I'm going to fall on my sword—pun totally intended—and take it on. I want you to feel comfortable talking about it, what you can and can't do."

"Intercourse, intercourse, intercourse."

"Stop taking the piss; I'm deadly serious." I cleared my throat dramatically as if making a proper speech. "There are three of us in this relationship—you, me, and your asthma, and your asthma has been calling the shots in your affairs for far too long. It's getting a little crowded."

He shook his head and frowned. "I'm not entirely sure where you're going with this, Guillaume, but carry on anyway."

I wasn't entirely sure either. But I'd made up my mind last night as I watched him sleep that we needed to confront the asthma head-on and not pretend it didn't exist or let it rule us, because it wasn't exactly going to disappear.

"Now, don't laugh, Marcel, and don't get all embarrassed on me. But I've made a list of sexual positions that you're comfortable with so you never feel I'm asking too much of you or feel obliged to have a go just to please me. Likewise, I need to know in advance what I can and can't expect you to be able to do, so I won't ever put you in a position when you feel you have to decline and have somehow let me down. Which you should never feel."

I was mildly embarrassed now I was saying it all out loud, and he was clearly amused.

"Are we going to need a safe word?" he asked.

"I'm taking this very seriously! Now, look here."

I brought the list up between us, and he hitched his glasses up his nose, squinting slightly at the variety of stick men I'd drawn in black ink on the page. One of the many things I'd learned about my man was that crude words made him flustered, so I thought I'd try a different approach so he didn't have to say them. He pointed to one of the sketches.

"Okay, so I'm guessing that's me lying flat on my back." He shook his head dubiously. "We need a cross next to that; it's a complete no-no. Not unless you're trying to kill me. I haven't lain completely flat for about twenty years."

He watched as I put a cross next to it. "You can put a cross next to lying flat on my tummy, too, to be honest. It's marginally easier on my breathing, but only if you're very quick."

I kissed the hair at his temple. "I'm not planning on being very quick, *mon coeur.*"

"All fours, however, that I can do. It's actually a very good position for opening up the ribcage, maximising functional lung capacity, and utilising the accessory muscles of respiration."

I obediently placed a big heart next to the picture of the stick man on all fours. And then another next to him standing, and another kneeling—I'd already enjoyed discovering the answers to those. The sketch of two stick men lying on their sides, curled around each other, was the recipient of two hearts; we knew this was a winner, even when Marcel was not at his best. Promisingly, the stick man I'd tentatively draped over the edge of the dining table was okay, too, as long as he'd had a nebuliser first. That could very easily be arranged, and I annotated my drawing accordingly.

My next image had a smaller stick man putting his mini stick inside a bigger stick man, whom I had drawn having an enormous stick of his own. The bigger man had a huge smile on his face. This one really made him laugh.

"Is this supposed to be me impaling you, Guillaume?"

"Yes, but only if you want to. I know it would be you having to do most of the work, and that could be tiring."

He chewed the inside of his cheek for a second, frowning slightly. "Can I think about it? I…ah, I like the idea in principle. In fact, I…I love the idea in principle. But, you know, I …ah, in reality…I might…my breathing…"

I stopped him with a finger on his lips. This was exactly what I meant by not putting him in an anxiety-inducing situation and bringing his asthma once more to the forefront. I wanted him to be so comfortable that, assuming he was well, he could have sex and never give his asthma a second thought.

"We'll come back to that one, *mon coeur.*"

He visibly relaxed as I moved on to the next—a stick man reclining, also smiling, on three raised pillows. A poorly drawn crystal chandelier hung above his head.

"What's this one?"

I brought his hand up to my mouth and kissed his fingertips. "This, my love, is your safe word. Chandelier. When you are too exhausted for sex but don't want to disappoint me. Say the word, and I'll understand."

He closed his eyes for a moment and swallowed. "I don't deserve you, Guillaume."

A solitary tear rolled down his cheek. I hugged him close, listening to the slightly wheezy but mostly comfortable breathing. I thought about our meetings in prison, and how he'd charmed me with his wit and his trademark stripy scarf. About our night at Rossingley, when I'd nearly dropped him as I carried him up the stairs. I'd taken to calling him *mon coeur* for a reason—it came from the Latin *cor*, which meant 'seat of feelings', and became *coeur*—heart. Which, in English, became courage. He had that in spades.

"You've given me more than I could have ever wished for, Marcel. It's me that doesn't deserve you."

★

Marcel's asthma settled back to baseline, and, hallelujah, pyjama yoga reappeared on the early morning schedule. He wasn't quite back to basking hippo level, or whatever the yoga move was called that practically begged me to climb between his lean spread thighs, but some of the simpler stretches, which still involved a satisfactory amount of skinny arse waving, continued to give me a breakfast boner.

"I know you're watching, Guillaume," he observed from the vicinity of his armpit. "As I've said before, you are extremely welcome to join in."

I adjusted myself under my dressing gown. "No, I'm good; watching is fine."

"You haven't seen my Breitling watch anywhere, have you?" he asked, shifting into what he'd informed me was a crescent lunge. "You know, the chunky silver one? I could have sworn it was on the bedside table before I went into hospital, but it's not there now."

I shook my head. We still hadn't unearthed his lovely signet ring, either, although I continued to search for it. Marcel owned several nice watches; the Breitling was particularly swish. I'd deduced fairly early on that my man was quite wealthy. Items such as the understated watches and the fancy Audi were clues, not to mention his rather fine house. But I also had the impression money didn't matter a great deal to him; it certainly didn't drive his work ethic—the mental satisfaction of completing tricky sums did that.

I promised to hunt around for it. Yoga session completed, he joined me in the kitchen, perched on my lap, and proceeded to demolish a croissant. Mischievously, he wiggled his bony bum on my hard dick, giggling.

"Yoga fetish, eh?"

I wiped some stray jam off his upper lip with my tongue. "Nope, a Marcel-doing-yoga fetish. And right now, I think I need to see that downward doggy stretch one more time."

Chapter Twenty-One

Marcel

Check me out! As somebody much younger and much cooler than me might have said. Although, maybe not. I didn't keep up with current vernacular. But nerdy, chronically ill Marcel Giresse was having full-on, penetrative sex with his hot lover on a pink yoga mat, in broad daylight, at a time when most men were brushing their teeth, donning scratchy suits, and heading out to work.

I took a couple of precautionary puffs on my inhaler first and then had it accessible next to me on the mat. But in retrospect, my only discomfort was mild indigestion from wolfing down the croissant because I was in too much of a hurry to get on with it.

Guillaume liked to take things at a snail's pace, and not only because of my asthma. Swivelling on his lap, I straddled him, and we exchanged open-mouthed kisses for what seemed like forever. He tasted of sweetened coffee and blackcurrant jam, and his overnight stubble would leave marks on my chin, not that I minded. Especially not with his erect penis rubbing up against mine through our PJs.

I could probably have ejaculated exactly like that, with only the friction and the kissing, and it was even more likely when he broke his mouth away for long enough to strip out of his soft pyjama top and divest me of mine. With the heat of his well-built chest against my pale puny one and the scratch of his nipple ring on my sensitive skin, warm pre-ejaculate dribbled onto the cotton of my pyjama bottoms.

"We need to add this position to the stick men repertoire," I breathed between kisses, and he signalled his agreement by pushing his groin up even harder against mine, spreading his legs wider, and rocking his hips up into me.

"My stick is going to explode inside my pyjamas if we don't get onto that yoga mat soon, Marcel."

We reluctantly pulled apart, but only enough so he could lift me off his lap and walk me backwards into the study, his lips scarcely leaving my face. As we shimmied out of our PJs, every molecule of my being, every single atom screamed to have him inside me again. I couldn't remember experiencing this needy sensation before, not even when I was a hormone-fuelled teenager, nor having sex with the callous young men of my youth.

I wanted so badly to be face to face when he was inside me, to feel his chest against mine, his mouth on mine. I wanted to be able to watch him when he let go and climaxed. But su-pine on the mat was not an option, not if I wanted to breathe at the same time, and especially not with any of his weight pressing into my chest. I could have had him lying on his back and me sitting on him, but we hadn't discussed that one, and it would require a lot of physical effort on my part. Yet Guillaume somehow managed to make being on all fours intimate as his warm body cloaked mine. With his lips licking a trail up my spine and settling at my shoulder, I forgot the indignity of having my naked bum in the air. So much, that I arched into him as he gently prepared my hole, whispering nonsense in my ear, telling me I was beautiful, that I was special, that I was his, and he was mine.

We'd dispensed with condoms in unspoken agreement, and when he entered me in one slick glide, a moan of lust and want escaped my lips, matching his contented deep sigh. And I couldn't lie that my chest didn't get a little tight with the fullness and burn. I hoped he was too wrapped up in the moment to notice my hand snaking to my inhaler for a sneaky puff, but maybe he did as he stilled, giving me a few seconds to adjust, stroking my back, telling me it was the smoothest, most gorgeous back he'd ever touched, which was kind of ridiculous but kind of sweet. And I forgot about my chest and my wheeze and my inhaler digging into my palm. *Mon Dieu*, my Guillaume was an awesome lover, not because of what he did, although that was rather marvellous, too, but because of how he made me feel.

There was no better way to start the day. Without a single touch to my penis, my balls tightened and my channel jerked around him as I ejaculated all over my pink yoga mat. He braced my chest with one hand and curled the other around my hip, pumping into me, harder than before, all attempt at rhythm abandoned, grinding out his joy, spilling hotly into me again and again, his face buried in my neck.

★

"You need to speak to your sister," he remarked afterwards as we cuddled together on the sofa. Lounging with my head elevated on some cushions in his lap felt almost as good as the sex itself.

"Perhaps a bit more of a gap between what we just did and the spectre of my sister?" I replied mildly, but he was right. Yesterday afternoon's argument had gone beyond our usual sibling bickering—I'd crossed a line. She could be bossy and domineering, and I didn't like her interfering so closely in my affairs, but over the years when I'd needed it, she'd been right by my side, and I liked to think I'd been there for her too.

"I'll drive over to her place tonight when you go to your football match," I agreed and stretched contentedly. "Dominic phoned to say he'd give you a lift— Why has he developed an interest in the Saint-Martin football team all of a sudden?"

Guillaume laughed his throaty chuckle, then dropped a kiss onto the tip of my nose. "Because of a certain prison guard who has taken a shine to him. I'm doing a spot of matchmaking."

We were quiet for a while, which was something I could add to the long list of things I liked about Guillaume. He was often surprisingly happy to do…nothing.

"Won't you get bored?" I blurted out suddenly, almost making him jump.

"When? At football? Nah, I love it. When I played professionally, I'd have run around all day for nothing—I didn't need paying."

I shook my head. "No, I don't mean at football. I mean…ah, here. With me."

He made to speak, but I shushed him. "What I'm trying to say is, ah…ah…is this enough for you? You have a lot of time on your hands, you know, working part-time at the bar and coaching Saint-Martin."

"You've been keeping me fairly busy." He smiled at me, amused. "Especially this morning,"

"I'm serious, Guillaume. I'm worried that it's not enough for you. There are so many avenues you could explore. I don't want to think I'm holding you back. You could coach at a bigger club, for example, in La Rochelle or somewhere."

Infuriatingly, he still smiled at me.

"Why aren't you saying anything?"

He flicked a lock of hair from my forehead, stroking it back. "Do you want me to go and coach in La Rochelle?"

"No! Of course I don't!"

He carried on with the dreamy hair stroking. Honestly, nothing had ever kept me from work before, and now it didn't seem to matter to me whether I sat at my desk or whether I parked myself here all day. His other hand performed a similar motion on my inner thigh, and my nether regions responded accordingly, despite their earlier workout.

"That's good, Marcel, because I don't want to coach in La Rochelle or work more hours than I do now. I've enough money, and I'm perfectly happy being here with you for as long as you'll have me. Not everybody is as ambitious as you are."

I'd have him forever; I couldn't contemplate a day when I wouldn't want Guillaume in my life. My feelings scared me. Grasping how much I loved him sucked all the oxygen out of my lungs. He sighed and reached down for a kiss.

"If it makes you happier, I have been giving my future a bit of thought, although it's still at the vague ideas stage. I've been thinking of perhaps buying or leasing a bar of my own."

Goodness, this was news.

"Not yet, but maybe in a year or so. Here on the island. I quite enjoy bar work, meeting people and chatting, as long as the chat isn't about me. If I sold my house in Marseilles, I'd have the money for it. I suppose it all depends on…on…"

He looked away.

"On what?"

His face took on a serious expression. "I hadn't planned on having this conversation yet. It's too soon, and you're too nosy."

I didn't push him, partly because I didn't want the hair and thigh stroking to stop. I knew the answer anyway.

It depended on us.

★

"Can I talk to you about something else, Marcel?" He looked anxious, not an expression I saw very often unless I was exceptionally wheezy. I nodded.

"It's about Simon."

Simon. That one name, and already my warm fuzzy enjoyment of being cocooned in Guillaume's lap faded. In fact, I felt a little queasy. The thing was, I knew what was coming. I would be the first to hold up my hand and admit to running a chaotic, messy household. It was no wonder I continually lost things, like my signet ring and my watch. But squirrelling myself away, leaving all that day-to-day bother to someone else was my *modus operandi*. Someone grateful to take it on. Someone who, on the one hand, behaved like a devoted friend and helped me out, and on the other, saw me as a soft touch. So if I turned a blind eye when Simon drank too freely of my wine, helped himself too readily to the contents of my kitchen cupboards, and frankly irritated the hell out of me, it was because I could then selfishly do my own thing. We'd developed a desperately unhealthy symbiotic relationship, which, since Guillaume had become part of my life, had run its course.

"I've been mulling over whether to mention it to you or not, but I think I should."

"If you're going to tell me he takes advantage of my generosity, there's no need," I replied defensively. "I'm fully aware of that."

"I'm not sure you are fully aware actually. There's a little bit more to it, unfortunately. I learned the truth a while ago, but I wanted to have concrete evidence first. Otherwise, it looks like I'm just bitching about the competition."

Guillaume probably had lots of choice thoughts about Simon, particularly as Simon was rude to him at every turn, but bitchiness wasn't his style.

"What evidence? What are you talking about? And Simon is definitely not the competition. In your football parlance, I would relegate him to a non-league team."

He sighed. "Don't be cross, but while you were in Paris, I did a little investigating. I collected a few receipts and things; they are in the annexe if you'd like to look at them. But, to put it bluntly, he's been doing worse than helping himself to your food. Sorry."

I sat up, the hair stroking forgotten. "What are you talking about?"

"I phoned the Audi garage. Your car had a normal, routine service before Christmas. There was never any problem with the carburettor. You never had a new pool filter fitted, either, because there is nothing wrong with the existing one. Old

Henri, who trims your hedges, hasn't put his hourly rates up since the Napoleonic era, but according to Simon, he's now charging twenty euros an hour. Whereas Henri actually bills you for eight. And the last dry-cleaning bill was significantly higher than…"

I tuned out. Goodness, I'd been played for a fool. I was more pathetic than I thought. It was farcical really; I'd welcomed a convicted murderer into my house who had never once asked me for anything or taken a single liberty, and all this time, one of my law-abiding, so-called friends had been systematically defrauding me. I couldn't have made it up.

"Okay, okay, I get the picture. Can we stop there please? I don't need to hear any more of my utter incompetency spelled out. Oh…heck. Really? Are you sure?"

He shrugged. "I've got emails from the Audi garage and the pool company. I spoke to Henri…"

"He needs a raise," I interrupted gloomily. "And back pay."

I paused. "Can you, ah… I don't know. Ah…could you sort it? I'm hopeless at managing him, at managing all of them. Oh, Guillaume, I'm a bloody useless fool."

My chest tightened, and I automatically reached for my inhaler. This was what happened when I unexpectedly faced confrontation. Anxiety. And anxiety led to asthma. The edges of my control were fraying; the conflict with my sister and Simon was, simultaneously, too much. I needed to curl up with my laptop and hide from the world. Or this world with people in it. Algorithms and spreadsheets and crosswords were fine. They didn't swindle me or give me asthma.

Neither did Guillaume. And it was as if he knew exactly what I was thinking. The hair stroking was back.

"Hey, Marcel, calm down. Have a couple of puffs. I'll deal with Henri. I'll do it today. I'll take over all the other stuff Simon did too. I'm already doing most of it already. And then he won't find himself in a position to be tempted to abuse your trust. But what you do with him as a person, as a friend, well, that's up to you."

I nodded sadly. Despite it all, I'd had some good times with Simon. As he'd smugly informed Guillaume, we did occasionally attend concerts and visit museums together, and he could be an interesting, informed companion. I was hurt by the discovery he'd been stealing from me, but what to do with the information, I had no idea.

"Guillaume, do you mind if…if I…you know…"

"Go and do your thing on your own for a while?" he interrupted, quietening me with a kiss. "I think it's an excellent idea, *mon coeur*."

Chapter Twenty-Two

Guillaume

I had several suggestions for how Marcel should deal with Simon, but none of them would have been acceptable to my sweet, naïve lover. I left him to do his thing for a while, mostly confident that I knew what decision he would arrive at, and I was absolutely right. Sure enough, he tracked me down in the annexe about six hours later. I was lying on my bed reading, having finished a lunchtime shift at the bar, and he flopped down next to me, wearing the same pyjamas he'd had on this morning.

"Have you shaved today?" I asked as he rubbed his stubbly chin against mine.

"Nope," he replied happily.

"Have you showered?"

"Nope. But I will before I go and visit Sabine."

"Are you going to get dressed as well?"

He shrugged. "Maybe, or I could put my pyjamas back on after my shower and wear my big overcoat over the top."

I laughed and tickled him until he yelped.

"Stop! Stop! You can't do that! Fifty-six percent of asthmatics have laughter-induced symptoms!"

I pulled him up the bed until he was safely reclining on the pillows, then pinned him down and straddled his belly. "Are you in that fifty-six percent?"

"Yes," he squealed, and I lifted up his pyjama top and blew a raspberry onto his navel, which made him squeal some more.

"Are you sure?" I did it again, harder. He was lying; I knew it; we laughed all the time together.

"No! Stop!"

"You're a grubby bugger, Marcel Giresse, Mr Important Director of Finance, did you know that? I've shared cells with men serving life sentences who cared more about their personal hygiene than you do."

"Yes, but they weren't as brilliantly witty, handsome, and charming, though, were they? You can't have everything, Guillaume."

I released him, mostly because I was worried it would lead to wheeziness, despite his playfulness. "What did you come here for anyway? I didn't think landlords were allowed to pop in on their tenants unannounced. Even brilliantly witty, handsome, and charming ones."

He propped himself a little higher and brought his knees up to his chest. "I came here to tell you what I've decided to do about Simon."

I nodded and waited.

"I'd like to think he didn't deliberately set out to steal from me. I imagine it evolved over time, little bits here and there, you know, rounding up the bill to the nearest ten euros or whatever, and pocketing the difference. He probably justified it as money earned, in a way, because he has helped me out an awful lot."

He stopped, deep in thought. I tended to agree; by being so open and casual about the arrangement, Marcel had certainly put temptation in Simon's way.

"But he was keen to help and so kind at the start that it made sense, especially as I was so ill. I think I should advertise for a formal arrangement with someone—a housekeeper—and pay them to do what he did. In retrospect, I should have done that years ago."

For as long as he'd have me, I wanted to share every single aspect of Marcel's life, not just his bed. And if that meant taking on tedious household chores he was incapable of performing himself, then I was the man to shoulder all of that too.

"Not happening, Marcel. You don't need or want anyone wandering through your house disturbing you while you're working. You've said yourself how much you value your privacy. And I'm keeping pyjama yoga all to myself. So, no housekeeper."

A worried frown creased his forehead. "I don't want you to feel obliged to do it all though; it's a lot to take on."

I smiled up at him. "No, it's not. Looking after you would be my pleasure."

He took my hand in his. "Thank you. But promise you'll tell me if you change your mind?"

No chance of that ever happening. "I promise, *mon coeur.*"

"I'm not going to say, or do, anything about Simon," Marcel continued with a sigh. "I do still want to be his friend because he's lonely, and he's not where he hoped he'd be in life right now. And…and anyone can make mistakes, can't they Guillaume?"

Fuck, yes, I knew all about making mistakes. So who was I to tell Marcel how to handle it?

★

Seeing as we were lying on the bed anyway, we indulged in some heavy petting before I persuaded Marcel into acceptable clothing to visit his sister.

After seeing him safely to his car, I waited for Dominic to pick me up, and then we headed out to football practice. At the speed Dominic drove his little red Honda Civic, it might have been quicker to jog there, but I'd begun to enjoy his peculiar company. He spent the journey outlining all the potential permutations of end-of-season league positions, depending on if we won, lost, or drew the remainder of our matches. He'd actually created a little computer program for that exact purpose, which was…very Dominic.

I might as well have been invisible when we arrived for all the attention he gave me once Antoine started limbering up for the match. Our previous conversation about role play had descended into farce. I was now well-informed regarding King Henry II's fatal jousting injuries in the sixteenth century, yet still had no idea of Dominic's attitude towards more personal role-playing activities. Funnily enough, it was quite a difficult subject to keep harping back to—even with Dominic—without coming over as plain weird.

"I see your hot mate's come to watch again, Guille," Antoine remarked. By now, I'd mastered not looking around in astonishment after this sort of comment about Dominic.

This evening, though, Antoine wasn't his usual perky self; I also thought I'd detected a whiff of stale alcohol when he'd entered the changing room.

"I think it's safe to say you've got yourself an admirer, Antoine."

"Did you feel him out about, you know, some let's pretend stuff?"

I rolled my eyes. "Yes, and I still have no idea. Although, if you ever succeed in getting that far, maybe a grumpy knight of the realm and a poor serf scenario might appeal to him as he appears to have a fondness for medieval history."

One of those conversations I never envisaged having with anyone ever, though I could see Antoine carefully storing away this nugget of information for future use.

"My wife's gone for good anyway," he informed me gloomily. "And taken the kids with her. It's not a big surprise or anything, but it still feels a bit shit."

That explained his low mood. I briefly put an arm around his shoulders.

"Sorry to hear that mate. I'm here for you if you want to talk about it or go out for a beer together sometime?"

He smiled weakly. "Yeah, maybe we should do that. You could bring your handsome friend. A night with him would definitely cheer me up."

I returned home from the match in an excellent mood. Another crucial victory in the bag, and the team had shot up the league table. According to Dominic's calculations, if we won or drew the remainder of our matches, we'd finish in the top five, a club record.

I was glad to see that Marcel's car was still missing as I peered into the garage—hopefully a sign that his evening with his sister was going well.

So, expecting to find an empty house, I was disappointed to discover Simon had made himself comfortable at the kitchen table with Marcel's copy of *Le Monde* and a glass of pastis. The feeling of disappointment was mutual.

"Oh, it's you," he said with a grimace, returning his gaze to the paper. "I was expecting Marcel."

"He's at Sabine's," I said shortly, helping myself to a glass of juice. "I'll tell him you stopped by."

"I'm prepared to wait," he countered. "I have matters to discuss with him."

Pompous arse.

"The pool company called," he continued. "We still have a problem with the filter. The old pump isn't man enough to handle the new design."

I sipped my juice calmly, waiting for the desire to punch him to subside. In Marcel's absence, I had to respect his judgement on this, and calling Simon out on his bullshit was not what he'd have wanted me to do. Hitting Simon was not an option either, however satisfying.

"I'll contact the pool company, Simon," I responded pleasantly. "I'll call them first thing tomorrow morning. PiscinePiscine in La Couarde, isn't it?"

"There's no need for you to get involved. I can manage it," he hastily replied. "Leave it to me."

"No, Simon. I'm afraid that's not going to happen."

I spoke carefully and firmly, with an edge of finality in my voice, shifting slightly into his personal space. Hopefully, he could still recall the last time we were alone together in this kitchen when he was seconds away from pissing himself.

"Simon? We need to get a few things straight around here. Marcel and I have agreed that, from now on, I am best placed to help him with this sort of thing. Speaking on his behalf, I can confidently reassure you that he values your friendship and enjoys the things you do together, but your kind services around the house are no longer required."

The mature, adult approach. Marcel would definitely approve.

Up until now, I'd always considered Simon a moderately good-looking bloke. He kept himself in reasonable shape, and while not my type, I could see that his sly, foxy features would be attractive to some. At this moment, however, he was downright ugly, his expression twisted in a hateful sneer. He stood and drained his pastis, then reached for his coat, eyeing me distastefully.

"You do know he's frigid, don't you? God knows I've been trying to fuck him for years without success. He blames his asthma, of course, and dresses it up as 'voluntary celibacy'."

He continued, spitting out, "But actually, he's fucking frigid. An uptight, frigid homosexual. Who knew they existed?"

He shouldered on his coat and picked up his cycling helmet. "So you're wasting your time, Guillaume. Find another mug to con. Marcel Giresse is a sexless, cold, queer bastard, who will take what he can from you. And in return, you won't get your hands on a penny of his money, or his arse for that matter. Consider this as friendly advice from someone who knows."

Funnily enough, my anger from earlier had vanished. I almost smiled. A picture of my sweet Marcel plopped into my head, the sated, sleepy expression on his pretty, pretty face when he lay in my lap after our lovemaking on the yoga mat this morning.

I'd stopped listening to this oily man, with his sneaky, penny-pinching ways. He was not worthy of my anger. I'd won; it was that simple. Marcel was right. Simon never was the opposition, not that I'd even understood I was competing when I fell in love with him. The pathetic man standing in front of me was merely a sad, desperate fucker, who'd been living parasitically off my vulnerable lover for way too long. I was intrigued though.

"If he's so cold, Simon, then why the hell are you still hanging around like a bad smell?"

Shaking his head, Simon gave me a scornful look as if I was too dumb to bother conversing with. "Isn't it obvious? It's because I love him, you utter prick. I always have."

At that moment, a tiny part of me felt sorry for him, this petty thief, this slimy individual. But only a tiny part. I opened the front door wide, the quicker for him to leave.

"Not that it's any of your business at all, Simon, but Marcel and I are sleeping together. And it's fucking brilliant. Now take your nasty comments with you and fuck off."

★

I woke much later to the soft whirr of a nebuliser. My still half-asleep brain registered that Marcel must have come to join me in the annexe, which was rather lovely. I would show my full appreciation next morning; right now, curled into him, I was happily snoozing.

Marcel evidently had other plans. A warm hand snaked its way under the duvet and found my waist, and light fingers danced over my hip bone. A waft of the slightly astringent scent of the nebuliser floated towards me, the white noise of the little machine lulling me back to sleep. That hand, though, making persistent overtures in very much the right direction, was difficult to ignore, and I rolled onto my back, lazily stretching out.

As the hum of the neb clicked off, Marcel's cool lips pressed against my neck. That hand had now honed in on its target, which was waking up much more quickly than my brain.

"Hello, *mon coeur*. I wasn't expecting this."

My voice was thick with sleep, and Marcel nuzzled into me, his warm, naked body blanketing mine.

Er…Marcel? Naked? No stripy grandad PJs? Bloody hell. Instantly, I was wide awake and running my hands down the length of his bare smooth back, over the swell of his bony pelvis until I cupped his skinny arse cheeks. Crouched over me in the darkness, he captured my lips with his, a hot chocolatey taste that was uniquely my Marcel.

"I wasn't either," he whispered, and I could tell he was smiling against my skin. "But…ah, I…I…my body seems to be telling me something otherwise. In fact, it's been nagging me all evening, and I…"

I chuckled against him, and he shifted, so he straddled my hips entirely, bracing me with his lean thighs, sitting up straighter. My dick brushed against the divide of his arse.

"I hope you don't mind, but I took the liberty of…ah… preparing a little first," he said in a breathy whisper. He followed it with a giggle and another brush against my dick.

"That was very presumptuous of you, Monsieur Giresse."

Taking hold of me in one hand, he lifted himself and very carefully took me inside, his eyes closed and lips parted, moaning slightly as he adjusted to the intrusion. God, he was beautiful; in the dark, I could make out the pale delicate skin over his collar bones and his angular jaw as he whimpered with pleasure. Once seated, he allowed himself a pause, a flash of bared white teeth visible in the gloom.

"Are you okay?" I asked, my voice shaky with the effort to stay still for him. "Your asthma, I mean. I don't recall us documenting this position in the Asthma Sutra."

"I know." He laughed, still panting slightly. He adjusted again, sitting up straighter still, a slight shift backwards. "But, oh…aah, that feels so…ah, goodness, Guillaume, I didn't know how much I'd like it like this."

Bending my knees and planting my feet firmly on the mattress, I thrust my hips up gently, steadying him with my hands at his waist. "Like this, Marcel? Is this good for you?"

"Goodness, yes. Exactly like that."

With his palms planted on my thighs for leverage, he experimentally rode me, raising and lowering himself, gaining confidence each time. Christ, I wished the bedroom was brighter. The sounds escaping from his throat and the glimpses I caught in the low light of his pale face and body as he fucked himself on my cock were almost enough on their own to send me over the edge. *Putain*, Simon couldn't be more wrong. There was nothing cold about my lover. He was about as frigid as the hot white sandy beaches of Marseilles in the height of summer. I couldn't get enough of how his arse encased my dick so tightly, as if a velvet glove was rhythmically squeezing my length.

Marcel's breathing became louder, wheezier, and as delicious as it was being ridden so perfectly, my few remaining working brain cells knew he needed to stop. Once again, imaginary discussions with concerned paramedics burst through my pleasure, and as if in tune with my thoughts, Marcel leaned forwards and groaned, supporting his weight on his arms either side of my head.

"Do you want to stop?" I asked with concern, although it would have been a Herculean effort on my part; I was heading past the point of no return.

"No, please, no, Guillaume," he gasped above me. "But...but...I'm afraid you're going to have to do all the work from here on in."

And so I did, digging my feet into the mattress and bucking up into him, relishing his hot, slick tightness and whimpering, needy sighs with every upwards thrust as he held on and enjoyed the ride. Rapidly losing grasp on my control, my legs trembled with the strain of driving upwards. With a laboured breath, Marcel flung his head back. A hot gush hit my chest and neck seconds before my own muscles tightened, and I shuddered into him.

Marcel didn't so much as collapse on top of me as he seemed to virtually pass out. I cradled him close, his chest heaving and singing like a bunch of flat sopranos as he fought to regain a measure of control over his laboured breathing. Which was fine by me because, hell, I needed a minute too. I felt every bit of my thirty-eight years. I definitely needed to improve my core strength if I was going to be lying on my back doing this regularly.

"You still alive?" I nudged him, and he nodded, his rapid breaths harsh in the still night.

"*Mon Dieu*, Marcel, that was bloody knackering," I managed to get out at last, pushing back damp locks of hair off my forehead.

I waited as he took some puffs on his inhaler and was able to speak.

"If you joined in with my yoga, instead of watching and playing with yourself under your dressing gown, then it might not have been such a problem for you."

"I do not play with myself under my dressing gown!" I protested, giving him a sharp poke. "What could possibly have given you that ridiculous idea?"

Shit, I'd been totally rumbled. I reached for the bedside light so I could look at Marcel properly and grinned as he gradually peeled himself off the sticky mess between us, wincing at the pull on his scanty chest hairs. It was time to regain the upper hand.

"You're very good at coming no handed," I remarked carelessly. "Particularly considering we're not spring chickens anymore."

I watched with satisfaction as he groaned and blushed a beautiful shade of pink. I could always rely on a spot of naughtiness to shut him up; throw in a crude expression and he became adorably mortified.

"It's...ah...a superpower I...um...I'm not especially proud of," he mumbled into my neck. "I'd rather thought I might grow out of it, but it appears that…I…I haven't. Do you mind if we talk about something else, please?"

I laughed and pecked him on the lips, wrapping him in my arms again. "Yes. Why don't you tell me how you got on with your sister this evening?"

He groaned once more and snuggled closer, hiding his head. "Guillaume, you seem to be developing a disturbing habit of mentioning my sister immediately after sexual intercourse. Should I be concerned?"

"Nah, she's not my type."

"What is your type?"

"Oh, you know, a bit too posh, a bit too skinny, a bit too much of a smart arse…trigger happy…"

Fuck, these were the best of times. Giggling with your man in the middle of the night, when you were so in love you thought every love song ever written must have been written especially for you. And when the sex you'd had was perfect, in all of its imperfections, because the person with whom you'd had it was wrapped in your arms and imperfectly perfect too.

We must have fallen asleep like that after Marcel assured me he and his sister had made up. I woke with a dead arm and a delicate, precious man lightly snoring on my chest. True love was putting up with muscle cramp and a need to piss. Bloody hell, moments like this were more fucking special than any-thing.

Chapter Twenty-Three

Guillaume

Marcel's next trip to Paris came around way too quickly for my liking. He'd been really well for several weeks, an early morning threesome with the nebuliser had become the exception rather than the norm, and *mon Dieu*, the sex was magnificent. Those stick men were receiving a hell of a workout. It didn't prevent me worrying though. His last trip to Paris had ended with that horrid episode in hospital, and even though visiting the capital and mixing with colleagues was a necessary hazard of his job, I'd be glad if he never had to travel again.

And we'd become even closer, our lives together seamlessly merged into one peaceful day after another. Days spent working, doing yoga (him, not me; I still preferred ogling, my hand wedged in my pocket), cooking together, short walks around the port or along the beach together, sleeping together, endlessly kissing together, and, well, being blissfully happy together.

Our lives were exceptionally quiet, some might describe them as dull, but after so many years in prison surrounded by hundreds of shouting, sweary, sweaty men, the calm rhythm and quietude of Marcel's house was everything I craved and more. When I wasn't at work, myself, I contentedly lay reading on the sofa for hours, surreptitiously watching him tapping away at his computer or listening with half an ear to his conference calls.

Dominic was a frequent visitor, Sabine, too, even though she preferred to drop in when I was at football practice or the bar, but that was okay; Marcel said time would prove to her I was trustworthy and decent, and we had to be patient.

Simon also remained a regular visitor, unfortunately, and Marcel being Marcel, he behaved as if he had no idea about the deceit and the petty theft. To all intents and purposes, he gave Simon the impression he was equally as happy to talk literature, politics, and art with him as much as ever. I couldn't lie; I tended to find pressing things I needed to do on these occasions, like cutting my toenails or rearranging my underwear drawer, which suited all three of us.

But Marcel had gone now. He'd left in his usual whirl of chaotic packing and forgetfulness, with promises to phone regularly and to not ignore his various alarms reminding him to eat, shower, and sleep. I spent my nights in the annexe. That cosy bed upstairs was too darned lonely on my own while I counted down the days until his return.

The last match of the football season provided a flutter of excitement though. A win would secure us fifth place in the league and a club record. Dominic came to cheer us on, armed with concise statistics regarding the opposition's key players, which, as well as being sweet and hilarious, vitally enabled us to mark their best player from the opening whistle. Interestingly, Dominic was working on creating an app for next season, which would hold data about all the opposing teams in one place. Saint-Martin had a secret weapon masquerading as a spectator dressed in a blue anorak.

We won the match comfortably. The only disappointment of the night was that Antoine hadn't turned up, without prior explanation, which was unlike him. He'd made no secret he was having a tough time with his soon-to-be ex-wife. I had a sneaking suspicion he was consoling himself by heavily tucking into the booze.

My suspicions were confirmed by a text, laden with spelling errors, received as Dom and I walked back to the car after the match. I relayed the message to Dominic.

"It's Antoine. He's drunk and over in Loix, contemplating the point of his existence on Grouin Beach. I think that's what he's doing anyway. Though he's pissed and using predictive text, so he could equally be in the Loire constipating a pint of Excalibur on a green beech tree. What do you reckon?"

Dominic frowned, giving it some serious consideration. "I think he's probably at the beach in Loix because the second option doesn't make grammatical sense. What do you think, Guillaume?"

How Simon could be so vile to such a gentle, sweet soul like Dominic, I have no idea. There is absolutely nothing to dislike about him whatsoever. I was even becoming quite fond of the warty thingy.

He frowned again. "I hope he's okay, Guillaume."

"I hope he's okay too. Shall we go and find out?"

★

It would have taken a few hours to drive to the Loire, so we were lucky that Antoine was, indeed, sprawled against a rock at one end of a damp and windy Grouin Beach, a mile outside the picturesque village of Loix. Having evidently finished contemplating his existence, he'd fallen asleep—we heard the snoring before we saw him and smelled the alcohol fumes before we reached him.

"He must be very tired, Guillaume."

Nope, no irony, 100 per cent sincerity.

"He'll get hypothermia sleeping here, Dom; we should wake him up and get him home."

It took a while to rouse Antoine to fully awake.

"What are you doing here, you sexy troll?"

I liked to think this was directed at Dom, not me, but it was difficult to ascertain as Antoine's unfocused eyes seemed to be roaming in several directions.

"Er…you texted me?" I replied.

"Did I?" He appeared to be pondering this for a moment. "Oh."

Dom was clearly fascinated, gawping as Antoine gradually re-entered the land of the living. After crawling into a sitting position, he farted noisily, then fumbled around for the bottle of red wine at his feet. He tipped it up to his mouth and then swore when it came up empty.

"What's the score, then, Antoine? We missed you at the match. Everything all right?"

Belching loudly, Antoine scratched his arse. "No. Everything's not all right. I'm cold."

Like a little furry knight in shining armour, Dominic stepped forwards. "Here, have my anorak. I'm plenty warm enough. It has a 900 goose down rating, and the fabric is 300 grams per square metre, so it will have you snug in no time."

He tenderly helped Antoine into his coat, which was a little tight on the larger man.

"Love your eyebrow, babe," slurred Antoine before belching emphatically. "Like a big fat hairy slug."

Okay, so this one definitely wasn't directed at me; I wasn't the vainest of men, but I was no stranger to a pair of tweezers.

"So what's happened then, Antoine?" I asked, sitting down next to him on the damp sand. "You want to talk about it?"

"I want to lick my tongue along it."

Christ. Why did I think coming out here to help Antoine was a good idea? I glanced up at Dom who was doing his jiggling like he needed to piss thing.

"Why don't you tell Dom and me what's happened and let us help?" I tried again. "And then maybe…maybe he might let you touch his…um…his eyebrow…brows."

Well, that bit of bribery worked. Dom sat on the other side of Antoine, and Antoine slung a heavy arm around his shoulders.

"Everyone hates me," he announced, each word merging with the next. He sounded a little like one of those old records played at the wrong speed, but mostly like just about every drunk bloke at the end of a heavy night propping up the bar. "My brother-in-law says I'm not to go back, my father-in-law says I'm not to go back, my mother-in-law says I'm not to go back, my sister-in-law says…"

I think I knew the words to this tune.

"They said I was a pervert, a ponce, and…a…a deg…a deg…deter…a detergent!"

Dominic was frowning, as indeed was I.

"I'm not sure they did, Antoine," said Dominic cautiously. "I don't think they would have called you a detergent."

"They did!" insisted Antoine, waggling a finger at us. "They said I was a pervert, a ponce, and a det…a detergent."

Arguing with a drunk was pointless. Unfortunately, no one had ever informed Dominic.

"No, Antoine. I'm sorry, but a detergent is a water-soluble cleansing agent which combines with impurities and dirt. I can't imagine that they…"

"I'm a detergent! How many times do I have to say it?"

He raised his voice, sounding more belligerent. I gave Dominic a firm shake of my head and brought my fingers to my lips. Thankfully, he got the message.

"I don't hate you, Antoine," I said calmly. "Your friends on our football team don't hate you."

I followed with a list of a few of Antoine's work colleagues whose names I could remember and finished with, "The bloke in 33M doesn't hate you."

"He does, actually," said Antoine with a flash of clarity. "He said we can't both be on our knees, and if I wouldn't take it in turns, then I could sod off."

I didn't have an immediate response to that.

"I don't hate you either," said Dominic and bravely gave Antoine's knee a little pat. Fumbling slightly, Antoine lifted his own hand and lay it over Dom's.

"Do you know what I do, Antoine, if people aren't being very nice to me?" he suggested tentatively.

Antoine raised his bloodshot eyes up to Dominic's concerned ones, waiting.

Flushing slightly at being the centre of attention, Dominic carried on, "I imagine myself in an important position—I don't know, like a headmaster or something, or a general in the army. Or the really scary boss of a big company. In a position of authority."

He suddenly had Antoine's full attention, and for a man who five minutes ago was almost comatose from alcohol, he appeared astonishingly alert. Dominic was getting into his stride.

"And I imagine that the person who is upsetting me is my inferior, like a normal soldier, or an underperforming employee. Or a shy school librarian. And they are scared because I'm in charge, and it's me who has the upper hand."

Dominic stared into the distance, his fist clenched, his mind clearly in the scene, picturing himself taking control, scolding, being a disciplinarian. I hoped to God it was Simon he was imagining cowering at his feet.

"And I shout down at them and tell them exactly what I think of them. I boss them about. And then…and then…I feel much better," he finished and nodded with satisfaction.

Antoine was riveted and stone-cold sober, hanging on Dom's every word, gazing up at him with awe, reverence, and, yeah, pure unadulterated lust.

"God, you're sexy. Can I lick your eyebrow now?"

Bloody hell. If I'd ever felt more like a spare part than I did at that moment, I've blanked it out.

"Hey, Dom," I murmured, touching his arm gently and rising to my feet. "I think…um… Do you know something? It's a fresh evening, and I'm…a little stiff after football. I could do with a run. I'll…um… Shall I leave you to get Antoine safely home, and I'll head off?"

I gave him as broad a wink as I could manage without Antoine spotting, then slightly nudged my head in his direction. Without explicitly stating: "Dom, that guy you fancy is heavily into role play, and you've provided his next wet dream," I didn't think I could have made it any clearer. Apparently, I was wrong.

"Are you sure, Guillaume? Honestly, dropping the both of you off is no bother. It's quite a long way to run."

Thank God that Antoine, recognising the golden opportunity I was placing in his lap, had regained some of his senses.

"Nah, Guillaume's fine. The run will do him good. He's getting lardy, aren't you, mate? That's what too much sex and home-cooked dinners does for you."

God, he owed me big time. "Yes, Antoine, you are absolutely right. I'll run really quickly; I'll see if I can burn a few extra calories."

"I think you look fine," butted in Dominic. "You're in great shape, considering your age."

Christ. Give me strength.

"Who are you having lots of sex with? Is it Marcel? I thought you two were just going out for drinks?"

Okay, my work here is done. These two could sort their own love lives out. I reckoned I'd taken it as far as I could. With a backwards wave, I sprinted off, leaving Dom busily calculating the distance I had to run and my average calorific consumption, while Antoine was no doubt wondering how he could get his peculiar fantasy to start whipping him into submission. As I turned the corner and caught a glimpse of them both still cuddling up on the beach, I grinned to myself and shouted back, "It's degenerate, Antoine! You're a fucking degenerate!"

★

I was still chortling to myself over the ridiculous scene on the beach when I pushed open the front door, all hot and sweaty, ready for a shower and decent food. Whereupon it became immediately apparent neither were happening any time soon.

Sabine was waiting for me in the kitchen and, joy of joys, so was Simon. My thoughts immediately leapt to concern that something dreadful had happened to Marcel, but from the self-satisfied look on Simon's face and Sabine's pinched, cool demeanour, I guessed not.

"What's up?" I asked, reaching for a glass and heading for the fridge. I lived here, I paid rent, I wasn't going to be intimidated out of my own kitchen.

It was only as I half turned, with my hand poised on the fridge door, that I noticed two objects had been placed in the middle of the otherwise clear kitchen table. One exquisite, darkly glowing amethyst signet ring and, next to it, a familiar sleek platinum Breitling watch.

A man with a different background to mine would perhaps have reacted with words along the lines of, *Great, you've found them!* or *Marcel will be so pleased; where the hell were they?* But after fifteen years of incarceration, though my heart might have been naïve enough to believe it belonged with a man as precious as Marcel, my head never had that luxury. Instead of either of those reactions, I said nothing and stared in disbelief as dreams of my wonderful future with him slid out of view.

I'd heard it said there is nothing worse than being falsely accused of something you haven't done and having no way to prove it. This wasn't strictly true. Being *correctly* accused of something you *have* done, then spending most of your youth behind bars as a punishment for it, is much, much worse.

Although, the wrong accusation staring at me from the kitchen table came a fucking close second.

Particularly when the accuser was the fucking thief himself, and you had no means of proving it. And even if you made that allegation, it was only your word against his. And your word counted for absolutely fucking nothing because you'd been labelled a thief and a liar, to add to the epithet of murderer, from the moment you stepped foot in the house. Nothing you could say or do would ever change that. Whereas his word, accompanied by his fancy vocabulary, his smart clothes, and his cultured background, counted for everything.

Guilty until proven innocent.

I didn't know how Simon had framed me, and I didn't care. But somehow, he'd persuaded Sabine that I'd stolen those high-value items of jewellery from a man I had grown to love more than life itself. Sabine, in full disapproving teacher mode and, to her credit, seemingly miserable, gave me twenty minutes to leave the premises. If I failed to comply, she would involve the *gendarmes*. Which, in retrospect, as I hoisted my holdall over my shoulder and headed out into the dark night, was probably a wise move. If I had stayed any longer, Simon would have felt the pressure of my big, strong hands around his neck. I couldn't be certain I would have stopped squeezing until it was too late.

I could have phoned Marcel. I probably should have phoned Marcel. I knew he cared for me; that much he'd made plain. But did he care enough? Would he have stood up for me against his sister and Simon and everything he knew and trusted? Everything that was safe? He'd known me—what? Four months? And he'd known his sister a lifetime and Simon four years.

A cooling shame replaced my anger at Simon and Sabine as I sat on the bus that transported me away from the island and away from my dream with Marcel. Shame for the life I'd had before I met him, which would follow me for the rest of my days, the poor choices I'd made when I'd been young and stupid, and shame for not having the balls to stand up for myself to Sabine and Simon. I ran from Ile de Ré not as a guilty man—I'd no more steal from Marcel than I would hurl stones at ducks on a pond—but as an unworthy, ashamed one.

I had no clue where I was heading. After the bus pulled into the terminal in La Rochelle, I alighted and wandered in a daze around the corner to the train station. I bought a ticket at random from the first kiosk. The train was mostly empty, and I blindly sat on a window seat and closed my eyes against the city lights as they whizzed past. If I ended up in hell, it wouldn't be far enough away.

Chapter Twenty-Four

Marcel

Hi, Marcel, let me know when you leave Paris so I can be at your place when you get home. Drive carefully, Sabine x.

An annoying text. Not that I minded Sabine popping over, especially as we'd kissed and made up, and she'd promised to try to be friendly to Guillaume. But I'd been planning sexy times within seconds of barging through the front door. We were going to start with acting out the first stickman scene in the Asthma Sutra and not stop until we reached the last. In theory anyway. The reality would be hopefully completing picture one, followed by a neb, a nap, then possibly a stab at picture two before we settled for cuddles on the sofa. But, hey, a man could dream, couldn't he? Having my big sister around kind of scuppered that little fantasy.

My sister *and* Simon were perched, waiting for me, on the sofa, like disapproving parents. Doubly scuppered. I tried to appear pleased.

"A welcoming committee! Hi, guys!"

After plonking my bag down on the floor, I flopped into the armchair opposite.

"Goodness, that was a rubbish journey. The motorway at Poitiers was closed for roadworks, so I had to take a massive detour through what essentially amounted to several farms and an enormous housing estate, and what with the rain and…"

"Marcel," interrupted Sabine cautiously. "We have some bad news, I'm afraid."

Oh God, something had happened to Guillaume. Something awful. He'd been run over, or had a massive heart attack, or…or…

I'd texted him before I set off. In fact, now I thought of it, I'd texted him last night too. I hadn't received a reply to that one, either, but I'd assumed he was working or sleeping or playing football or… We weren't in each other's pockets; we weren't teenagers who needed constant reassurance. I trusted him implicitly; we trusted each other, and… Christ, why hadn't he answered my texts?

"I found these," Simon announced smugly and pointed to my signet ring and favourite watch lying on the coffee table.

"Great! Guillaume and I hunted everywhere for those! Where on earth did you find them?"

I happily seized the ring off the table and slid it onto the third finger of my right hand.

"Simon found them in a dressing table drawer. In the annexe," continued Sabine carefully. Why was she talking in that annoyingly calm teacher voice as though explaining a difficult concept to a ten-year-old? She'd said something about bad news. What bad news?

She took a deep breath. "Guillaume had your ring and your watch, Marcel. Simon discovered them wrapped in a pair of his socks. He must have stolen them from you."

I heard the words, and I saw her lips moving, but nothing was making sense. "That's ridiculous! And why the hell were you going through Guillaume's stuff, Simon?"

"Because I had reason to believe he'd stolen them," he replied pompously. "So I took the liberty of having a look around."

Oh, for goodness' sake. I'd had enough of Simon trying to damn Guillaume, and now he'd roped my sister into this farce. "He wouldn't steal from me. He's not a thief."

Unlike some people I know, I nearly added but stopped myself.

"Let's get him here." I stood and started for the kitchen, which led to the garden door to the annexe. "I'll go and fetch him now. It's not fair to accuse someone of a crime behind their back. And I think it's about time we all sat down and had a frank discussion, anyway, don't you?"

"He's not in the annexe," said Sabine, also standing. "He's…he's gone. I sent him away. It was either that or get the *gendarmes* involved, which is what Simon thought we should do. But because I know how fond you were of him, I gave him a choice. And he chose to leave."

I sat down again, more of a flump, really, as my legs had independently made up their mind they could no longer support my body before my brain had reached the same conclusion. A sudden image of Guillaume filled my head. It was from Christmas Day when he'd hugged me close to him, outside a ladies' lingerie shop of all places. As his hazel-flecked eyes had gazed down at me, I'd known at that moment, with a visceral clarity, that this man would be my forever, that those muscular brown arms were my rock, my safety net, my harbour, my home.

And I'd never told him.

My voice sounded as if it were coming from very far away when I spoke. As if I were watching myself from a corner of the room, seeing myself implode. Nonetheless, I was surprisingly calm and deliberate.

"Simon, I'd like you to do something for me."

"Anything, Marcel, tell me how I can help."

"I'd like you to get up off my sofa, drop your set of keys to my house in the bowl on the table by my front door, and then let yourself out. And I'd rather that you never attempt to contact me again."

"But…Mar…"

"Please, Sabine. This is my house. Simon? Go. Now. Otherwise, it will be me calling the *gendarmes*."

I managed to hold it together until he left before burying my face in my hands and rocking. It physically hurt. The loss of Guillaume burned in my guts and my chest as if I'd been branded. I sat like that for goodness knows how long, and Sabine had the good sense not to speak to me. At least not until my traitorous lungs decided to join the party and remind me of their inadequacies.

"Which inhaler do you want?" she asked as she rummaged in my bag. "Blue? Or a neb?"

We started with blue, although I knew the neb would follow, especially after Sabine pegged the oximeter to my finger, and we numbly read the numbers displayed. While I still could,

I texted Dominic, already knowing the answer. He hadn't seen or heard from Guillaume either—he'd spent the last twenty-four hours with his boyfriend. Boyfriend? At any other time, I would have pressed for details.

"That's it. He's gone. He won't come back, you know."

"If he hadn't done it, he would have stayed. Only guilty men run."

I was scornful. "No, they don't. Men like Guillaume run because they have no alternative. Do you really think the *gendarmes* and the law would give him a fair hearing? Because you certainly haven't."

"I don't know why you're so bothered! I mean, I get that you liked him, but he's stolen from you! You should be fucking furious and reporting it to the police yourself!"

Shaking my head, I leaned back and closed my eyes to prevent the tears from falling, twisting the signet ring around my finger. "I trusted him. I trusted him with my life. He'd never steal from me."

Kneeling on the floor in front of me, she took my hands. "Hey, Marcel, don't get all upset. It won't help your chest. I know that's what you want to believe, but it isn't true. Simon said all along he wasn't to be trusted, and you should have listened to him."

I roughly pushed her hands away. "Let me tell you something about your precious Simon."

And so I did. I told her about the receipts, the money transfers, and how he'd been pilfering from me for years and I'd been too dumb to notice. He'd been in the house on Christmas Day when I mislaid my signet ring and again when the Breitling went missing and I was in hospital with Guillaume at my bedside. And I cried, and Sabine cried, and then I had a nebuliser and another nebuliser after that. And then she drove me to the hospital because crying and talking had become incompatible with breathing.

As the clever doctors and nurses set about keeping me alive by administering oxygen, taking their blood tests and setting up drips, I couldn't help thinking it was an absolute…expletive…waste of time. Continuing to breathe in and out was pointless. Guillaume was gone. Even industrial-strength salbutamol, intravenous steroids, and a theophylline infusion wouldn't mend a broken heart.

Chapter Twenty-Five

Guillaume

I missed Marcel in the way I might miss both my arms. Or my liver. Every breath I took ached and every tear that rolled down my cheek held a precious memory of the short time we'd shared.

I briefly considered what would have happened if I had stayed at the house and awaited the arrival of the *gendarmes*. An arrest, of course, followed by an invitation to make a statement down at the local *gendarmerie*. Fingerprints probably. The entire process would have started out politely, all very low-key. After all, Ile de Ré wasn't exactly a crime hotspot. The alleged theft of an expensive ring and a watch was possibly the most exciting event that had happened all week. What to expect next would have been outlined clearly, in simple terms. I might have even been offered a bloody cup of coffee.

But then, whichever lacky would type my details into the database—with half a mind on the job, the other half on whatever was on the telly that night—would have paused in their task as an alert flashed against my name. Maybe they would have rechecked their spelling, whispered in the ear of a colleague, asked them to come and look too. Immediately, everything would have changed. The offer of coffee withdrawn, the room a lot less friendly, the officer more senior, and so on. And within a short space of time, someone would have recalled a couple of unsolved burglaries in empty holiday houses, a theft from an unlocked car on one of the campsites, that time their brother's cousin's boss had had his bike nicked. And on and on and on.

Reuben left countless messages on my phone, pleading for me to get in touch with either him or Lucien, to reassure them I was alive and well. Unfortunately, I was still both. How could I face Reuben now? Love and trust went hand in hand; you could not fully embrace one without the other. Like a delicate pane of glass, trust, once shattered, was broken forever.

I knew what Reuben would say. He'd urge me to get myself on the next flight to England, and whatever had happened, we'd sort it out together. And even though his boyfriend, Freddie, would say all the right supportive things, even though he'd pretend he wholeheartedly accepted Reuben's faith in my innocence, those tiny seeds of doubt would have been planted. He might be a blond catwalk model, but the suspicious viscount wasn't so dumb that he'd ever trust me again. And Lucien? I couldn't ever contemplate facing Lucien.

Dominic called, too, sweet man that he was. Even Antoine left a message. I'd miss them both in a funny sort of way. Nothing from Marcel though.

In the end, I threw away my phone charger, and when the battery went flat, I stuffed the phone in my bag and forgot about it.

I alighted from the train in the chilly early hours of the morning in a downmarket district south of Bordeaux, figuring I could lose myself in the big city. After I'd aimlessly wandered the empty streets, dawn found me cold, wet, and the only customer in a scruffy suburban café. I knocked back a bitter expresso, followed by another. The proprietor, eyeing me suspiciously, sipped at a hot chocolate. The familiar aroma made my eyes hot with tears. I left abruptly after throwing a few coins onto the table. After several more hours slouched on a damp park bench, staring at nothing, I bought a bottle of brandy. I checked into an unremarkable hotel, locked my door, then lay on the double bed in the dark, drinking myself to oblivion.

Cheap brandy tastes shit on the path to my stomach and even shittier on the way back up. Not as bad as the bottle of pastis I chased it down with though. That was like swallowing and regurgitating pure battery acid. For three days and nights, I lay on that lumpy bed in a drunken stupor, feeling sorry for myself. No matter how much alcohol I imbibed, I might as well have been swigging Marcel's blasted hot chocolate for all the good it did at drowning my sorrows. He was there every time I closed my eyes and every time I fucking opened them too.

I hadn't expected him to call me. Not really. I couldn't face him again, not ever. The thought of those kind blue-grey eyes ever looking into mine and me seeing the tiniest amount of doubt reflected in them would be unbearable. I didn't blame him for not attempting to find me. I had brought this sorrow upon myself by believing, for even a second, I could step into his world and somehow carve a place at his side. For a wonderful, precious, few months, I'd had a dream, and I'd followed it, only for a measly piece of shit like Simon to bring me straight back down to earth.

On day four, even I couldn't bear my own stink, so I showered, shaved, and checked out of the hotel. I didn't have a plan; most likely, I'd roam the streets and then check into a different hotel. I'd lost the will to live, but unfortunately, I hadn't gained the will to die. The alcohol hadn't worked, so I was going to have to wallow in my own head until I pulled myself together.

Bordeaux boasted sixty-six kilometres of tram network. According to the panel I read in the shelter as I waited to aimlessly board yet another of them, the city was proud of its ground-level power supply, thus avoiding ugly overhead cables ruining the beauty of the eighteenth-century architecture. Typically French, all about the aesthetics. I became peripherally aware of another person studying the panel next to me, and I moved to the side slightly to give them more room. Instead, they tapped me on the shoulder.

"Monsieur Guilbaud?"

So surprised, I nodded confirmation before I'd really looked. Which was bloody annoying because the woman at my right shoulder, and indeed, the woman at my left shoulder, too, was dressed in the neat blue serge of a *gendarme* uniform, complete with a white braided *kepi* atop both of their heads. I briefly contemplated running, but from what? Myself?

I'd been a guest in the back of a police car on precisely three occasions. The first was when I was thirteen, and my mate Marco and I thought it would be a splendid idea to take out the windows of the school sports hall with a catapult. I discovered the hard way that it wasn't. I spent that journey trying not to piss myself, unsure if I was more scared of the burly uniformed blokes in the front seats or my mum, who was going to give me the bollocking to end all bollockings when she came to collect me.

The second time was after I committed premeditated murder. All I could recall from that trip was the look of profound horror on my mother's face as they pushed my head down into the car, and we drove away. I wasn't sure if she ever really properly looked at me again.

And the third time was now, travelling from the outskirts of Bordeaux back up the motorway to La Rochelle. I wasn't handcuffed, which was nice of them, or possibly naïve, but I guessed they could tell from my abject demeanour I really didn't give a fuck what happened next. I could have tried running when we stopped at a set of traffic lights, but I'd never escape or outrun being Guillaume Guilbaud, murderer, and now liar and thief, so there wasn't a lot of point.

To be honest, the *gendarmes* were fairly pleasant to me, in an abstract, professional sort of way. They showed more interest in dissecting someone in the office's recent affair with a married man, so I zoned out and stared at the passing bleak fields of bare vines instead.

After an hour or so, we pulled into the parking lot of a run-down-looking *gendarmerie*, badly in need of a lick of paint. I walked between my two escorts into the building, and they stood patiently at my side as a man behind a glass shield checked my identity card. It all felt extremely casual, which puzzled me slightly, and then the female officers disappeared and left me with the guy, who wordlessly led me down a couple of depressingly shabby corridors and into an interview room. Opening the door, he gestured for me to enter and then closed it behind me, taking his leave.

The grey, soulless cubicle smelled of stale cigarette smoke and coffee, and was reminiscent of every single police interview room I'd ever encountered. Except for two vital differences:

my hands weren't cuffed, and the room was already occupied. Impatiently waiting for me, his arse perched on the desk, was an exceedingly familiar young man, and I stared at him in disbelief.

Reuben Costaud, accomplice to murder, ex-con, obsessive gardener, cat owner, and boyfriend of a suspicious viscount, stared back.

"Guillaume, at last. Thank God."

Surely, I was hallucinating. Too much booze, too little sleep, too much grief.

He slipped off the desk, crossed the space between us, and before I had a chance to utter a single word, crushed me against him. That mass of wiry hair, that familiar firm body. I breathed him all in, and exactly like my release from prison, he was going to have to prise me away before I'd let go.

"Reuben, what the hell are you doing here?"

He let out a low bark of laughter and let me cling on a little longer. "I've come to give you a bollocking and then take you home, you fucking stupid *connard*."

"I'm not going back to Rossingley with you. I'm not. I can't. Sorry."

"*Putain*, not that home. Your home with Marcel. Your real home."

It was my turn to laugh, although there was no humour in it. "Haven't you heard? I've burned my bridges there. Thanks, but I'll be heading on back to Bordeaux when the *gendarmes* have done whatever they're planning on doing with me here."

I stepped away from him and rubbed my face. Christ, I was tired. The *gendarmes* could dump me in a cell, then throw away the key for all I cared.

"Guille, the *gendarmes* aren't doing anything with you. You're free to go."

I must have given him a very confused, disbelieving look.

"It's true! I'm here to take you back to Marcel. He needs you. He's…he's not been doing so well."

Talk about a dagger to my heart. I clutched at him. "What's the matter with him? Is he ill? Is it his asthma?"

"Hey, chill. Calm down. Yeah, of course it's his asthma, but he's improving. It's been a rough few days, but he was discharged from the hospital this…"

"What do you mean, discharged? He's been in hospital again?"

Reuben sighed theatrically. "Well, yeah? Why do think I've been fucking trying to call you, like, a thousand times? And Lucien's been trying to call you, and Sabine, and Marcel's other mate, and Antoine, your kinky prison guard friend! *Merde!* Marcel has been really ill, and you fucked off in the middle of the night! We all thought you were lying dead in a ditch or something!"

"So where is he now? Who's looking after him?"

Reuben detached my fingers from his upper arm, rubbing where I'd gripped him so tightly.

"He's tucked up in bed, I imagine. Like I said. Lucien is with him."

Okay, so the immediate crisis was over. He was in safe hands. While I hadn't gained the will to end my life, knowing that Marcel was no longer alive might be enough to send me over the edge.

"I'm…I'm glad he's better. Truly I am, like you wouldn't believe. But I'm not going back." I hefted my bag onto my shoulder and turned for the door. "I can't face him; I can't face any of them. Sorry."

"*Putain!* Of course you're going back. Marcel is waiting for you at home."

Home. A port in a storm. Where the heart is. *Mon coeur.* Marcel had been all of those things and more. How could I ever look him in the eye again?

I shook my head. "I can't go back. Tell Marcel I'm sorry. For everything."

"Guillaume!" barked Reuben in a growly tone I barely recognised. It was accompanied by a foot stamp and a sharp finger poking into my chest. "If you walk out of that door and disappear again, I'll personally hunt you down and come after you. With…with my hedge trimmer. I'll rip you into such tiny shreds you'll wish you'd never been born. And then…and then…I'll mulch you into compost and grow fucking spiky hawthorn bushes over you. Really spiky ones that will pierce into your soul."

Bloody hell. Psycho gardener. I'd never witnessed this side of him before. I've always been bigger than Reuben and stronger, but in that moment, he was furious and breathing fire, with his hands clenching and unclenching at his sides. Though a tad dramatic, they weren't idle threats.

"Don't you dare walk out that door. Sit down, and shut the fuck up."

I wavered.

"Do it!" he screeched. "Now!"

Not sure what would happen if I didn't, I obeyed.

"Okay, *connard,* you listen to me. I've had the whole story from Sabine. How the hell could you possibly think Marcel would ever, for even a second, believe any of that shit? That you stole that stuff from him? Do you not credit him with any intelligence? He's fucking heartbroken, man! So heartbroken, in fact, that his asthma took over, and he stopped bloody breathing!"

"What?"

"Yes." He poked me again. "He. Stopped. Fucking. Breathing. The shock of everything, I guess. Fortunately, Sabine had already reached the hospital by the time it got that bad."

Oh, God, this was awful, worse than I could ever imagine. I buried my face in my hands. That I could ever be the cause of Marcel's pain and illness. Reuben was right. Even if Marcel hated me, even if they all believed I was nothing better than a two-bit thief and a liar, I had to go back and see him. I needed to check with my own eyes, to be sure he was truly alive.

"*Putain*, Guillaume! He fucking adores you. How could you not have noticed? He told Lucien he wanted to spend the rest of his life with you, loving you, and you fucking walked out before you gave him a chance to trust in you!"

"Do you think I stole those things?"

"Of course, I don't! Neither does Lucien, nor Freddie. Why the hell would anybody think that? Now, if someone accused you of killing that *branleur*, Simon, then, yes, I'd not have bet against it. You're a coldblooded murderer for sure, but you're not a petty thief."

Well, that was the mother of all backhanded compliments.

He paused a moment and grabbed my hands across the table, holding them tightly. Psycho gardener had vanished, thank God, and my sweet Reuben had returned.

"Let me take you back home to a man who loves you," he pleaded gently. "Neither of us have come this far to run away when the going gets tough, have we? You told me I deserved my wonderful life at Rossingley, and you deserve yours with Marcel. We've served our time, *mon ami*. The rest of our lives are ours for the taking, okay?"

He squeezed my hands even more tightly. "He needs you. He really does. You've broken his heart. And, you stupid *connard*, you need him."

Christ, I wanted it so badly I could almost taste it. I had to believe him. My voice was hardly above a whisper.

"Are you sure? Are you sure Marcel needs me? That he wants me?"

Reuben's tone gentled. "I'm not going to bother replying to that, Guille. You know the answer already."

Shaking his head at me, he turned for the door. "Shall we get out of here? I don't like police stations very much."

I laughed and stood. "Me neither. They scare me." I cast my eyes over cracked plaster walls, stained brown from years of damp. "Especially grotty ones like this."

Reuben was right when he said the *gendarmes* had no interest in me. The guy at the front desk gave a lazy wave of his arm as we strolled out of the front door. Reuben saw me frowning and held up a hand.

"Don't ask me—ask Marcel," he commented by way of inadequate explanation.

"Does your boyfriend really believe I'm innocent?" I asked as we reached the car. "He's fairly suspicious of me at the best of times."

Reuben grinned. "Don't be silly. Freddie loves you! You know that! Especially as you live many hundreds of kilometres away from me."

He winked broadly. "Anyway, I have a feeling that very soon he's going to be my fiancé, not my boyfriend. He told me he's waiting for the perfect moment to get down on one knee and ask for my hand in marriage. Tell me that's not the most romantic thing you've ever heard."

Romantic, yes, and one of the funniest too. Reuben Costaud marrying a member of the British aristocracy? Fuck, he'd travelled a hell of a long way from the backstreets of La Chapelle.

"Does that mean you are going to become a viscountess? Viscountess Reuben of Rossingley?"

"Don't be an arse." He giggled. "Of course not, but I am going to expect quite a lot of bowing and scraping in my presence from now on."

Reuben gave me an enormous hug before dropping me off at the end of the road leading down to the old port and Marcel's house. He was due to meet with Lucien, who'd been multitasking—combining looking after Marcel with viewing a few properties on the island with an estate agent—and they'd arranged to meet so they could view them together.

"Because, you know how it is, Guille," Reuben explained. "Sometimes a vast country estate and a swanky pad in Mayfair aren't quite enough. Lucien has decided he wants to have a holiday house here on the island close to Marcel so he can keep an eye on him. I told Freddie it was an excellent idea, and they are going to buy one together."

"Is that so you can keep an eye on me?"

"Exactly, *mon ange.*"

★

Marcel's house was silent when I opened the front door. But then it always was, and that's exactly one of the things about it I'd grown to love. Of course, the thing I loved the most about the house was the owner, and I found him propped up on several cushions on the sofa, fast asleep. He wouldn't have been on his own for long. I knew from Reuben that Lucien had only just left.

I watched Marcel sleep awhile, an activity that had become one of my favourite pastimes of late. He wasn't at his best; that much was clear. His pale features were even paler than usual, purple smudges visible under his eyes even from this distance. He seemed younger and thinner, too, his grey chinos hanging loosely from his narrow frame. Some things never changed though; the collar of a blue stripy pyjama top poked out from above his soft navy sweater.

I still had my bag at my shoulder, and I placed it soundlessly on the floor at my feet. Torn between wanting to wake him and letting him sleep, I compromised, watching him for a while longer before delicately sliding under the pile of cushions supporting his head so that he was in my lap. He stirred to wakefulness as I stroked his hair.

"You came," he said sleepily. "I missed you, my love."

"I missed you, too, *mon coeur*," I answered, leaning in to kiss his forehead.

"You also missed all the excitement," he said softly, giving me a small smile.

His voice had that hoarse, dry quality I remembered from after the last time he'd required round-the-clock oxygen therapy in hospital. The skin of his lips and nostrils was chapped and cracked too; I'd find him some Vaseline later. There was a jitteriness in his hand movements as he rubbed his face, a side effect of the superstrength bronchodilator medication. I recognised that after his last hospital admission too.

"Reuben said that you stopped breathing," I replied. "I'm so sorry I wasn't there, Marcel. I'm even more sorry that I caused it."

Inadequate words, but they were all I had. He shrugged dismissively. "They're all being dramatic. I prefer to think that I…ah, that I took a short rest from it for a while. The effort to continue breathing seemed pointless without you."

Christ, my love for this man would fill the Olympique de Marseilles stadium a hundred times over. *Mon coeur.* If ever I were to face a battle, I'd want Marcel on my side, not because he would be skilled with a weapon or handy with his fists, but because he had more courage than anyone I'd ever met.

"Did you ever used to wish you were back in prison?" he asked as I continued to gaze down at him. "You know, in the first few weeks when you were adjusting to being out."

"No." It wasn't a difficult question to answer. "There was nothing or no one left in there for me. I used to miss the routine, I suppose, and the regular football, but nothing else. Whereas Reuben missed it massively when he left—he was homesick for months, at least until he became settled at Rossingley. He would actually have been granted parole sooner, but he didn't apply for it so that he could stay with me. I was all the family he'd ever known."

"I've read up on the emotional consequences of long periods of incarceration, Guillaume," Marcel said, those blue-grey eyes not leaving mine. "I expect you have too."

I nodded in affirmation, waiting.

"I looked out for the signs, and you never displayed any of them. None of the anxiety or depression or anger. You always gave the impression that you knew exactly what to do and what you wanted. As though you picked up your life, albeit it a changed one, almost from where you had left it fifteen years earlier."

His gaze was unsettling, and I ran my fingers through my hair. I recalled my weeks at Rossingley after my release, those sleepless nights and nightmarish days. Without Reuben's love and that mundane outdoor labouring with a bunch of ordinary blokes in the estate grounds, I think I'd have gone crazy. I recalled the fear too. The same fear that had visited me these last few days in Bordeaux—the insane, gut-churning conviction I was about to be accosted by the police and hauled back to jail. I'd held it together those first few weeks after my release, clinging by the tips of my fingers. Even when I was here, living with Marcel, it hadn't quite faded. Every stranger who walked into the bar, every unfamiliar spectator at the football matches had my heart racing. Reuben would have understood it, of course; he would have seen my outward normalness for a sham because he'd experienced it himself. I'd never spoken about any of this with anybody until now.

"I felt all of those things at the beginning," I confessed, even now aware of a panicky sensation building in my chest at the recollection. "I wasn't sure I would cope, to be honest. And then…and then you came to Rossingley, and I could see a future maybe. A way forwards."

"You hid it very well," he observed with the smallest hint of a smile, which turned into a hacking cough.

Christ, this latest bout of illness was all my fault. Not waiting for him to finish, I headed for the kitchen and returned with a glass of water. He eventually settled in my lap again.

"I know why you ran, Guillaume. I understand."

Reaching up, he smoothed a finger over my lower lip. "You don't have to explain."

"I want to…I…"

Fuck, this was hard. I had to use a word that I hated admitting to myself but had to try to express anyway. There couldn't be any dissembling or lies with Marcel. He'd see through them. I reckoned he saw everything.

"I was scared, Marcel. Scared that you wouldn't believe me, scared that I wasn't good enough, scared that I didn't deserve you. I should have trusted you more, I guess."

He brought my hand to his face and held it there, my palm against his cheek, then turned his mouth into it and kissed it softly.

"But how could you trust me when I never told you that you could?"

He looked up at me, not letting go of my hand. "We should have had this conversation a long time ago, Guillaume. My problems are so visible. Me and my asthma call the tune, and everything else follows. But it's not the visible we need to watch for—it's the hidden stuff too. You were coping so well, too well, I think. You made it so easy to believe you were fine. I should have worked it out sooner. Tell me if I'm wrong."

I pulled him up higher in my lap and brought my legs up, too, so that he was sprawled on top. Even with all the pillows bunched under my head, and although he was lying on his belly, he was upright enough to find his breathing comfortable. But the touch of his hand wasn't enough. I needed to feel more of him. Wrapping his arms around my neck, he pressed into me, his head on my shoulder. Too thin, too wheezy, too bloody wonderful for words.

"Fuck, I love you, Marcel," I whispered into his silky dark hair. "Please try to love me back, *mon coeur.*"

"No trying required," he whispered in reply. "Loving you is totally effortless. I think I've loved you since you manfully carried me up two flights of stairs at Rossingley and then apologised for kissing me. It was the most romantic and wonderful moment I've ever experienced."

Seems we'd fallen in love with each other on the same day. Who knew? Reuben was right all along—Rossingley did have magical properties.

"Marcel, how the hell did you find me in Bordeaux?"

"Ah, yes…I wondered when you'd come to that."

He giggled softly. "Do you remember the second time we met at the prison? And I told you, ah, a touch arrogantly in retrospect, that I was very important?"

"You *are* very important," I agreed, leaning up and kissing his nose and then kissing it once more because I could.

"Well, after I started breathing properly again, I got in touch with the *chef de service* of the La Rochelle police department and asked her a small favour. Using her detective cunning, or rather her large computer database, she had a couple of members of her staff track down your bank card usage. And *voila*, you were located buying vast quantities of cheap brandy not far from the centre of Bordeaux."

"Marcel! That's an abuse of your position!"

He smiled mischievously. "I know."

"Aren't you going to get into trouble?"

"Nope." He grinned. "We came to a little…ah…a little arrangement. For the last five years, she has had her application for funding for a new *gendarmerie* turned down. The existing one is dreadfully scruffy, so I'm told. This year, she's going to have a pleasant surprise because she's going to be granted enough funds to build a police station that could rival the Louvre."

He was crazy, absolutely crazy to have jeopardised his career for me. But Christ, I'm so glad he did.

"You remember you stated there were three of us in our relationship, Guillaume? You, me, and my asthma? Well, you were wrong. There were more than that, too many more. Simon, of course, although he shan't be bothering us again. My sister, even Dominic."

I didn't know the details about how he'd ended his friendship with Simon, and I didn't care. Sabine was a different matter; I still didn't want to be the cause of a rift between brother and sister.

"We're good when it's only the three of us aren't we?" he continued. "So, if it's okay with you, that's how it's going to be from now on—unless we can persuade my asthma to disappear and find another set of lungs to haunt. From today onwards, the only people in possession of a key to my front door are you and me."

He paused before carrying on, and I used the opportunity to let my hands roam over his narrow back, hitching up the hem of his pyjama top. As my warm palms met his smooth skin, he wriggled with pleasure.

"Tell me about Sabine," I murmured as my hands explored farther south.

He sighed contentedly. "Yet again, you've mentioned my sister while simultaneously massaging my bum."

I laughed and squeezed his skinny arse even more.

"Sabine and I have had a long talk. She's going to step away from me for a while to concentrate on carving out her own life. She needs to move on and find a love of her own, maybe. She's signed up to a dating agency. So we can expect to be on standby for babysitting duties from now on, at least once a week."

I wanted to listen to Marcel chatter until the end of my days. I wanted to feel the soft swell of his arse until the end of my days too.

"And, Guillaume, you won't have heard the news! Excitingly, Dominic has a new boyfriend. So he won't be bothering us too much either. Antoine, one of the prison guards. I don't suppose you know much about him?"

I laughed at the thought of explaining to Marcel exactly how much I knew about Antoine and his peccadilloes. I would explain, but not today. Today was all about us and how we weren't going to be swinging from the chandeliers.

The persistent squirming above me and the stroking and press of Marcel's body on mine was absolutely delicious, so we ceased talking for a while and kissed breathlessly because that was the only sort of kissing Marcel ever managed. Without his lips leaving mine, we somehow wriggled out of our sweaters, and I pushed up Marcel's pyjama top, relishing the heat of skin on skin. Still not enough, I unfastened both of us and dragged my jeans down to my thighs so I could feel the fullness of his hard shaft against mine, wetness from both of us enhancing the push and slide.

"I…ah, I can't recall if this is in the Asthma Sutra or not." His breath ghosted against my ear. "But it *should* be…goodness, I…"

"We're going to be very busy stick men over the coming weeks," I murmured back and was rewarded with a breathy giggle. "Sticky men too!"

With my hands cupping his arse, I pulled him closer still, arching my hips up to meet his downward thrusts, our cocks digging into each other's bellies. From his loss of rhythm, I could tell Marcel was close; I reckoned if I could reach down and get my hand around the both of us, then, fuck, I'd be right there with him.

There had probably been a warning rattle at the door, but I'll be damned if I'd have heard it, not with Marcel grinding his bony hips into mine, words of love dripping from his lips with every thrust. We froze instantly, Marcel's ecstatic whimpers abruptly stopped, and the look of horror on his face no doubt matched my own as a familiar voice drifted towards us.

"…Gosh, Reuben darling, did you see how gorgeous the view was from the master bedroom of the second villa? Freddie will go utterly wild when he sees it. All the while the estate agent was prattling, I was imagining Jay draping me over that divine Juliet balcony and…"

"Fuck, Marcel, that's Lucien! Quick, get off me!"

Marcel wriggled up, but only onto his elbows, catching his breath before glancing in the direction of the hallway, then back down at me. Biting his lower lip, he gave me a helpless look. "Oh, goodness. I…I'm not entirely sure that I can…I, ah…I appear to have…um…activated my… my superpower all over you."

My first reaction was to offer my congratulations because Lucien's unexpected interruption had left me hanging with an aching cock and swollen balls. Whereas the damp, sticky sensation spreading across my groin, confirmed that the contents of Marcel's own balls had indeed been emptied all across my belly.

I had a theory about his superpower, which I hadn't yet got around to expounding, and I wasn't inclined to do it in front of the aristocratic audience about to burst into the room. But basically, I had been reading up on Marcel's orgasms. Well, not Marcel's in particular. I didn't think anybody had written about those, although maybe they should as, from my reading, I had a feeling they were probably spectacular. This was not entirely due to the sexual prowess of his lover. I'd been specifically reading about breath play—I'd come across a couple of guys in my time who got off on it. While it wasn't for me, I reckoned Marcel was unwittingly enjoying its heightened sense of arousal every time he came. Autoerotic asphyxiation, or whatever they called it. Hence, his no-handed superpower, despite being in his midthirties. What with the reduced oxygen reaching his brain cells while getting jiggy, I reckoned my bashful sickly lover was achieving better orgasms than anybody.

But now was really not the time to outline my hypothesis because, fuck, I was about to greet the sixteenth Earl of Rossingley with my trousers round my knees and my groin and belly covered in Marcel's spunk. And my lover still sprawled on top of me, giggling uncontrollably into the crook of my neck.

"Get up!" I hissed.

"I can't get up! Our penises are hanging out, and there's semen dribbling everywhere!"

Too late anyway, the front door had closed, and they were heading our way.

"I thought you said that only you and I had a set of keys!"

"Ah…yes." He had the good grace to look slightly sheepish. "I obviously ah…overlooked that Lucien also owned a set."

An elegant, pale figure, swathed in a lavender-coloured tailored suit appeared in the entrance, followed by my oldest friend.

"Oh, hello, Marcel! I'm back. Guillaume too!"

Lucien leisurely surveyed the scene, his lips twitching. "I say, Marcel, you do seem to be on the mend."

He'd switched to French, for my benefit. I closed my eyes. Christ, we were never going to live this down. There was no way I could look at Reuben. No doubt my face was beetroot red.

"Gosh, don't get up on my account, my darlings. I'll take a seat over here."

"Lucien, *darling*," warned Marcel, "I'm um…kind of…ah, busy here? If you'd like to go and help yourself to a cup of tea in the kitchen or something? And maybe take Reuben with you?"

Even with my eyes shut tight, I could sense Lucien's delight radiating from across the room, which I bet was nothing compared to Reuben's.

"Oh no, *darling*," replied Lucien. "I want to show you the brochures from the properties we've been viewing. There are a couple of splendid ones. We're absolutely fine here, aren't we, Reuben?"

"Absolutely," responded Reuben, the little fucker. "Perfectly fine. Tip-top."

"Don't you two have a plane to catch?" groaned Marcel, still lying on top of me. I'd managed to hitch his chinos back up over his skinny white arse, but my jeans and underwear were still hanging somewhere around my knees. The mess between us was cooling unpleasantly.

"Lucien has chartered a plane," Reuben responded with satisfaction. "We'll leave when he's ready. There's really no rush at all."

Christ, these two were a right bloody comedy duo. "You're going to make one hell of a viscountess, you little shit," I growled, and he laughed.

"One episode of coitus interruptus, Guillaume, that's all this is. You made me have ten years of no bloody coitus at all! This is payback time, *mon ami*!"

Eventually, our guests were persuaded to avert their eyes sufficiently long enough for us to unglue ourselves from each other and cover up. And, after poring over brochures of insanely gorgeous villas, the sort that only oligarchs and Lucien Avery could afford, they took their leave, with me firmly locking the front door behind them. And putting the safety bolt across it, too, to be sure. And then wedging a dining chair under the handle.

★

With the front door secured, all that remained were the three of us. Marcel, his asthma, and me. Over the next few hours, in the still of the night, we became a tangled joy of limbs, gentle touches, and whispered words of love. And, yeah, an inhaler or two.

Caregiver, lover. Lover, caregiver. It was one and the same, wasn't it?

Epilogue

Marcel

One Year Later

I'd waved the fitness freaks off to do their thing a couple of hours earlier. Then I set the table for lunch and enjoyed a peaceful hour or so at my desk.

Their plan was to cycle over to the little town of Ars for a coffee and then a wander around the outdoor market before cycling back to our house for a late lunch. Hopefully, armed with a delicious selection of cheeses. Not an inch of Lycra in sight, thank goodness. Lucien and Freddie would rather lose an arm than be seen wearing that sort of get-up.

The Rossingley Six, Lucien had dubbed us, which made us sound like a gang of criminals. Two of our close-knit group were, which was endlessly amusing to the six of us and to pre-cisely no one else. Lucien and Freddie had bought a stupidly luxurious pad on the island and, as they'd become quite fond of chartering planes, they were frequent and most welcome vis-itors, although I'd insisted Lucien return my door key.

My health had been stable for a while, which was a relief, as today's gathering was particularly special. I had no intention of inviting my asthma to the party. While my health wasn't good enough that I could join them on cycling trips, occasionally, when the weather was fine, Guillaume would bundle me up in my scarf and drag out our old tandem. I could freewheel behind him and enjoy the flex of his muscles as he did all the work, as much as I enjoyed the beautiful scenery around us. He was as healthy as ever, of course; his football team had won the league this season, unsurprisingly, as he ruled the players with a steel rod.

And talking of steel rods… I was seriously considering publishing the Asthma Sutra as a guide for all other sufferers of chronic respiratory incompetence. Guillaume and I had devoted considerable time and effort expanding our repertoire. While my safe word was employed on an almost weekly basis—my Guillaume had an extremely healthy sexual appetite—my days of ever believing sex was something to dread and avoid were a thing of the past.

A rattle at the garden gate alerted me to their return. Jay was first to arrive, his handsome bulk filling the path. Safe, solid Jay—Lucien's bedrock. He was followed by 'his girls', Lucien and Freddie, as twin-like as ever, despite the age gap. Though, goodness knew what my dear, dear Lucien was wearing on his head—some sort of purple cloche hat. It matched his purple eye shadow. And beautiful Freddie, whose charm and humour always made me smile, strolling down my garden path as if it were a Milanese catwalk. Then gorgeous Reuben, his wild spirally hair having taken on a life of its own after cycling against the breeze. He laughed as he threw his arm around my lover's broad shoulders. My lover, my Guillaume, the only man I have ever and will ever love.

As Guillaume approached, he ran his eyes over me, his usual quick assessment—more expert than any doctor. I walked into his open arms.

"Okay, *mon coeur*? Did we leave you to your own devices for long enough?"

A gentle tease rewarded with a gentle kiss. Followed by a much firmer one.

"*Merde*, Guillaume, put him down. I'm going to lose my appetite."

The wide selection of cheeses ensured we would still be nibbling on leftovers at Christmas. Jay eyed them hungrily as I laid out a platter. To stop him picking, I handed him the champagne to uncork, and with much jostling and chatter, everyone found their seats around the dining table. Lucien led with a toast.

"Darlings, to the Rossingley Six. I salute and love you all."

If there was a general undercurrent of excitement, it was because all gathered were in on the secret, except for Guillaume. We met like this frequently, but today's get-together was a little more special than usual. After we had eaten our fill, we would be meeting others—my sister Sabine and her boyfriend. My niece Clara. Antoine and Dominic, and a few other friends Guillaume and I had picked up along the way.

Together, we would set off, at my regal pace, my arm nestled into Guillaume's. Our route would meander across the cobbled port and up one of the winding side streets. It would take me a while to traverse this short distance—the others would have time to stop for a coffee at one of the pretty cafés and still arrive before Guillaume and me.

Our destination was a little registry office tucked into the side of the much larger Saint-Martin town hall. The high walls of the island's prison, only a stone's throw away, overshadowed the town hall, which seemed fitting. Tourists aplenty still flocked to admire its grandeur. Guillaume and I hardly noticed it anymore.

Very soon, my wonderful Guillaume and I would exchange vows, to love and cherish each other, both in sickness and in health. I could hardly wait. In the inconspicuous little registry office, before all of our friends, I would make an honest man of him.

Acknowledgements

With thanks to the Wells family for introducing me all those years ago to the exquisite island of Ré, home to Marcel and Guillaume. And to my friend, C.M., who doesn't read romance novels, therefore has no idea her beautiful house overlooking Saint-Martin port has been appropriated by Marcel.

As always, I'd like to also thank my publisher, NineStar Press, and above all, my editor, Elizabetta, for her endless patience and encouragement.

About Fearne Hill

Fearne Hill lives deep in the southern British countryside, a stone's throw away from the private country estate providing her inspiration for Rossingley. She looks after varying numbers of hens, a few tortoises, and a beautiful cocker spaniel.

When she is not overseeing her small menagerie, she enjoys writing contemporary romantic fiction. And when she is not doing either of those things, she works as an anaesthesiologist.

Email
fearne.hill@fearnehill.com

Facebook
www.facebook.com/fearne.hill.50

Facebook Group (Fearne Hill's House):
www.facebook.com/groups/11724592699 38382

Twitter
@FearneHill

Instagram
www.instagram.com/fearnehill_author

Other NineStar books by this author

The Last of the Moussakas

Rossingley Series
To Hold a Hidden Pearl
To Catch a Fallen Leaf

Coming Soon from Fearne Hill

To Melt a Frozen Heart

Rossingley, Book 3.5 (Holiday)

"Mingle. *Go on*! Shake some hands and cuddle some babies. You're a politician; you're supposed to be good at this sort of thing."

Bah, humbug.

I huffed a sigh, feeling like a timid five-year-old clinging to my mother's skirts at a birthday party. As Freddie had observed, I was good at this sort of thing, but only with the right kind of people. My kind of people. Old Etonians, Harrovians—even Wykehamists at a push, as long as they didn't drone on about their dull civil service careers. People with whom I shared the uncommon language of Oxbridge, the City, Henley, croquet on the lawn, Wimbledon. Actually, not Wimbledon. Tennis was a sore subject these days, ever since wife number two ran off with the tennis coach. A shame really; he'd worked a minor miracle on my topspin backhand.

Freddie had a point though. I had docilely traipsed after him all evening. Scratch that, I'd traipsed after him for the last four days. When he invited me to join the clan at Rossingley for the Christmas parliamentary break, I'd leapt at the offer, overwhelmingly and pathetically grateful. There were no two ways about it. The alternative would have been gloomy as hell, whereas at least here I swung from feeling bloody brilliant to inexplicably tearful.

My son and Reuben were splendid company—as were Lucien and his husband, Jay. And I'd fallen head over heels in love with Lucien's babies from the moment they were born, surprising myself as much as anyone. The stupid and unpredictable tears came when my son Freddie and his friends were so damned nice to me. I didn't deserve any of their relentless kindnesses—and not from Freddie especially. I'd been a rotten father, utterly rotten, and yet my precious, big-hearted son had forgiven me anyway.

So I had no reason on earth not to be jolly and full of Christmas bonhomie. But I was a modern-day Scrooge. I liked to think I'd learned from my past and more recent mistakes, yet I couldn't seem to bloody start the last chapter, the tear-jerking finale, Scrooge's vision of a future filled with joy and happiness. Witnessing first-hand how competently these delightful young men managed to combine ambitious careers with successful personal lives was, frankly, extremely depressing. I'd failed miserably at the latter, costing me two wives and almost losing my dear son. Real life, unlike romantic fiction, didn't guarantee a happy ending, even if the principal villain had recognised the error of his ways.

Grumpy and irritable, I surveyed the happy spread of humans gathered in the Rossingley drawing room with mild distaste. It was no wonder I was struggling to find my place at this ghastly affair. Ever the libertarian, Lucien didn't care two figs for inviting the landed gentry to his inaugural Rossingley Christmas drinks party. He'd chosen instead to cram his elegant drawing room with grubby villagers. Even the barmaid from the Rossingley Arms was here, leaving nothing to the imagination as far as her bosom was concerned.

And that second glass of fizz had given me rotten heartburn. I glanced at my watch. Only another bloody three hours to go. Perhaps I could slink undetected…

"Where do you think you're going?" Freddie demanded, rounding on me. Gosh, that boy was more and more like his departed mother, rest her soul. It was as if his sharp blue eyes could read my every thought.

"Um…to the little boy's room?"

He sighed with exasperation, the tiniest of frowns denting his flawless smooth forehead. He'd inherited his perfect skin from his mother too. "You know as well as I do where the loo is, and it's not over there! I'm not letting you duck out of this, Daddy. Do what you're told; it's good for you. Go. And. Mingle! You never know, you might actually meet somebody you like."

Humph. It was all right for Freddie, with his astonishing handsomeness and natural social grace (mother's genes again). All he had to do was flutter his eyelashes and men and women seemed to materialise from underneath the sideboard. All of them hoping the glamour would somehow rub off. Whereas I stood alone, approaching my sixtieth birthday next month with trepidation and wishing I'd an antacid in my pocket. I could have done with notching my belt on a slightly looser hole too. At least with my height, my ever-spreading bald patch wasn't so obvious. And maybe I could discreetly adjust my belt, seeing as nobody had so much as cast a glance in my direction anyhow. Surrounded by Freddie and Lucien's cohort and raucous villagers making the most of the earl's free fizz and sherry, I felt myself entirely invisible.

"Maybe I'll go and find Marcel," I decided gloomily. Lucien's oldest pal was always good for a chinwag. I could tease him about France's stagnant economic growth.

But that wasn't good enough for my son either.

"Daddy," he tutted. "Talking shop to Marcel doesn't qualify as mingling. You've known him since he was about ten years old. He's practically family." Freddie cast his steely blue gaze around the room, squinting over people's heads. "Anyway, Guillaume has taken him upstairs for a short lie-down. Allegedly, he overdid things with the ramble around the estate this afternoon. That's their excuse anyway."

Lucky Marcel. Both in having a valid excuse to escape and a delightful partner with whom to make his escape. Not that I wished for a debilitating chronic disease. Or coveted his rather exotic lover, Guillaume. I'd put a tight lid on shenanigans like that years ago.

Buggering around (quite literally) with the shirt lifters in the school dorm was but a hazy memory—it had almost been a rite of passage. And there had been absolutely no reason at all not to carry on at Cambridge; indeed, it was par for the course amongst our hedonistic set. Naturally, I'd thrown that nonsense into the bottom of my trunk and shoved it to the back of the attic years ago, along with the old school tie and my threadbare rugger shirt.

After all, I'd had a reputation to build. And I'd succeeded, had dedicated the last thirty or so years crafting my career. But more recently, I'd been seriously asking myself the question: For what? Two failed marriages and the prospect of facing the latter quarter of my allotted threescore years and ten alone? Seems I had achieved everything I always wanted and yet nothing I actually needed.

Thank God for Freddie and my nephew, Lucien. If they hadn't taken pity on me and invited me to stay then I'd be wallowing on my tod in London with a quart of Scotch, reruns of

Dad's Army, and the extensive romcom oeuvre of Hugh Grant for the entirety of the Christmas parliamentary break. Even an evening with Lucien's village rabble was preferable to that purgatory.

Glumly, I surveyed the gathering. Still no sign of my saviour, Marcel. Freddie wandered across to join Lucien over by the mantel, where he indulged a gaggle of village women as they cooed over baby Eliza and cast covert glances at Lucien's peculiar attire. Tonight, my nephew had chosen a tangerine-coloured silk tunic and taken a liberal approach to eye makeup, still managing to look strangely beautiful. God knows what the tweedy villagers made of him.

Near the buffet table, Lucien's equally eye-catching but soberly dressed husband, Jay, with a sleeping Arthur casually draped over his broad shoulder, was deep in conversation with the estate manager, Will Beecham. While excellent at his job, just like his father before him, Will was dull as ditch water. I could have joined them, but the talk would likely have been centred around crop rotations or soccer, subjects I neither cared for nor understood.

Which left young Reuben, of whom I'd become increasingly fond, principally because he let me witter on about my orchids without interrupting and kept my wayward Freddie on an extremely short leash.

Swallowing a hefty glug of Lucien's delicious vintage fizz, which may as well have been battery acid judging from the effect champagne had on my insides these days, I eased my way through the throng over towards Reuben.

Big mistake. Freddie's boyfriend was surrounded by the ragtag group of degenerates he insisted on referring to as friends, known to anybody with a modicum of decorum as

Lucien's ex-con gardening crew. Judging from the state of his trousers, one of them looked as if he'd actually joined the party straight from the potting shed. Goodness knows what devilment he'd deposited on Lucien's cream carpets.

With a fresh flood of social anxiety, I loitered in an awkward, self-conscious limbo between Reuben's chums and a raucous cluster of women. Me, the Rt Hon Charles Duchamps-Avery MP, of the Rossingley Duchamps-Averys, hovering like an ingenue wallflower. Hesitating on the periphery of a group of men, most of whom would struggle to locate their nearest polling booth, let alone discuss the finer points of the global impact of the UK's post-Brexit trade policy. Ignorant, or at the very least uncaring, that unemployment figures had risen by 1.2 per cent in the past six months, or that the pound had fallen against the dollar 0.38 per cent in the last forty-eight hours. They didn't give a flying fuck about the macroeconomics of the electric car industry. And why should they, when they could discuss the opening of a new microbrewery in the next village, or that old Pete Evans was currently languishing in Allenmouth Hospital with a nasty chest infection and wasn't expected to come out alive?

Even if the waves suddenly parted, even if Reuben noticed me at his shoulder and welcomed me into the group, I would have remained tongue-tied. I literally had nothing of value or interest to impart to these ordinary folk. Shockingly, I had found myself in the extraordinary position of being a misfit. An outsider. An anachronism. And depressingly, my Damascene moment was occurring here of all places, in the bloody stately home in which I was born and raised. All these happy, excitable souls, laughing, chattering, and scoffing sausage rolls in the exact same drawing room where, too many years ago to calculate, I'd showed off my first Beethoven piano recital to my proud parents. Where I'd brought Freddie's mother to announce our engagement. Lucien and Freddie had moved with the times, effortlessly it would seem. Sadly, I had not.

"Hello, I'm guessing this isn't your scene either."

I turned, prepared to look down (Freddie inherited his height from me), but found myself tilting my gaze slightly upwards, into narrowed grey eyes. The voice was low and devoid of the local country burr. Automatically, I held out my hand.

"Charles Avery, how do you do." God, I sounded pompous.

The stranger's steady gaze was eerily serene; if I had to choose one adjective to describe his eyes, I'd plump for 'knowing'. As he leisurely scrutinized my face, I had the uncomfortable sensation he'd already extracted and filed away my deepest secrets merely from the act of me returning his gaze.

I pumped his cool hand, pathetically grateful to him for rescuing me, although I wasn't entirely sure from where he'd materialised. Possibly the nineteenth century, if his outfit was anything to go by. The man was tall and thin—elegantly so. A faded burgundy velvet smoking jacket hung from his angular frame; he had carelessly tied a paisley silk cravat around his neck. A Bohemian type, the likes of which I hadn't encountered since my Cambridge days. Indeed, we were of a similar age.

Measuring oneself against one's peers is a deeply embedded facet of human nature. As reflexive as breathing. It begins on the school playing fields, where we note and celebrate the fastest, the strongest, the fittest. Then, as we pass through the years, more successful young men display their rank by purchasing sportier cars, receiving bigger bonuses, and securing prettier wives. Followed by more expensive divorces.

With all that nonsense behind me, these days I found myself measuring success in terms of hair follicles. And against this fine figure of a man, I fell woefully short. A luxuriant silvery mane swept back from a high forehead hung down his back, neatly secured with a black hairband.

"George," he returned eventually, holding the handshake fractionally longer than comfortable. "George Samwise."

That assessing gaze travelled the length of my body, raking over my bland country casuals—the clothing equivalent of tofu—with the open regard of one's tailor sizing up for a new suit. Yet this man didn't wield a tape measure, and I wasn't in a private Savile Row changing room, dressed only in my underwear. Regardless, his grey eyes stripped me naked. With a jolt of shock, I realised I was being, as Freddie would have put it, *checked out*.

Connect with NineStar Press

www.ninestarpress.com

www.facebook.com/ninestarpress

www.facebook.com/groups/NineStarNiche

www.twitter.com/ninestarpress

www.instagram.com/ninestarpress

www.ingramcontent.com/pod-product-compliance
Lightning Source LLC
Chambersburg PA
CBHW060242100726
47907CB00003B/739